BLEEDING in the Eye of a BRAINSTORM

A MONGO MYSTERY

by GEORGE C. CHESBRO

SIMON & SCHUSTER
New York London Toronto Sydney Tokyo Singapore

SIMON & SCHUSTER
Rockefeller Center
1230 Avenue of the Americas
New York, NY 10020

SIMON & SCHUSTER and colophon are registered trademarks
of Simon & Schuster Inc.

Designed by Hyun Joo Kim

Manufactured in the United States of America

10   9   8   7   6   5   4   3   2   1

Library of Congress Cataloging-in-Publication Data

Chesbro, George C.
    Bleeding in the eye of a brainstorm : a Mongo mystery / by George
C. Chesbro.
        p.   cm.
    I. Title.
    PS3553.H359B57   1995b   95-17732
    813'.54—dc20   CIP
ISBN 0-684-81495-1

Bleeding in the

Eye

of a Brainstorm

A MONGO MYSTERY

CHAPTER 1

*O*h, *woe was me. Alone and lonely on Thanksgiving eve, I was* feeling sorry for myself, an unpleasant and enervating state of mind I thoroughly despised, and so I decided to seek out a little company and distraction as an anodyne. In New York City, if you are a chess player, you need never lack for reasonably respectable, like-minded souls at any hour of any day of the year if you know where to look, and so I headed for the Manhattan Chess Club in their new digs in a renovated four-story brownstone on West 46th Street, a ten-minute walk from the similar brownstone my brother Garth and I owned on West 56th Street.

I arrived at the club with its glowing twin globes flanking the entrance without having had my brain, heart, or spinal column aerated by an ice pick, which in this killing season on the city's streets was not something to be taken for granted. The crowd was sparse, even for the night before a holiday. Normally, you'd find upwards of a dozen grandmasters and international masters interspersed with sixty or seventy weaker players of all shapes, sexes, ages, and colors, but tonight there was less than half that number. I attributed the low turnout to the fact that even the rabid chess players, among the most compulsive of God's creatures, who usually frequented these haunts were reluctant to leave the safety of their homes in the midst of a horror that had caught the attention and chilled the hearts of even those quick-stepping New Yorkers who thought themselves inured to the threats of random violence and sudden death in their everyday

lives, whether from stray bullets, muggers, or unlicensed killer taxicab drivers.

For the past week a really serious maniac had been stalking the
streets of the city, and this one was no garden-variety mass or serial
killer. The man or woman had a startlingly simple MO, striking in an
instant like a poisonous snake whenever, wherever, and as often as an
opportunity presented itself, night or day, whether on a crowded
subway platform, a lonely street, or in a knot of pedestrians moving
along the veins and arteries of the city's sidewalks or momentarily
clotted at a corner waiting for the light to change. There was no
apparent similarity or connection between any of the victims, and
pleasure- or rage-driven impulse seemed the only motive. The murder
weapon was an ice pick, thrust quickly and deeply into the base of the
skull or spinal column, or through the rib cage to prick the heart.
Death was not only instantaneous, but relatively bloodless. By the
time the victim had collapsed to the grass, gravel, or concrete, the
killer had moved on, sometimes alone into the night, at other times
through milling, anonymous crowds in the middle of the day. In this
one week seventeen people had died—men and women, old, middle-
aged, and teenagers. Thus far no young children had been victims,
but the police theorized this was only because young children were
usually accompanied by one or more adults, and their abiding fear
was that the first child victim would undoubtedly be a little boy or girl
momentarily left alone on a swing or in a sandbox on some play-
ground.

Knowing that the stranger walking toward or behind you, or standing at your side, could end your existence in the space between two
thoughts was not only enough to give pause but to induce panic in
most people living in a huge, congested city of strangers like New
York.

I looked around the main playing rooms for some action. There
were a number of games in progress, and a few individuals sitting
alone at tables and analyzing positions who might have been amenable to a friendly challenge, but I didn't see anyone I knew at the
boards, and in my current snit of self-pity and loneliness I wanted to
play with someone with whom I was familiar.

Finally I found someone who just sneaked in under that descriptive wire in an adjoining room where one of the club's assistant directors was conducting a three-round, game-in-sixty-minutes tournament for unrated players of unknown strength, usually beginners. By the end of the evening they would have earned a provisional rating, based on their wins and losses against other players in the tournament, which was supposed to be a rough numerical description of their relative playing strength, and which would allow them to play for cash prizes in tournaments sponsored by the United States Chess Federation, the country's governing body for the international sport.

Theo Barnes, who was on my very long, very eclectic list of acquaintances, was dressed in faded jeans, high-top black sneakers, and one of the garish, baggy, short-sleeved Hawaiian shirts he always wore year-round, regardless of the weather. Barnes was someone I'd once relieved of a few dollars one lazy Sunday summer afternoon in "Hustlers' Alley" at the southwest corner of Washington Square Park down in the Village, one of several sites in the city where people came to play chess. Barnes was no beginner—I rated him at about expert strength, which placed him in a very small percentile of the country's chess-playing population. But neither was he a tournament player, and as far as I knew he was not even a USCF member. Barnes, whom I judged to be about thirty years old—although his pockmarked face and generally grubby appearance made him appear older—was a street person, a chess fanatic and strong natural player who preferred the raucous, manic, motor-mouthed sprints of speed chess in Washington Square Park to the tight, nerve-racking, disciplined, long-distance-run style of play necessary for successful tournament competition and subsequent ascension in the ranks of titled players—National Master, Senior Master, International Master, and Grandmaster. He lived, so I was told, in a leaky basement, cooked on a hot plate, and stored what few clothes he owned in cardboard boxes that ringed the mattress he used as a bed. Nevertheless, I considered him a successful man; in my view, a man or woman who can manage to earn a living, however meager, doing exactly what he or she wants to do—something which he or she would otherwise be doing anyway, for nothing—is a success. Barnes supported himself by hustling chess-playing tourists, the vast majority of whom were "patzers" who seriously overestimated their own skills while underestimating those of the ragtag band of players in the park who might be carrying on simultaneous conversations with half a dozen kibitzers gathered around the concrete tables while offering a running commentary—usually derogatory—on an opponent's moves, all the while making moves and punching the button on a chess clock with lightning speed. Five bucks a game.

Theo Barnes was definitely not the Manhattan Chess Club type, and I assumed that he, like not a few other New Yorkers, had been driven indoors from his usual open-air haunts by fear of the Iceman, as the killer had been dubbed, none too creatively, by the media and police. Less clear to me was what Barnes was doing standing around watching a beginners' tournament instead of working the rooms and trolling for potential marks, however scarce they might be in this place, to at least earn back his admission fee.

He glanced up, saw me coming over, and started. That made me curious, since I could think of no reason why I should make Theo Barnes nervous. He retreated a couple of steps, then, apparently deciding that escape was impossible, turned back toward me with a decidedly sour expression on his cratered face. By moving away he had revealed what he had apparently not wanted me to see—namely, that he had been standing behind one of the players in the tournament, closely monitoring his play. The man at the table was about thirty-five, with a boyish face and a high forehead. His brown hair was raggedly cut, as if by somebody with dull scissors who'd been in a hurry. His narrow, aquiline nose looked as if it might break easily, and he had thin lips. Even in profile he looked to me slightly dazed, and he would occasionally touch his cheek and shake his head, as if to help him to focus his concentration on the game. He had on baggy slacks which looked like they had come from the same Salvation Army center where he had gotten his cracked plastic shoes. His shirt, however, had definitely come out of one of Theo Barnes's cardboard boxes; it was a blaring Hawaiian print with an old ketchup stain on the right sleeve.

I found the situation, if not surpassingly strange, at least mildly curious. Theo Barnes was self-centered to a point just outside the city limits of sociopathy. For the grungy chess hustler to take an interest in what anyone else was doing was most uncharacteristic; and for him to give away or lend something that belonged to him was downright extraordinary. The man with the chopped brown hair and narrow mouth obviously had no money, so he wasn't a potential mark, and he just didn't look like the type who would be part of the hustler's very limited social circle. Then again, neither did I.

Then again, again, crack private investigator that I am, upon reflection I was fairly certain I could divine the root of their relationship. I didn't particularly care what he was up to, but it did explain why Barnes wasn't all that happy to see me. He reluctantly came over to me when I beckoned to him, grudgingly accepted my handshake.

"How're you doing, Theo?"

He considered the question carefully, like a chess move in a slower-paced game than he usually played. He apparently hadn't showered in a few days, for he was slightly rank, and also hadn't shaved for the same period of time. His long, stringy blond hair was greasy. He certainly looked like a bum, which was not a disadvantage in his chosen profession, but if you looked in his face you knew he was more than that. His pale blue eyes, if perhaps a bit too wide and manic, glittered with intelligence, and were unclouded by the use of drugs or alcohol.

When he had finally finished calculating all the possible variations on his answer, he replied, "I'm okay, Frederickson. How are you?"

"Actually, I'm feeling a bit out of sorts, and I'm looking for company. To your good fortune, Theo, I've chosen you. Let's play some blitz."

"I don't play chess with masters, Frederickson."

"Aw, come on. A couple of ten-minute games. We don't have to play for money."

"I never play chess except for money. What, you think I do this for my health?"

"Okay, I'll give you odds. Your ten minutes to my five. A buck a game."

More considerations, more calculations, thoughts skipping like stones on water across the cold, pale blue surface of his eyes. Finally he said, "My five minutes to your one. Fifty bucks a game."

"That's a little fast, and a little steep."

He smiled thinly, revealing surprisingly good teeth considering the fact that he probably hadn't been able to afford a trip to the dentist in years. "Come on, Frederickson. Be a sport."

"I don't mind being a sport, Theo; what I'm trying not to be is a sucker. I like your game; you never saw an unsound pawn sacrifice you didn't like."

"If you want a game with me, Frederickson, those are the odds I want."

Theo Barnes obviously wasn't going to amuse me with a chess game, at least not under reasonable conditions, and so I decided to amuse myself by trying to rattle his cage a bit. I looked over at the player wearing Barnes's Hawaiian shirt just in time to see him glance up at a clock on the wall. Then he reached into his shirt pocket, carefully removed a rather large black-and-yellow capsule. Holding the capsule between his thumb and forefinger, he unselfconsciously popped it into his mouth, swallowed it without water.

"Who's your friend, Theo?"

"What friend?"

"The one wearing your shirt."

"How do you know it's my shirt?" he asked without bothering to turn around.

"I was hanging out watching the action the day somebody dropped their hot dog on it."

"He's . . . a student of mine."

"No kidding? I didn't know you took on students. From the looks of him, he'd be hard pressed to pay for a meal, much less a chess lesson. You doing pro bono chess teaching these days, Theo?"

He flushed slightly, and this had the effect of making the scars on his face even whiter. Although I wouldn't have thought it possible, his eyes grew even colder. "That's my business."

"The New York Open is coming up. It looks to me like you're trying to load a sandbag."

"Maybe you should mind your own business."

"I'm surprised you're willing to be seen with him here. Most of these players know who you are, and what you do."

"Not everybody is as nosy as you are, Frederickson. And I still think you should mind your own business."

He was, of course, absolutely right, and so I proceeded about my own business, challenging one of the men analyzing in another room to a game. He turned out to be a Peruvian grandmaster. To an average player looking on, the game probably would have appeared close, with the contest about even right up to the point in the endgame when I finally tipped over my besieged king. In fact I'd been thoroughly outplayed, put at a positional disadvantage which had only grown worse right from the opening.

My brief, sour conversation with Theo Barnes and sound thrashing at the hands of the grandmaster had purged my loneliness and restored my normal taste for solitude, and so I headed home, trying to concentrate on my surroundings so as not to get stuck with an ice pick, but at the same time compulsively replaying in my mind, as chess players always do when they have lost, the moves in my last game, trying to figure out where I had gone wrong. As a result, I wasn't paying much attention to what was directly in front of me, and I almost fell into the lap of the person sitting on the stoop of my brownstone. I whooped in surprise and alarm, then almost tripped over my own feet as I hurriedly back-pedaled to the curb, where I stood and stared into the chiaroscuro pattern of light and shadow at the middle-aged woman who had taken up temporary residence at the entrance to my home.

The woman's gray hair was severely pulled back from her oval face and secured in a ponytail by a rubber band. I thought she might be in her mid-fifties, but it was hard to tell because what could have been exposure to sun, wind, cold, and rain had weathered her skin to the point where it looked like worn leather. She wore no makeup, and her full lips had a purplish-blue tinge from the cold of the late November night. Her eyes, in the moment I had looked into them when I almost stumbled over her, had appeared to be a pale violet. Her clothes must have come from the same Salvation Army bin as those of Barnes's "student"—a long, flaring polyester skirt that was much too big for her and draped down over the steps, and a wool sweater with holes in it. It wasn't enough for the night and she was trembling, but I sensed that her shaking was as much from fear and anxiety as from the cold, for there was a desperate, haunted expression on her face.

My first reaction was that I didn't have the slightest idea who the woman was, or what she was doing on my stoop. But as we stared at each other in the night across the great territorial divide of the sidewalk, I experienced a chill that had nothing to do with the temperature as I slowly began to realize that I had, in fact, seen the woman before—in another context, and with her behavior and appearance so totally different as to suggest she might have blinked into existence on my stoop from an alternate universe instead of only a half block or so to the east. The woman sitting and shivering on my doorstep was none other than Mama Spit.

Mama Spit, as she was called by all the residents and store owners in the neighborhood, usually resided on a steam grate two hundred yards or so closer to the Hudson River. There she had sat, year-round, for the better part of two years, wrapped in a filthy blanket, wearing a filthy black wool seaman's cap I had never seen her remove, cursing and spitting at passersby—even those who tried to give her money. I was one of those who tried to give her something each time I passed by, which was unavoidably quite often since she was stationed just down the block, change from my pocket or sometimes a dollar bill, other times a piece of fruit or a sandwich wrapped in wax paper. I was always given a receipt of verbal abuse and spittle for my contributions, but she had never thrown my offerings back at me, as she did on most other occasions when people tried to give things to her. I had developed a strategy; when passing her from either direction, I'd always wait, well out of firing range, until she'd spat at two or three other pedestrians, then, when I knew she had to be running a bit dry on ammunition, I'd dart in, drop my offering of food or money, then hustle on out of there until I was again safely out of range. On one particularly cold day during the past winter I'd given her one of my brother's old parkas, which she had worn well into the spring. She'd apparently really loved the down-filled coat—which, of course, hadn't kept her from spitting and cursing at me when I made subsequent money and food runs past her. And then one day the parka was gone, presumably stolen right off her body by some other homeless person, leaving Mama Spit nothing in return but her old filthy blanket and a black eye and bruises on her face.

At least once a month, religiously, I called Social Services to request that something be done to help Mama Spit, get her into a hospital, or at least off the streets. Each time I was told by one bureaucrat or another that Social Services was aware of Mama Spit and her situation; she had been diagnosed a hopeless paranoid schizophrenic, but since she was not considered a threat to herself, and cursing and spitting were not deemed a serious threat to others, she could not be forcibly removed from the streets against her will. Now it seemed that Mama Spit, for whatever mysterious reason, had abandoned her grate, seaman's cap and filthy blanket, bathed and dressed in clean clothes, and apparently begun the first, tentative steps of a journey from self-destructive behavior, if not from the underlying madness. She'd made it as far as my stoop.

I cleared my throat, said, "Uh, can I help you?"

Mama Spit half turned, raised a trembling hand, and pointed to where a small sign on a first-floor window proclaimed: *Frederickson and Frederickson, Investigations.* "You're Mr. Frederickson?" she asked in a quavering voice.

"One of them, yes."

"My name's Margaret Dutton, Mr. Frederickson. I know I've been terrible to you. I've acted terribly toward everybody. I . . . do remember some things. But you've always been good to me. I remember you gave me money and food. You're a kind man." She paused and abruptly put both hands to her mouth as if to stifle a sob, or a scream. After a few seconds she put her hands back in her lap, took a series of deep breaths, then continued quickly, "This is awfully hard for me, Mr. Frederickson, so I guess I'm just going to have to come out and say it if it's ever going to get said. I'm feeling much better now. I went to the Salvation Army center today. They let me shower, and they gave me these clean clothes. But I don't have any place to stay. They wanted to take me to a shelter, but I'm afraid of shelters. I went to a shelter once, and a man hurt me. I was . . . I was wondering . . . if you could take me in for just a little while, until I can get back on my feet. I promise I won't be any trouble at all. You have a big house, and I promise I'll stay out of your way. I'd be so grateful if you'd just let me sleep in a hallway and use the bathroom so I can stay clean. I know places where I can get food. I'm going to get a job as soon as I can, and find my own place to live. Then I'll pay you. I just need someplace where I can stay clean and be safe at night for a little while. I know it's an awfully big thing to ask, but . . . there's nobody else."

Well. The Ultimate Theory of Cynicism—namely, that no good deed will go unpunished—might not have been specifically hypothesized for New York City, but it was constantly proven there every day; the streets were filled with the bloody litter of good intentions and the decaying corpses of good Samaritans. I would be an absolute fool to take into my home a psychotic who'd spent the better part of two years sitting on the sidewalk, dressed in filthy rags, spitting and cursing at people, just because she'd managed to clean up her act for a few hours, a remission of her madness I had to presume was only temporary and which could evaporate at any moment. Performing this good deed could have decidedly bad consequences, like having the house trashed, getting hurt, or even killed if Mama Spit was in brief transition to another, possibly more dangerous psychotic state.

On the other hand, it was Thanksgiving eve, and everyone I loved and who loved me was out of town; Garth and his wife, Mary Tree, were on a skiing vacation in Zermatt, and the woman I was sure I would one day get up the courage to ask to marry me, Dr. Harper Rhys-Whitney, was on an extended tour of South American universities, lecturing to fellow herpetologists and assorted snake charmers. I missed her terribly. If I couldn't be with the people who lived in my heart, I figured I might as well celebrate the holiday by playing Indian to Mama Spit's Pilgrim, offering a bit of kindness to another human being who certainly needed it. I really couldn't refuse, for I couldn't very well leave the woman alone out on the streets with a mass killer on the loose, and Mama Spit had made it clear that she'd opt for the streets rather than go to a shelter.

Besides, I'd been an absolute fool on more than one previous occasion, and survived.

"Come on, Margaret," I said, going back across the sidewalk to her and extending my hand. "Let's get you inside where it's warm."

CHAPTER 2

I put Mama Spit up in Garth's unused apartment on the third floor. His bedroom door had no lock on it, but I probably wouldn't have locked the woman in if it did. I had no choice but to give her the run of the place, along with a supply of fresh linens, a broad grin, and a hearty "good night" that served to mask the fact that I was already having second and third thoughts about my little gesture; I was hoping I wouldn't come up the next morning to find the apartment transformed into something resembling a cell in Bedlam. I went up to my own apartment on the fourth floor and double-locked the entrance door behind me. Willing to accept my fate and whatever dire consequences might result from my act, which in itself made me feel rather pleased with myself, I slept soundly, and awoke on Thanksgiving morning to silence and sunlight streaming in through the window. I considered it a good omen; at least Mama Spit hadn't burned down the house.

I showered and shaved, had coffee while I perused the slim Thanksgiving edition of *The New York Times*. The news had the effect of slipping a gray filter over what otherwise looked to be a fine day in the snow-powdered city; three more people had been stabbed to death during the night, two in the Bronx and one in Queens. I dressed, went down to my office on the first floor and did some paperwork, then went out and bought a carton of coffee, with milk and sugar on the side, and a toasted plain bagel with cream cheese. These I took with me up to the third floor of the brownstone. The door to Garth's apartment was still closed. I knocked, but there was no answer. I opened the door, went in, and looked around, but there was no sign of Mama Spit. There was no damage that I could see, but there was a different look to the place that at first I couldn't quite put my finger on. Then I realized that what was different was that the place looked cleaner. Not that the apartment had been that dirty to begin with, but everything had been dusted, and there was the faint, not unpleasant smell of furniture polish in the air. Over on a chair were rags and a can of polish Mama Spit must have found in Garth's utility closet.

I found her in the bathroom, with more supplies from the utility closet, down on her hands and knees scrubbing the bathtub, which had been clean to begin with. The tile floor, sink, and toilet bowl were already gleaming. On the shower curtain rack over the bathtub hung a shapeless cotton bra, frayed pink panties, and mismatched wool socks with holes at the heels and toes.

"Good morning, Margaret."

She started, then quickly turned and smiled shyly. "Oh! Good morning, Mr. Frederickson! I didn't hear you come in."

"I'm sorry if I startled you. I knocked, but there was no answer. I wanted to make certain you were all right."

"Oh, I'm fine, thanks to you." She paused, glanced up at the underwear hanging above her head, reddened slightly. "I apologize for having my dainties on display. I washed them out, and they're not dry yet. I didn't want you to think I was a dirty person—I mean, the real me."

For some reason, her words touched me. Suddenly I found I had a lump in my throat, and I turned away as I felt my eyes fill with tears. "If I'd ever entertained such a notion, Margaret, you've certainly disabused me of it. My God, you've cleaned the whole place. You must have been up before dawn."

She nodded eagerly. "I wanted to get off to an early start. I have to try to earn my keep. You'll see I'm a good cleaner."

"I already see that."

"It's been an awfully long time since I felt all right in my head, but I remember that I liked to clean when I did. I'll clean your apartment too. I'll keep the whole house clean."

"That isn't necessary, Margaret."

"But I really want to, Mr. Frederickson. And I'm going to start looking for a job first thing tomorrow morning."

"Every time you call me 'Mr. Frederickson,' I have to stop myself from turning around to see who you're talking to. Why don't you just call me Mongo. Nearly everybody else does." I held out the paper bag to her. "Here. I brought you coffee and a bagel. I hope you like cream cheese."

Her eyes went wide and filled with tears, and her hands trembled as she reached out for the bag. "Oh, thank you," she said in a quavering voice. "I am hungry, but I didn't dare ask . . ."

"Well, if you're still hungry after you eat that, I'll take you out for a proper breakfast. But if you can hold out, you might want to save your appetite. I'd like you to join me for Thanksgiving dinner at my favorite restaurant."

"Oh, my," she said in a small voice, looking down at the floor. She wiped her hands on the front of her frayed sweater as more tears came to her eyes, rolled down her leathery cheeks. "I can't go into a restaurant with you dressed like this."

"You're dressed just fine. The owner's a friend of mine. He won't object; if I thought he would, he wouldn't be a friend of mine, and that wouldn't be my favorite restaurant. I'll lend you some money, and tomorrow you can go out and buy some different clothes. For today, what you're wearing now is perfectly okay."

"Oh, Mr.—Mongo. It's too much! I've already said I'm going to pay you for letting me stay here. I can't take anything more from you."

"We want you to look good when you go job hunting, right? You can add it to your bill and pay me back in installments when you start working."

She choked back a sob, nodded, then wiped the tears from her eyes and looked up into my face. "Does this mean I'm . . . doing all right? You'll let me stay here a little while longer, until I get my job and apartment?"

"Let's take one day at a time, Margaret. Up to now, I'd say you're doing wonderfully. I'll be back to pick you up at two."

*   *   *

The Gentle Peacock was on Restau-
rant Row on 46th Street, not far from the Manhattan Chess Club. The
sight of a middle-aged woman in bag-lady clothes accompanied by a
middle-aged dwarf would have turned heads in most expensive restaurants around the country, but this was New York City, and people
barely glanced in our direction as Peter Dak, the owner, escorted us
to our seats at a table by the window and personally took our drink
orders. I ordered a scotch on the rocks, and Margaret asked for
iced tea.

"Oooh," Margaret sighed, closing her eyes and breathing deeply
through her nose. "There are so many wonderful smells in here!"

"This is a Thai restaurant, the best, and Thai cooking is all about
spices. Their special Thanksgiving dinner isn't exactly the traditional
turkey and stuffing with all the trimmings, but I think you'll enjoy it."

"Oh, I know I will. I've never eaten Thai food before, at least not
that I can remember. I can't remember too much, but I think I'd know
if I'd ever eaten food that smelled this good."

"What kinds of food do you remember eating, Margaret? Where do
you originally come from?"

She stared out the window for a few moments, as if searching for
her past in the ghostly reflections in the glass, then turned back to me
and said, "Down South. Atlanta. My parents died, and I think that's
when I came to New York City . . . Lord, it must have been twenty
or twenty-five years ago. Then I got sick. This kind of thing runs in my
family. The state couldn't find any of my relatives, so they put me in
a hospital. The doctors there put me on some kind of medication that
helped me to get my thoughts straight, and then they let me go. But
the medication made me sick to my stomach, and my mouth was dry
all the time, so I stopped taking it. The rest of my life during all those
years is just kind of a blurry soup with bright spots of color and sounds
floating around in it. I remember terrible things happening to me in
the shelters, and I remember feeling this awful rage in me all of the
time. I remember living on that grate, and cursing at people . . . and,
of course, I remember you. But it's impossible for me to describe how
I *felt*, other than angry all the time, or how I saw things that were going
on around me. Most of the time I couldn't tell whether what I saw was
real or imagined. I'm still not sure what was real and what was

imagined. I heard voices. Now I know the voices were only in my mind, because they're not there any longer, but they certainly seemed real at the time."

"I understand."

"I guess maybe I don't really want to remember, because most of what I do remember makes me hurt and feel ashamed."

"Then we won't talk about it. You said the state couldn't find any of your relatives; that doesn't mean you don't have any. Do you think you might still have some family living?"

"I suppose so, back down South."

"Maybe they can help you now."

"I don't think so. I went to live with an aunt and uncle right after my folks died, but we didn't get along. They were the ones who suggested I move away in the first place. I've probably got cousins, or whatever, but I don't see how they'd want to help me after all these years. Besides, I don't think I want to ask. I'll be all right, Mr. Mongo."

"Just Mongo, Margaret."

"All I need is a little time to get myself started. I know I can be a very capable person when I'm not out of my head."

"I believe that. You're also a remarkable person. I've spent some time around mentally ill people—my brother, Garth, once suffered a psychotic episode, and he was put in a hospital. With most outpatients, you can tell they're on some kind of medication, but you don't show any of the usual side—"

"Oh, I'm not on any medication," Margaret Dutton said quickly—perhaps, I thought, too quickly.

"You're not? Your doctor . . . ?"

"I'm not seeing any doctor," she interrupted tersely, averting her gaze. Suddenly she seemed tense and uncomfortable.

"Margaret, what's wrong?"

"Nothing. I'm just not seeing any doctor or taking any medication."

"How could that be, Margaret?" I pressed gently. "How else would you be able to function like you are? You've been living on a grate, dressed in rags, for the better part of the past two years. Now, suddenly, here you are, cleaned up and attractive, conversing with me in a perfectly rational manner. I've never heard of a person suffering the kinds of symptoms you showed making such a remarkable recovery without medication, and it's even more remarkable that it happened in such a short time. How do you explain it?"

I waited. Finally she looked back up at me, and in her pale violet eyes there was a kind of naked plea. And fear. "I can't explain it, Mongo," she said very softly, in a frightened child's voice. "I woke up yesterday morning and I . . . just *felt* better. The voices had stopped, and I just suddenly seemed to be able to think clearly. I knew I had to get up off the sidewalk, go someplace to get cleaned up, and start taking care of myself. That's all. The rest is like I told you. I went to the Salvation Army, and they let me take a shower and gave me these clothes. Then I left, not really knowing where I would go or what I planned to do; the only thing I knew for certain was that I didn't want to go to any shelter. Then night came, and I got cold and afraid. The only person I could think of who might help me was you. Your lights weren't on, so I sat on your stoop and waited for you to come home."

"So all of this—the silencing of the voices and your ability to think rationally—just *happened* to you overnight?"

"Yes. I know it sounds odd."

It sounded not only odd but totally unbelievable; her story bore no resemblance to any of the anecdotal reports of remission in schizophrenics I'd read in the psychiatric literature I'd perused when Garth was sick. But I certainly wasn't prepared to call Margaret Dutton a liar, and the anxiety and plea for belief and understanding in her eyes were so strong that I decided I wasn't going to ruin her mood and meal, which I was clearly threatening to do, by pressing her any harder. I changed the subject, complimenting her on how nice her hair looked.

I ordered the same thing for both of us, and the first course arrived almost immediately. It was a clear soup with a mint leaf floating on top and a few tiny pieces of chicken paddling around near the bottom. But the fact that you could see the bottom of the bowl was the only clear thing about this soup, which contained a dozen ingredients, required hours of simmering for proper preparation, and produced on the palate a slowly unfolding, silent explosion of subtly blended flavors.

"Oooh," she exclaimed once again after she had first smelled the bouquet, then taken her first taste of the soup. "There are so many wonderful things in this—I mean, besides the chicken."

"You've got that right. Like it?"

"Oh, yes." She took another sip, closed her eyes, slowly swallowed. "Besides the chicken, I can taste the basil, pork, at least three different kinds of fish, and maybe nineteen or twenty spices I don't know the names of."

I blinked, set down my soup spoon, leaned back in my chair, and studied her. In the soup there were indeed chicken, basil, pork, at least three different kinds of fish, and nineteen or twenty spices I didn't know the names of either. I was suitably impressed. "Margaret, you can actually smell and taste all those things separately?"

"Well, Mongo, I just did, didn't I?" she replied in a strong voice as she beamed proudly. "I can smell all sorts of things. For instance, your friend who owns this place is wearing an aftershave lotion that's very strong. I don't know what it's called, but it smells like lemons and limes. He must like citrus smells, because the soap he uses smells like oranges. When you came in to see me this morning, I could tell that you'd showered with Dial soap and used witch hazel as an aftershave."

Well, now. I hadn't smelled anything on Peter, and I was surprised she could pick out anything as banal as aftershave lotion among all the pungent, exotic aromas in the restaurant—but I did use witch hazel as an aftershave, precisely because its bouquet didn't linger long, and I didn't like to smell like a perfume factory. And I had washed with Dial soap. I said, "That's very impressive, Margaret. You've got quite a sniffer on you."

She nodded in agreement, then brushed back a strand of gray hair that had fallen across her eyes. "I know. Sometimes it isn't so much fun. There are a lot of bad smells in the city, but I'm learning how to kind of ignore the really nasty ones and concentrate on the nice ones, like bakeshop smells."

"Have you always had this ability?"

"Oh, no. Only since yesterday morning. I started to get real good at smelling things at the same time I started to feel better."

By the time we ended our meal with simple orange sherbet and mint tea, my initial surprise and curiosity surrounding Margaret Dut-

ton's olfactory acumen had turned to utter astonishment. All through
the six courses following the soup she had carried on a running
commentary on the ingredients in the dishes, many of which she could
name, most of which she couldn't; when she couldn't identify some
particular taste or smell, she would content herself with telling me
just how many ingredients were in that particular dish. I didn't care
to interrupt the flow of our meal by constantly calling Peter over to
verify her proclamations, but I knew enough about Thai cooking to
suspect she was right about most of the ingredients she could name.
As I paid the bill, I mused on the fact that Mama Spit not only had
undergone what seemed a near-miraculous, overnight transformation
from raving psychotic to a thoroughly pleasant and lucid woman by
the name of Margaret Dutton, but also had turned into something akin
to a human bloodhound.

CHAPTER 3

*O*n Friday morning I lent Margaret two hundred dollars to go out and buy herself underwear and some changes of clothing from what she was wearing. And I told her to be very careful; during the night the ice-pick killer had claimed two more victims, one on a street in the Bronx and another at a subway stop in lower Manhattan.

She returned before noon with a good basic wardrobe of corduroy slacks, a skirt, a print dress, two blouses, changes of underwear, sturdy but comfortable shoes, and a cloth coat, all of which she'd bought at a church thrift shop on the Bowery. She even brought me back change. She'd also found herself a job, just as she'd said she would, responding to a Help Wanted sign posted on a building on Seventh Avenue, in the garment district. I recognized the address, and didn't like it; it was a sweatshop turning out knockoff designer jeans, no place for Margaret. I told her she could work for me, as my secretary's office assistant, until we could come up with something better, perhaps a job utilizing her extraordinary senses of taste and smell, which had to be of value to *some* enterprise, perhaps a perfume manufacturer or product-testing laboratory. I would pay her what I paid the temporaries Francisco occasionally hired when the paperwork in the office began to pile up. In addition, I would provide her with room and board and forgo payments on her loan, which she insisted she would repay, until she had saved enough money to go out on her own. In the meantime, I would check with some of the city officials I knew and inquire into the availability of low-income housing. The only proviso was that she would have to sleep in a spare bedroom in my apartment if and when Garth and Mary were in the city and wanted to use their apartment. She was grateful, and it took me fifteen minutes to get her to stop crying. Despite my protestations and reminders that she already had a job, Margaret insisted that she was going to spend the weekend scrub-a-dubbing the house from top to bottom. By the time she had finished, the brownstone was cleaner than the professional cleaning service had left it when Garth and I had first bought the property. I almost felt as if I were exploiting the woman, and I suspected I was going to miss Margaret Dutton when she moved on.

On Monday morning she was downstairs at the office promptly at nine o'clock to meet Francisco, who proceeded to teach her how to use the multi-line telephone and do a little basic filing. I went back into my own private office to prepare for an eleven o'clock meeting with the board of directors of a corporation for which Garth and I had been doing some in-depth vetting of potential CEOs. There was a fax from Garth, who for some reason had assumed I would be away over the weekend. My brother usually wasn't very particular about what he wore, but a monthlong skiing vacation in Zermatt, with its glitzy après-ski nightlife, was apparently bringing out the finicky in him; the good news was that he was indeed learning how to ski and hadn't broken anything yet; the bad news was that he had forgotten to pack a favorite sweater, which he believed was in the apartment in the brownstone, and he didn't see how he could possibly manage to make it to New Year's without it. Would I send it to him? Well, sure. I couldn't have my brother skiing and partying in Zermatt half naked.

I finished typing and reviewing the report I was to give, then trotted up to Garth's apartment. It didn't take me long to explore the drawers and closets and determine that the sweater he wanted wasn't there, but when I turned to leave the bedroom I noticed something that was there, and it disturbed me very much. I went over to the nightstand next to the bed where Margaret had been sleeping and picked up a plastic bag containing perhaps two dozen or more rather large black-and-yellow capsules which resembled nothing so much as a pile of dead mutant bumblebees with their heads, wings, and legs chopped off. I shook my head in frustration, then punched the intercom on the wall. When Francisco answered, I asked him to send Margaret up to see me. Then I went into the living room and sat down on the sofa with a sigh.

She saw the bag of pills in my hand as soon as she entered, and the blood drained from her face. "Oh, dear," she said in a small voice, putting a hand to her mouth.

"Sit down, Margaret," I said, indicating a chair directly across from me. "I need to talk to you."

She slowly came across the room and sank down in the armchair, clasping her hands in her lap. She had begun to gnaw at her lower lip, and her pale violet eyes were fixed on the bag of capsules. "I haven't taken one yet today," she said in the same small, weak voice.

"What are these, Margaret?"

"I . . . don't know."

"You lied to me, Margaret. You told me you weren't on medication. Why?"

Now she looked up into my face, and her eyes swam with the same fear I had first glimpsed in the restaurant on Thanksgiving when I had started to question her. "It's not like medication, Mongo. I mean, I didn't get those from a doctor."

"Where did you get them?"

She again put a trembling hand to her mouth, and her eyes filled with tears. "I'm not supposed to tell. I was warned not to tell anybody about the pills, or something very bad would happen."

"Something very bad has already happened, Margaret. If a doctor didn't give these to you, then they're probably illegal—some street drug you brought into my home. I have a very special hatred for street drugs, Margaret; they cripple, and they kill. There's no telling what this stuff is, or what it can do to you. You're a guest in my home, and that makes me responsible for what you do here and what happens to you. It also makes me responsible in the eyes of the law for what you bring in here. You say you don't know what these are? The drug doesn't have a name?"

She shook her head.

"How did you get these pills? You don't have any money, so you couldn't have paid for them."

"A man gave them to me just before the young people caught him. They killed him and threw him away."

Her voice had grown even fainter and slightly hoarse, so I wasn't sure I'd heard her correctly. "What?"

"I was sitting in my blankets on the grate, Mongo, like always. It was last Tuesday night. The streetlight was broken, and it was dark. I was still awful crazy then, so I can't remember everything exactly the way it happened, but I'm sure it was real. I'm sure it really happened. The pills prove that, don't they?"

"Tell me what happened, Margaret."

"A man came running around the corner and up the block toward me. He stopped in the middle of the block and looked around, like he was afraid of something, or somebody was chasing him. Then he saw me in the shadows and came running over to me. I started spitting and cursing, and I even hit him in the face when he put his hands on me, but it didn't do any good. He looked real scared, but he also looked determined, like he was going to do something to me no matter what I did to him. That made me real scared. He took that bag of pills out of his coat pocket. Then he put one of them in my mouth. I didn't want to swallow it, but he put one hand over my nose and mouth so I couldn't spit it out or breathe, and he rubbed my throat with his other hand. That made me swallow the pill. Then he put the bag under my blanket. I started spitting and cursing at him again, but he held my head in his hands and spoke real loud and slow in my ear so I had to hear what he told me. He said I'd feel better after taking the pill, and that I should remember to take one at the same time every day if I wanted to keep feeling better. He said I shouldn't tell anybody about the pills, or something bad would happen to me. I don't know for certain if what I heard next was the man talking or one of the voices in my head, but I seem to remember him saying something about meeting some woman under a Christmas tree, and she'd give me more of the pills. Then he started running up the block, but he stopped when he saw this boy standing on the corner up ahead of him. Then this girl comes around the corner at the other end of the block, and they both start walking toward the man. He tried to run across the street, but the boy cut him off. He kept trying to run away, but the kids—they looked like teenagers—kept cutting him off. Finally they grabbed him. The girl took something out of her purse and put it to the back of his head. I think it was a gun. I didn't hear any shot, but I think she killed him; he slumped all of a sudden, like he was dead, and the kids had to hold him up by his arms. They dragged him away into the next block. I couldn't see much by just the light from the streetlamps, but it looked like they just kind of threw him away. They tossed him into the air, and he disappeared."

I sighed, averting my gaze from the woman's pain-filled eyes, glanced down at the bag of capsules, which suddenly seemed to weigh very heavily in my hand. My good intentions had bitten me on the bottom, and I was greatly saddened. Margaret Dutton's apparent resurrection from madness hadn't been so miraculous after all, had in fact represented only a transition from one psychotic state to another which, in its way, was even more bizarre than her Mama Spit persona. Her story about being given the capsules by a man who was then shot and "thrown away" by a couple of teenagers was obviously a fantasy. Margaret Dutton was still delusional, which probably meant that her ugly alter ego was lurking just below the surface, waiting to spit, as it were, into action. I had no training in psychiatric nursing, the brownstone was no mental hospital, and I would be doing her absolutely no favors by keeping her with me. I couldn't let her keep the capsules, I couldn't, for both our sakes, allow her to keep living in Garth's apartment, and I couldn't simply toss her back into the rough ocean of the streets. Just exactly what I was going to do with Mama Spit was something I was going to have to think on.

"We're going to have to discuss this further, Margaret," I said, rising off the couch and heading for the door. "But not now. I have to go to a meeting. I don't want you to worry; I'll see that you're taken care of. You can go back to work now, if you want to. If you're too upset to work, you can just stay up here and rest. We'll talk more later, or in the morning."

I went up to my apartment and locked the bag of black-and-yellow capsules in my safe. Then I walked the ten blocks to my corporate client's headquarters on Avenue of the Americas. The board of directors was impressed with my report, but had in fact already decided on their choice even before I delivered her clean bill of health. They gave me a generous check, and I was out in less than forty-five minutes.

It wasn't yet noon. There was plenty of work to do back at the office, and I had tentatively planned to take a late-afternoon flight to Pittsburgh to take the preliminary steps in a HUD investigation that had been farmed out to Garth and me by a Senate subcommittee. But the situation with Margaret Dutton was forcing a change in my travel plans, and I didn't want to go back to the office, for fear I would have to spend the rest of the day looking at the anxiety and supplication that were so clearly mirrored in the woman's expressive eyes. I hadn't even started to think about what I was going to do with her, and so I decided to play hooky for the rest of the day.

Normally, having not found Garth's missing sweater in his apartment, I would have called or faxed to tell him to forget it, that he'd just have to make do between now and New Year's with the half dozen or so other sweaters he'd taken with him. But the sun was shining, the wind was up, it was surprisingly mild for late November, and the water in the Hudson would still be relatively warm compared to the air; the possibility of getting in just one more sail on my brother's fourteen-foot catamaran was too great a temptation to resist, and the quest for Garth's sweater was just the excuse I needed to remove myself from the city and my distractions.

I drove out of New York and up the Palisades Parkway to Garth and Mary's home in Cairn, a small, very artsy town on the banks of the Hudson thirty-four miles to the north. I found the sweater he wanted in the bottom drawer of a dresser in his bedroom, threw it on the back seat of my Volkswagen Rabbit. Then I stripped and put on the black rubber wet suit I kept there, went down to the boathouse beneath the eaves of the music room, then huffed and puffed the cat down across the beach to the shoreline. I set sail, and with eighteen-knot winds was soon streaking across the vast expanse of river between Haverstraw and Piermont that the early Dutch settlers had dubbed the "Tappan Sea." There was nobody and nothing else on the river, and conditions were ideal, if perhaps just a bit nippy. I whizzed back and forth across the river between Cairn and Westchester for almost four hours, dumping only once when a wind shift crossed my stern while I was flying a hull. I ran the cat back up on the beach behind Garth's home just as the blood-red sun was sinking behind the craggy, black outline of Hook Mountain, to the south.

I felt at once completely relaxed yet exhilarated. I took a long, hot shower, then drove south to Nyack for dinner and a movie at Cinema East. By the time I got out of the movie and headed back toward the city I was ready for sleep, for I had decided what I was going to do about Margaret Dutton.

First, I would turn the capsules I had taken from her over to the police, who would probably tell me they were some new kind of illicit drug; how and where Mama Spit had gotten them would undoubtedly remain a mystery, for she obviously couldn't remember. Then it was going to be time for a lot of tender, loving care and attention to the woman's needs. Margaret would no doubt be disappointed in me for in effect turning her out, but it was my hope that she would continue to trust me; as long as I stayed by her side and walked her through the process every step of the way, I thought she might at last be amenable to letting the city's Social Services Department help her. I was going to have a serious chat with a social worker friend of mine to map out a detailed plan for getting Margaret into a controlled clinical setting and keeping her there, at least until she was officially released as an outpatient under the supervision of doctors. And Frederickson and Frederickson would subsidize some of the cost, if it came to that.

When I got home I barely had enough energy to brush my teeth and strip down to my shorts before collapsing into bed, pulling the blankets up over me, and immediately falling asleep. I didn't sleep long. Muffled screams and what sounded like crashing, overturned furniture first materialized in my mind as a dream about the demolition of some theater where there were still people inside, and then yanked me into consciousness when I realized the sounds were real, coming up through the floor from Garth's apartment below me. I jumped out of bed and without even stopping to pull on my pants raced out of the apartment and down the stairs, through the door of Garth's apartment, and into the bedroom. What I saw stunned and horrified me.

Mama Spit had returned with a vengeance. The flannel nightgown I had bought her was half torn from her body and hanging from her shoulders in shreds. Her hair tangled and matted with sweat, Margaret Dutton was once again caught in the throes of madness. Alternately screaming and muttering obscenities, she was slapping at her body and stomping her feet as she slowly circled the nightstand, which she had placed in the center of the room. She would occasionally halt her mad dance and snatch at the empty space on the wooden table where her bag of capsules had been before I'd taken them away. The bedspread and carpet were spattered with blood; bright crimson arterial blood oozed from her eyes, ears, nose, mouth, vagina, and anus. Margaret Dutton not only had snapped back into violent insanity but was slowly bleeding to death from every orifice in her body.

She glanced over to where I was standing just inside the doorway gaping at her, paralyzed with shock. She screamed, spat blood in my direction, and charged, but by then I was already on the move. Heart pounding, thoughts tumbling around in my mind in a kind of prayer that I knew what was wrong and was not too late, I sprinted back up the stairs to my apartment, my safe. For a few terrifying moments I couldn't remember the combination, and I forced myself to stop and take a series of deep breaths to calm myself. The combination came to me. I opened the safe, grabbed the bag of capsules, and raced back downstairs.

I took her low, around the waist, literally tackling her and driving her back on the bed. There I climbed up on top of her and sat on her chest, pinning her arms to her body with the insides of my thighs—no easy task since she was thrashing wildly, probably weighed as much as I did, and was a foot taller. As she opened her mouth to scream at me, I popped one of the capsules down her throat. Then, just as her first benefactor had done, I clamped one hand over her mouth and used the fingers of the other to gently knead her esophagus, encouraging her to swallow. She finally did, and then I lay down on top of her, wrapping my arms around her body to keep her from flailing, burying my face to the side in the bloody bedding to avoid the fusillades of blood and saliva that spewed from her mouth. I held on tight and waited for something to happen—or stop happening.

Gradually she stopped struggling, and her breathing became deep and regular. I carefully eased my weight off her, raised my head to look into her face. She was sound asleep, and the bleeding from her eyes, ears, nose, and mouth appeared to have stopped. I rose and went into the bathroom, looked at myself in the mirror, and saw that I was covered with Margaret Dutton's blood. I turned on the shower, used towels soaked with warm water to gently clean the sleeping woman's face and body as best I could, then covered her with a clean blanket.

I hurried upstairs, quickly showered and pulled on sweats, hurried back downstairs. Margaret Dutton was still fast asleep. The woman had lost a considerable amount of blood, and under normal circumstances I would already have called an ambulance. But I was not dealing with normal circumstances. Until I understood what was happening, and until I could determine exactly what was in the black-and-yellow capsules, I was very reluctant to involve anyone else, especially medical personnel or the police. Notifying the authorities might not at all be in Margaret's best interests; something very bad might happen, just as the man who had given her the capsules had predicted.

I pulled a chair over next to the bed and sat down in it to wait and watch over Margaret until morning.

CHAPTER 4

argaret awoke around ten o'clock looking very tired and pale, and with two swollen black eyes—the only external legacy, as far as I could see, of the copious amount of blood that had leaked from her during the night. "Oh, my," she sighed in a hoarse, small voice as she turned her head and saw me.

"Are you all right, Margaret?"

"I . . . I don't know. I feel so tired, Mongo. I don't know what's wrong with me. I had . . . this terrible nightmare."

"Yeah. Me too. I know about your nightmare, Margaret. I shared it. That's why I'm here."

She pulled back the blanket covering her, started to try to get out of bed, stopped when she saw the blood-soaked bedding beneath her. "Oh," she said in the same weak voice. "I must have gotten my monthly. I'm sorry."

"There's nothing for you to be sorry about. I'm the one who's sorry."

"But I've ruined your sheets and blankets. And I think I'm late for work."

"Don't you worry about the sheets and blankets; I've got more. And you're not going to work. I'm your boss, and I'm ordering you to take the day off. I'm going to change the bed and give you one of Garth's sweatshirts to wear, and then I want you to get right back into bed and stay there. I have things to do, but I'll have Francisco look in on you

from time to time, and he'll bring you your meals. If you need anything, just press the blue button on that intercom on the wall next to
you. That will connect you to the office downstairs, and Francisco will
come right up, or take care of whatever it is you need. Okay?"

Her swollen eyes went wide. "Something bad happened, didn't it?"

"Yes. Something very bad happened. I know now you were telling
the truth about what happened on the street and how you got the pills.
I apologize for not believing you, Margaret."

"But I was still crazy then. I don't know how much of what I told
you was real."

"I think it was all real enough." I paused, pointed to the bag of
capsules I had replaced on the nightstand after removing a few.
"There are your pills, Margaret. I've borrowed a couple, and I'll try to
put them to good use. The man who gave them to you was right when
he said you have to take one every day. I helped you take one during
the night while you were having your nightmare, so you might want to
wait until this evening before you take the next. Then be sure you
keep taking one every day at bedtime, until you hear differently
from me."

"Then you're . . . not going to make me leave right away?"

"No, Margaret, I'm not going to make you leave right away."

I gave her a bath towel to cover herself, helped her out of bed and
into the chair, then brought her one of my brother's old, baggy sweatshirts to wear as a nightgown. I changed the sheets and blankets, then
helped her back into bed and tucked her in. Her eyes were already
closing, but she seemed to be breathing and moving without pain or
undue difficulty, and I judged that she would be all right.

"Thank you, Mongo," she sighed.

"You're welcome. You should eat soon. Nap now, and Francisco
will wake you in a little while and give you some breakfast; I hope you
like liver, because that's what you need to eat. Then you can sleep as
long as you want. I'll see you later."

My first stop was a nearby commer-
cial testing laboratory owned and operated by a chemist and pharma-
cologist, Dr. Frank Lemengello, who was also a friend. The tall,

handsome, sad-eyed black man who was going into another room
when I entered the main office was not a friend; neither was he an
enemy, at least I didn't consider him one, but he was a bit more than
just an acquaintance. He was most certainly a victim, in this case of
his own past hubris, arrogance, and greed, aspects of his personality
that had been thoroughly squeezed out of him by the courts, serious
hang time on Rikers Island, and the opprobrium of his ex-colleagues
in academia.

Dr. Bailey Kramer had once been a rising star in the international
science firmament, a brilliant organic chemist lauded for his pioneer-
ing research on some curious chemical beasts called mega-long-chain
polymers. But Bailey Kramer had wanted to make some big money in
a short time, and he'd taken a hard fall. In the course of an investigation into industrial espionage in the pharmaceuticals industry,
Garth and I had uncovered the fact that Bailey Kramer, renowned
researcher, was also the brilliant sole creator and hopelessly inept
wholesale distributor of a certain illegal, cheap, and highly addictive
"designer drug," a new amphetamine, that had begun turning up on
ghetto streets around the country. We'd turned him in.

I had never seen an individual so thoroughly crushed, humiliated—and sincerely contrite, contrition being an exceedingly rare
quality in the usual kinds of people who are involved in the making,
buying, and selling of illegal drugs. Even the prosecutor had felt
pity—an even rarer quality among New York City prosecutors. After
agreeing to turn state's evidence and testify as a key witness against
the others involved, he had been given a relatively lenient sentence.
He had served time, been a model prisoner, and then been released
on early parole. I'd gotten him his present job after I'd discovered him
driving a taxicab, underemployment I'd considered a waste of knowledge and talent for society as well as Bailey Kramer. I didn't think
that Kramer had lost sight of what I'd done for him, but neither did I
think he'd forgotten what Garth and I had done *to* him. I could
understand how his feelings toward me might be mixed.

Not so his boss, who simply considered me a rather good fellow.
"Hey, Mongo!" Frank Lemengello boomed as he entered his office.
"How're you doing, my friend?"

"I'm doing the usual. How about yourself?"

"I'm doing the usual too. Bring more river water for me?"

"Not this time. What about Kramer? Is he working out?"

The burly scientist finished pumping my hand, then rolled his eyes toward the ceiling. "Are you kidding me? Model employee. He's working out just fine. But it sometimes feels strange having an assistant who knows ten times more about your work than you do. He's taught me a lot. I'm giving him top dollar for a technical lab assistant, but I can't afford to pay him what he's worth."

"Don't worry about it. There isn't that much demand in industry or the academic world for organic chemists who are also convicted drug dealers. Actually, he's probably making almost as much money with you as he did as a research professor, and he's making a hell of a lot more than he was as a taxi driver. Besides, he likes what he's doing."

"Bailey told you that?"

"He hasn't told me anything; he doesn't much like talking to me. But he's a scientist, and he's doing science, which is something he probably thought he'd never be doing again."

The heavily muscled, curly-haired scientist shrugged his broad shoulders. "What we do here is pretty cut-and-dried. It must be boring for him."

"He's got an attitude problem?"

"Not at all. Sometimes it's hard to tell if he has any attitudes or emotions. He's always polite, but he doesn't seem to care much to talk to me either, so we don't talk. I just let him go on about his business, which he does just fine. This a social visit, Mongo, or have you got something for me?"

"I've got this for you," I said, taking one of the black-and-yellow capsules out of my pocket and handing it to him.

He rolled the capsule back and forth between his fingertips, then examined it against one of the bright fluorescent lamps in the ceiling. "Hmm. No brand name on the casing, not even a lot number. The gel feels just a tad thicker and heavier than what most American manufacturers use. I'd guess this was made in Europe."

"Ever seen one like it before?"

"Nope. Black-and-yellow is an unusual color combination; can't say it looks very appetizing. Patients and drug addicts usually like whatever they're taking wrapped in more soothing colors."

"I haven't seen anything about black-and-yellow capsules in police or FBI bulletins. Have you seen anything like this mentioned in the trade or professional journals?"

"Nope, can't say I have. What do you think this is, some kind of medication, or a street drug?"

"That's what I'm hoping you'll be able to tell me. It could be either. I want you to tell me all the ingredients in that thing, and then give me your best guess as to what effect taking it could have on the human mind and body."

"Where'd you get it?"

"I'd rather not say right now, Frank. I wouldn't want to influence your analysis."

He stopped studying the capsule and looked at me, raising his thick eyebrows slightly. "What, are you kidding me? I'm a chemist, not a palm reader. My spectrograph doesn't give a damn where what I feed it comes from, it just gulps it down and burps readouts. But there are tests, and then there are other tests. If you could give me some idea of where it came from, it could give me a clue as to what it might be. That could save me time, and you money."

"I don't mind paying for your time, Frank," I said, turning and heading for the door. "Just run a full analysis on whatever is in that capsule, and give me your opinion on what it does. Can you have something for me tomorrow?"

"No problem."

"Thanks, Frank."

My next stop was the public library. I read *The New York Times* every day, but the *Times* wasn't big on reporting what it considered routine street crime in the city, and I had seen no mention of anybody being shot on 56th Street. With the mounting toll being taken by the ice-pick killer, whose victims, as of that morning, now numbered twenty-five, it was more than likely that one more old-fashioned shooting hadn't made the news. When I found no mention of any killing in my neighborhood in the Thanksgiving editions of the *Daily News* or *Post*, I reluctantly headed for the Midtown North precinct station house.

The commander of the precinct was one Captain Felix MacWhorter, and our relationship dated back to the days when Garth was an NYPD detective. MacWhorter hadn't liked Garth or me then, and he still didn't like us—the reason I had tried the library first. I didn't know why. I suspected there had been bad blood between Garth and MacWhorter over something, but Garth had never said anything to me about it, and I hadn't inquired, so I put it down to a personality conflict between two cops which, by reason of family ties, had included me. I had never exchanged more than a few words with the man, but I had always felt his hostility. I didn't plan on exchanging any words with him now. I was on my way to the desk to talk to the booking sergeant, who was a friend of mine, when MacWhorter spotted me through the glass wall of his nearby office, rushed out, and intercepted me in the middle of the stained tile floor. I hadn't done more than walk into the building, and already I could see that he was angry. His green eyes flashed, the tendons in his thick neck were straining at his shirt collar, and his face and the flesh of his scalp showing through his close-cut, thinning brown hair were pink.

"What do you want, Frederickson?" the big man growled.

"Take it easy, Captain. I'm just visiting my local outpost of peace-keepers."

"We're a little busy, and we don't give tours. I don't want you in here wasting the time of any of my men."

"Hey, hang on a minute. I'm a taxpaying citizen, I don't have any outstanding parking tickets, and I have as much right to come in here as anybody else."

"Other taxpaying citizens aren't all private investigators who are always trying to use the police station as a reference library whenever they want some information. And other private investigators don't suck up to cops and ask the cops to do their work for them."

"You must have this confused with another planet, Captain. Every private investigator I know sucks up to cops all the time, and most of them, including my brother, used to *be* cops. If we couldn't get cooperation from the police from time to time, we'd all be out of business. Sometimes that cooperation works both ways. So why the attitude, MacWhorter? How come you've got such a hard-on for Garth and me?"

Shadows moved in MacWhorter's emerald eyes. "The Frederickson brothers just piss me off. The media thinks both of you walk on water."

"You've never seen us do that?"

He was not amused. "If a cop fires his gun at a suspect in self-defense during the commission of a crime, he's more than likely to end up before some civilian review board. The two of you leave corpses piled up all over the world, and you're treated like heroes. The cops solve thousands of crimes a year, and most of the time we get shit on; you bust two or three off-the-wall cases, and you wind up rich and famous. Now the two of you don't even get your hands dirty; you spend all your time doing donkey work for fat-cat corporations and collecting fat fees. If your brother had any real balls, he'd still be a cop, instead of a pussy who went running to you when he got into trouble and ended up cashing in big as your partner."

I glanced around me. Cops, perps, and suspected perps had all stopped whatever they had been doing and were staring at the sight of a six-foot-two-inch, two-hundred-twenty-plus police captain and a dwarf carrying on a one-sided, heated colloquy in the center of the station house. Angel Gonzalez, the booking sergeant, averted his gaze and bowed his head slightly in embarrassment. Captain Felix MacWhorter, who was obviously more than just a tad jealous of Garth, was looking to embarrass me, not Angel, but all he had managed to do by his reference to my brother was get me riled a bit.

"You've got your fat head up your fat ass, MacWhorter," I replied in a voice that wasn't as loud as his but was of sufficient volume to be heard by everyone. "If the NYPD hadn't thrown Garth to the wolves, he'd still be a cop—and I'd have been killed a long time ago. Garth had the guts to stand up to a bunch of corrupt Feds, and the NYPD brass didn't. First they caved, and then they cut Garth loose. My guess is that you don't have a clue about what happened back then, so I don't want to hear any more of your horseshit. Fuck you and have a nice day. I'll take my business downtown."

"Hey, Frederickson!" MacWhorter shouted as I headed for the door, smiling at a couple of hookers who were sitting on a bench to my left, staring at me. When I didn't react, he tried again, louder. "*Frederickson!*"

Now I stopped, turned back. MacWhorter's face and scalp had gone from pink to a beet red, which gave me a certain satisfaction. He was apparently tired of crossing words with me in public, because he

motioned with his head toward his office. I went in. He followed
behind me, shut the door and closed the blinds, then turned to where
I stood, leaning against his desk.

"I know you've got friends in all sorts of high places, including One
Police Plaza," he continued. "Do you really think I give a shit if you
go over my head to get whatever it is you want?"

There was still fury in his voice, but he'd turned down the sound
level, and that was a welcome relief. "You don't know whether I want
anything, Captain," I replied quietly. "You never bothered to ask.
You just went apeshit when you saw me. You keep losing it like that,
and One PP is going to be packing you off to a police shrink."

MacWhorter continued to glare at me, but the green fire in his eyes
gradually cooled. He took a deep breath, then abruptly brushed past
me and sat down behind his desk. "You want something. What is it?"

"I just came in to verify that a man's body was found within a block
or two of my home a week ago, last Tuesday night. That's something
any citizen would want to know. He would have been shot. I checked
in the papers, but there wasn't any mention of it."

"Did you see it happen?"

"No. If I had, I'd have reported it."

"Then how do you know a man was shot—if a man was shot?"

Now I had to be very careful what I said. Becoming an NYPD
commanding officer is not the easiest thing in the world. MacWhorter
might be a hothead on occasion, and harbor all sorts of twisted feelings about Garth and me, but I knew from casual conversations with
other cops that he could also be cold and calculating. His irrational
outburst in the other room notwithstanding, he was by no means a
stupid man. There might not be much hair on his head, but there
wasn't any moss growing there either. This could be round two of the
fight he had tried to pick with me a few moments before, a variation
on a theme. There were all sorts of nasty rhythms, like obstruction of
justice or withholding evidence or even illegal possession of a dangerous drug, MacWhorter would almost certainly love to tap out on my
skull if given the opportunity, and I was going to have to do some
serious bobbing and weaving if I hoped to act in the best interests of
my houseguest.

If the police, or any other city agency, found out about whatever it was Margaret Dutton was taking, the black-and-yellow capsules would undoubtedly be confiscated pending analysis and investigation, and no amount of pleading or claims that without them she would suddenly plummet back into madness and spontaneously bleed to death would be heeded—until it was too late. And there was no doubt in my mind that that was exactly what would happen to the woman if she did not ingest a capsule every twenty-four hours. She would die. Horribly.

"Frederickson?" MacWhorter continued quietly. "It seems a simple enough question. What's taking you so long to answer it? What makes you think a man was shot in your neighborhood last Tuesday night?"

"Somebody saw it."

MacWhorter raised his eyebrows slightly. "An eyewitness? Who?"

"Mama Spit," I replied evenly, watching him.

His lips drew back from his teeth in a thin, wry smile, but there was no hint of amusement in his eyes. "Mama Spit? You've got to be kidding me. Mama Spit wouldn't recognize her own hand if she was holding it in front of her face."

"Even schizophrenics can have their lucid moments, Captain."

"Oh, can they? Well, thank you, Dr. Frederickson. I didn't realize your degree was in medicine."

"You know it isn't."

"Did Mama Spit say Martians did it?"

"She said a couple of teenagers did it—a boy and a girl. They might be young, but they were cool and professional. They trapped him, pinched him in when they came at him from opposite ends of the block. So now, if there was somebody killed on my block, you have a description of the killers."

MacWhorter was no longer smiling. Now he was studying me very carefully, like a cobra measuring a small, furry candidate for lunch. I hoped I could successfully play mongoose. "If Mama Spit is the eyewitness, why isn't she here?"

"Like you said, most of the time she wouldn't recognize her own hand. Schizophrenics may have their lucid moments, but they're still only moments."

"And she told you all this during one of those lucid moments?"

"Yes."

"If Mama Spit saw these killers, why didn't they see her? Why didn't they kill her?"

"It's possible they didn't see her; the streetlight was out, and she was back in the shadows. Or maybe they did see her, but weren't worried about some homeless woman who was probably crazy."

MacWhorter mulled it over for a time while he drummed his fingers on the desk, finally said, "All right, Frederickson, there was a man killed in your neighborhood last Tuesday night. He was shot once in the back of the head, and then tossed into the Dumpster in the street down by Carnegie Hall."

So Mama Spit had been absolutely right when she'd said he'd been tossed into the air and disappeared, been thrown away. I said, "It sounds like a professional job, an assassination. Did you find the slug?"

"Twenty-two, but tinkered with to lower mass and velocity. It didn't even exit from the skull."

"No mess."

"That's right."

"Unusual. Definitely the work of pros."

"I'd say so."

"What was the victim's name?"

"Unknown. If he had any identification, his killers took it with them. He had a dollar and seventeen cents in his pockets."

"What about his clothes?"

"Not exactly designer label. He wasn't killed for his money."

"Fingerprints?"

"No match with anything on file."

"Age?"

"Around fifty. Caucasian."

"Did the M.E. do an autopsy?"

"On a homeless stiff with a bullet hole at the base of his skull? They cut him to remove the bullet, but that's all. Why do you ask? It sound to you like he might have been poisoned?"

"Sorry. It was a stupid question. Thanks for your time, Captain."

"Hold on, Frederickson."

I'd made it as far as the door, and when I turned back I didn't at all like what I saw. Captain Felix MacWhorter had a very hard look on his round, florid face, and that did not bode well. It seemed I was not a very clever mongoose; I had been all too willing to meander into close quarters with this dangerous opponent, lulled by his seeming reasonableness and willingness to share information. I had asked too many questions too soon, and now he was loaded up with a few sharp questions of his own. I smiled. "What is it, Captain?"

"You lied to me," he said in a voice that had suddenly gone as cold as his eyes.

"I lied to you? I don't know you well enough, or like you enough, to lie to you."

"You told me you came in here to find out if a man had been killed near your place last Tuesday night. I told you there was. If you'd been telling the truth, that should have been the end of the matter. But you verify that there's been a homicide victim, and then you *really* start asking questions. Christ, you even want to know if there's been an autopsy."

"Just idle curiosity."

"Bullshit. You're working a case, Frederickson, some angle, just like you and your brother usually are when you stop by here to see if the police can make things easier for you. I want to know what you're working on, including the name of your client, and I want to know what you think it may have to do with this particular homicide. I want to know why you're in here asking all sorts of questions about a murder victim who ended up with a city Dumpster for his grave."

"I'm not working on any case," I replied evenly. "There's nobody paying me any money to look into this, and I'm not sticking my nose into any police business. I investigate things for a living, and when something like this happens virtually on my doorstep, I just get naturally curious."

"More bullshit. I know as sure as I know my ass is sitting in this chair that there's something you're not telling me, something I should know. That's obstruction of justice, and I don't have to tell you that's a serious matter. Actually, I think I'll be rather glad if it turns out you're trying to fuck me around, because I'd love to nail you. Somebody should have clipped the wings of the high-flying, shithead Frederickson brothers a long time ago."

This dim-witted mongoose's mental feet were getting tired from all the tap dancing I was having to do in front of the venomous fangs flashing in my face, but I just kept smiling; the object now was safe retreat, not to trade insults with the mysteriously—but seriously— aggrieved Felix MacWhorter. "You've got both Garth and me wrong, Captain. I don't understand why you're so hostile. Did Garth do something to you? I know I didn't. So where's all this pique and piss coming from?"

"Where's Mama Spit?"

"I don't know what's happened to Mama Spit," I replied evenly, considering this a not completely untruthful statement.

"You're lying!"

"Damn it, MacWhorter, if you think I'm lying, go check out her grate for yourself. You know which one it is. Maybe witnessing the killing unnerved her. For whatever reason, Mama Spit has moved on. If you don't mind, I'd like to move on too."

"I know you're lying to me, Frederickson. If I find out you're stunting on this one, if I catch you withholding evidence and ob- structing justice, I'll have your license. And I'll press charges. I'll bring you down."

"Have a nice day, Captain."

I used a pay phone on the corner to call the office to see if Margaret was all right. Francisco had just left her; she'd eaten breakfast, including some liver, and was now sleep- ing. Her pulse wasn't exactly beating at jackhammer level, but it was steady. I thanked Francisco, hung up, and then, as if I didn't have other, more important things to ponder, I thought about Captain Felix MacWhorter as I rode the subway downtown to Washington Square Park.

I couldn't understand MacWhorter's animosity. The one man who would know if there was a valid reason, my brother, hadn't seen fit to discuss the matter with me when I'd once asked him about it, so I'd subtly checked around with other cops. The line on MacWhorter was that he could undermine his considerable intelligence by being pig- headed, but for the most part he was a good cop, respected and honest, one who'd never been involved in any scandal or charged with corruption. He ran a clean operation in the most high-profile precinct in the city, and any cop who wanted to make a little extra money on the side by going on the pad was well advised to steer clear of his command. He certainly had nothing to fear from Garth or me, and he didn't seem like the type to be so apparently jealous of an ex-cop's good fortune, so I figured maybe he was just overreacting in an attempt to protect his turf from a notorious set of brothers with a residence in his precinct and whom he must perceive as smart-ass interlopers and headline grabbers.

My concern with MacWhorter's hostility was for professional reasons, not personal. Private investigators do indeed need to keep lines open to the police for information that might not be available to reporters or the public, but, as I'd told the commander, providing useful information was a two-way street, and it was not unusual for a private investigator involved in a criminal case to provide the police with important leads they might not otherwise have found, or which would have proven expensive and time-consuming in terms of man-hours to develop. MacWhorter knew this as well as anyone, but in my case he had made it clear he did not want to play the game.

It wasn't that I didn't have a goodly number of reliable and friendly police sources in the five boroughs, including uniforms and detectives in Midtown North, who were happy to barter information with me. But MacWhorter was the precinct commander in *my* neighborhood, and I wanted to be able to freely approach him when the need arose. Perhaps it was simply a matter of local pride, in addition to the fact that I didn't need any NYPD captain angry with me and constantly looking over my shoulder.

I was finally able to put MacWhorter out of my mind when I reached the Washington Square Park station. I emerged from underground into bright, cold sunlight and walked to the southwest corner, where I found Theo Barnes and his "protégé" with the brown hair, high forehead, and plastic shoes sitting at adjacent stone chess tables hustling tourists just as I'd known they would be. I stayed back for a time and watched.

The "protégé" was now wearing a threadbare wool jacket that I recognized as Barnes's over the same Hawaiian print shirt, also belonging to Barnes, I'd seen him wearing the week before at the Manhattan Chess Club. If anything, he was even faster on the chess clock—actually a two-faced clock with a separate push-button control for each player—than Barnes, who was no slowpoke, moving his hand with lightning speed to stop his clock and start his opponent's each time he completed a move. He may have been playing in a beginners' tournament at the Manhattan club, but he looked to me to be no less skilled than his mentor; during the half hour or so that I watched him, he easily dispatched seven opponents, pocketing a five-dollar bill each time. Only once did I observe more than three minutes elapse on his clock. Finally I stepped out from behind the tree where I had been standing and lined up behind three two-legged pigeons, two men and a woman, waiting to challenge Theo Barnes.

"Your money's no good here, Frederickson," Barnes said as my turn came and I stepped up to the table. He didn't even look at me as he returned the pieces to their starting positions on the board. "Go play somebody else—unless you're willing to give me the odds I mentioned before. My five minutes to your one, fifty bucks a game."

"Let me see if I can't change your attitude toward my money," I said, reaching for my wallet. I found a ten-dollar bill and laid it out on the stone battlefield between the marshaled white and black armies. "Here's ten bucks, twice what you'd normally win in one game. A game between us would probably go the limit, ten minutes. So I'm willing to pay for ten minutes of your time, twice what you'd usually make."

"Five minutes," he said, picking up the bill and stuffing it into the pocket of his worn leather jacket. He pushed the button on his side of the two-faced clock, and the clock on my side started ticking. "That's all you'd have in a ten-minute game. The rest would be mine. So talk."

"Not here," I said, reaching out and stopping the clock.

"Hey!"

"At two bucks a minute, I want to be able to savor the sound of your voice in relative privacy. Let's go sit down on a bench."

"I can't leave. I'll lose my table."

Click.

I went to my wallet again, took out two twenties. I held them up for Barnes to see, but did not put them down on the table. "I'll make it worth your while. Fifty bucks for you, and fifty for your partner over there if he'll talk to me too."

Click.

Barnes combed the fingers of both hands back through his long, stringy blond hair as he stared at the bills. "Where's the rest of the money?"

"That goes to your partner, if he'll talk to me. If you two have some kind of management agreement, you can work out the commission with him."

"All right," he said as he pushed his button, then snatched up the clock and started to walk away. "Let's go."

"Hey!" I shouted as I hurried after him. "Travel time shouldn't count! You should at least stop the clock while we're walking!"

"Time is money, Frederickson!" he called back over his shoulder. "It's going to take me a while to get my table back!"

I made sure we walked fast, but not far, a couple of dozen yards beyond the playing area, where all I had to compete with to be heard was a country band and two singing jugglers. We sat down on a stone bench, and Barnes placed the clock between us. I had four minutes left on my clock before the minute hand tripped the red flag at the top.

He held out his hand. "Let's have the rest of my money."

I gave him the two twenties, and quickly said, "First, I want to make sure you don't lie to me, Theo. I goddamn well know what you're up to. You've found yourself some very gifted but unknown natural talent, and you're giving him a crash course in what competitive chess is all about. You put him in that tournament at the Manhattan Chess Club to get him a provisional rating, but that rating is going to be well below his real strength. You're going to enter him in one of the lower-class sections at the New York Open, and you figure he has a good chance to win his section, even against the other sandbaggers who've been deliberately losing rated games and dropping their ratings for that tournament. You figure he's got a good chance to pocket eight thousand dollars, which I assume you'll share."

Click.

Theo Barnes didn't appreciate my observation, and blood rose to his pockmarked face. "You're full of shit, Frederickson. But even if you're right, I'm not doing anything illegal."

Smack.

"Right. But if I find out you've lied to me, I'll go to the tournament directors and blow the whole thing. They don't like sandbaggers. He'll be forced to enter the Open section, and he's not going to get very far playing against grandmasters. What's his name?"

Click.

"Michael."

Smack.

"Give me a break, Theo. Michael what?"

Click.

"Michael Stout."

Smack.

"Tell me about him."

Click.

Barnes laughed, then grinned at me as if he'd just executed some marvelous combination that would give him a forced checkmate. "You're not going to get much for your fifty bucks, Frederickson. I don't know a damn thing about him except his name, the fact that he's the most gifted natural chess player I've ever met, and he'd never played in a single tournament before he met me. Who gives a shit about anything else? He *will* win his section of the Open. You can bet on it. The people he'll be playing are probably two or three hundred rating points below him in real strength."

Click.

"Where does he come from?"

Click.

"I don't know."

Click.

"How did you meet him?"

Click.

"Your flag's going to fall pretty soon."

Click.

"It hasn't fallen yet. I'm paying big bucks for this little game, Theo, so answer the damn question."

Smack.

The chess hustler shrugged, then leaned back on the stone bench and crossed his legs. "He just came walking into the park a couple of weeks ago. He saw us playing, came over and stood around watching. He was wearing rags, and he looked like shit—scared, maybe a little dopey. But he was paying real close attention to what was going on. At first he was standing back quite a ways, but after a couple of hours he started coming closer—like a few inches at a time. He was real interested in the games. Finally he ended up actually standing between two tables, looking back and forth at the games on either side of him. We were busy playing, so nobody gave a shit where he stood as long as he didn't interfere with the paying customers. Then he lines up at the table where Buster Brown is playing. It comes his turn, and he takes sixty-seven cents out of his pocket and challenges Buster to a game. Can you believe it? Well, there's nobody else waiting, so Buster takes him on. Damned if the guy doesn't beat Buster."

Click.

"Buster isn't that strong."

Click.

"You've got that right. Buster's only a C, maybe low B player. But he talks trash, he's intimidating, and he's pretty good at speed chess, where the other guy is under pressure. Still, he's just been beaten by this dopey-looking guy, and we're all laughing our asses off at him. Buster Brown doesn't like that. He gives the guy sixty-seven cents, challenges him to play for double or nothing. They play again, the guy beats him again. Well, before you know it he's got ten bucks in his pocket. That's enough to interest me, so I challenge him to a game for the ten bucks, figuring I'll blow him away. Then the son of a bitch beats *me*! How would you rate my strength, Frederickson?"

Click.

Smack.

"Any questions you have get answered on your time, not mine. We've never played a serious game, but I'd rate your strength in the mid-nineteen hundreds, close to expert."

"I like you, Frederickson."

"I'm aware of that, Theo. You're a man who wears his heart on his sleeve."

"You're a player. You don't let the fact that you're little get you down."

"That's very good, Theo. A real howler."

"What?"

"Play me the rest of the story."

Barnes shrugged. "He ends up beating every one of us, over and over. By the time it got dark he's won close to a hundred and fifty dollars. Now we're not laughing anymore. Some of the other guys are getting downright pissy. Nobody hates being hustled more than a hustler, and that's what we figure he's been doing. I mean, like maybe this guy is a grandmaster from Liechtenstein or someplace like that, and he's come downtown to pick up some pocket money while he makes fools of the poor, dumb local yokels. Buster Brown's getting ready to clean his clock, but this guy—"

"Michael Stout."

"Yeah; that's who I'm talking about. He swears he hasn't played chess in years, not since he was a kid. He didn't say where he'd come from, only that he'd been kind of out of it—those were his words—for a long time. He swore he wasn't very good when he did play. He swore he'd never played in any tournaments, and had never heard of the United States Chess Federation or FIDE. By this time Buster Brown's got his fist up against the guy's nose, but the guy sticks to his story, says he doesn't have any idea why he's suddenly so good; he says he just discovered that afternoon that he was able to glance at a position on the board and know what each player had to do in order to defend or win. Well, who's going to believe a total bullshit story like that? Buster Brown still wants to punch his lights out. But, you know, there was something about him, something about the way he kept swearing that this fucking fairy tale was all true, that made me kind of start to think that maybe he was on the level. I mean, I've got a good bullshit antenna, and I wasn't picking up liar vibes."

"I'm constantly amazed by your fine-tuned sensibilities, Theo."

"Yeah. So, anyway, I get Buster Brown out of his face, and him and me cut a deal. What the hell. The guy's already taken thirty-five bucks from me, so I didn't have anything to lose by checking him out. If he was telling the truth about never having played in competition, he'd make the perfect sandbagger. We could clean up in at least one big tournament—and maybe even two or three, if they came close enough together, and if we could get him into the lower-class sections before his adjusted rating from the first tournament was published. He

didn't have a place to stay; he'd been living on the street, picking food
out of trash cans and riding the subway all night. The deal was that
he could stay with me, and I'd teach him the ropes about hustling so
he could start to earn his keep. We'd get him signed up with the
USCF, put him in a beginners' tournament where he'd intentionally
lose most of his games to ensure him a low provisional rating, and
then enter him in the C or D section of the New York Open, and
maybe a couple of others around the country if they offered decent
prize money and fell within the next month or so. I was to be his
manager. Since he was flopping at my place and eating my food, it
seemed only fair that I get a percentage of his winnings at tournaments, or at hustling down here. Hell, I was giving him career training and a job. That's it, Frederickson. I don't know a goddamn thing
about where he comes from or what he used to do. I think he may be
either sick or psycho, or something like that, because he's on some
kind of medication. He takes these pills—big suckers. But I don't
give a damn about that just so long as he keeps his shit together long
enough to earn us some big money. How come you're so interested?"

Smack.

"I assume you did check him out, and he wasn't a USCF member
or a Liechtenstein grandmaster."

Smack.

"Right. We wouldn't have been at that tournament last week, and
he wouldn't be living with me, if I'd found out he hustled us. I'd have
put Buster Brown back on his case."

Smack.

"Theo, I think you did a decent thing by taking him in, and by
looking out for him now. But just out of curiosity, what percentage of
his earnings do you take?"

Smack.

"Uh-uh. Your flag's down."

So it was. I got up off the bench and walked back toward the stone
chess tables.

CHAPTER 5

*I*f the man with the boyish face, brown hair, high forehead, blue
eyes, and slightly dazed expression had missed a couple of
meals while he was living on the streets, he was rapidly trying to
make up for it. He'd already wolfed down two cheeseburgers, a
mound of french fries, a side order of coleslaw, and two large Cokes
at the small luncheonette across from the park where I had taken him.

"I've never met a dwarf before," Michael Stout said, sipping at his
chocolate ice cream soda. "I've never even seen one, except in pic-
tures."

I smiled, said, "It looks like you're surviving the experience."

"You're a nice man, Mr. Mongo. I haven't met many nice people
in New York; most can't even bother to be polite."

"Just Mongo will be fine."

He pointed to the fifty-dollar bill resting between us on the marble
tabletop. "That's an awful lot of money. You're a friend of Theo's, and
you're buying me lunch, so you don't have to pay to talk to me."

"It's all right, Michael. It's worth it to me. I'd like to ask you a few
questions."

"Sure. But I don't see how anything I have to say could be worth
fifty dollars. I know money doesn't grow on trees."

"Theo tells me you only picked up on chess a couple of weeks ago.
Is that true?"

"Well, I only began to *understand* the game a couple of weeks ago,
and I'm learning more every day—even playing here, where the peo-

ple who pay to play aren't that strong. But I learned the moves of the pieces as a child."

"Can you tell me how this sudden understanding of the game came about?"

He gave it a lot of thought while he sipped at his soda. He ate some of the ice cream left at the bottom, then looked up at me with his wide, innocence-filled blue eyes and shook his head. "No, I don't think I can."

"Give it a try, Michael. For instance, on the day when you first met Theo, Buster Brown, and the others, had you come down here to the park to play chess?"

"No. I was doing what I did every day, just wandering around."

"And then you saw Theo and the others playing, and you were interested. So you stopped and watched."

"Yes. I remembered how I liked to play as a kid. I watched people playing for a while, and—this is what I don't know how to explain—I just suddenly understood all sorts of things about the game that I'd never been taught. You hear people talking about how good players can think nine or ten moves ahead, but it wasn't like that at all. I could look at a position and know what was a good move and what was a bad move, and why. If one player made a bad move, then I could see what moves the other player could make in order to win. Suddenly I just understood certain principles of the game, and the right moves flowed from these principles. Sometimes I could see the right moves all the way to the end of a game. I don't want you to think I'm bragging, Mongo, but beating Theo and the other people who play here regularly isn't hard; beating the people who want to bet with me on a game is usually even easier. Actually, getting used to playing with a clock, and remembering to hit it after I'd made a move, was a lot harder in the beginning than actually playing."

"How do you come to be in New York, Michael? How long have you been here?"

Michael Stout was guileless, his emotions transparent, and now it was as if a curtain had dropped down somewhere behind his expressive blue eyes. Clearly uncomfortable with the question, he quickly averted his gaze. "I, uh, just kind of ended up here."

"Where did you come from?"

"Well . . . uh . . . that's kind of hard to say. Look, maybe I should—"

"Were you in a mental hospital, Michael?"

His eyes darted back to my face. The curtain behind them had abruptly been raised, and onstage, front and center, were alarm and anxiety. "Why do you ask that?"

"You told Theo, Buster Brown, and the others that you'd been 'out of it' for a long time. I thought you might have been in a mental hospital."

He pushed the remains of his ice cream soda, and the fifty-dollar bill, away from him in a slow, deliberate motion. "I don't mean to be rude, but I don't want to talk anymore. I think I'd better be getting back to the tables. Theo will be wondering where I am."

I took a second black-and-yellow capsule I had brought with me out of my shirt pocket and set it down in the center of the table where the fifty-dollar bill had been. Michael Stout was halfway out of his chair, but when he saw the capsule he let out an audible gasp and collapsed back into the chair as if his legs had been cut out from under him. The expression on his face was not only one of shock but something very close to terror.

"What's the matter, Michael?" I asked quickly. "I'm not going to hurt you."

"But you have one of the pills! You're not one of us!"

"One of whom, Michael? One of what?"

His gaze left the capsule, came back to my face. He stared at me for a few moments, mouth slightly open and eyes still filled with fear, then slowly shook his head. "I can't tell you, Mongo. I'm not supposed to say anything to anybody."

"Michael, I know you're in trouble. You're in danger. I think there are people stalking you who want to kill you, and it has something to do with these pills. I want to help you. I got this one from some-body—"

"Who?!" he interrupted, his eyes growing even wider. "Which one?"

"You don't know her; she's not one of you either. They were given to her by a man I'm sure knew he was about to be killed, and he gave his bag of capsules to the first person he came across who he thought could be helped by them. Right after he gave them to my friend, he was shot on the street. My friend suffers from severe psychosis—she's schizophrenic. Is that what you are, Michael—a schizophrenic who's able to function normally on this particular medication?"

He stared at me, clearly frightened, for what seemed a long time, then slowly, reluctantly, nodded his head.

"Do you know that if you stop taking this medication, even if you skip just one dose, you'll lapse back into madness, and maybe die?"

"Mongo, I can't *talk* about it!"

"You can talk about it to me. I want to help you—you, and my friend, and however many more there are of you in the city. But I can't do that unless you tell me everything. Now, do you know what will happen to you if you stop taking the capsules?"

I wasn't sure he was going to answer me, but after another long pause he finally nodded his head again. Now he had the startled expression of a deer caught in headlights. "I just know I have to take one every day or I'll end up nutty again."

"What are you supposed to do when you run out of the supply of capsules you have now? I don't know how many you have, but my friend only has enough to last her another couple of weeks or so. How can she get more?"

Michael Stout swallowed hard, said quietly, "Dr. Sharon is trying to get us more. We're supposed to meet her on Christmas Eve at the big Christmas tree by the skating rink uptown."

"You mean Rockefeller Center?"

"Yes, I think that's the name of it. Besides the Christmas tree, there's a big statue there."

"Who's this Dr. Sharon?"

"Sharon Stephens. She's a psychiatrist. She was the only nice one there."

"Where, Michael? A mental hospital? Is that where you came from?"

He nodded in a timid, birdlike fashion.

"What's the name of it?"

"Rivercliff. It's about a four-hour drive from here, north up the Thruway."

"How did you get to New York City?"

"Dr. Sharon brought us, in a bus that belonged to the hospital. She helped us get away. Raymond was running around with a surgical saw and scalpel killing everybody. She took as many of us with her as she could, and she brought us here. There were twelve of us on the bus, besides Dr. Sharon."

I suddenly realized I was breathing rapidly and shallowly, and my stomach muscles had knotted. I took a deep breath, slowly let it out, then leaned back in my chair and tried to relax. "All right, Michael," I said in what I hoped was a soothing, reassuring tone, "let's slow down and back up. You trust me, right? You believe I want to help you?"

"Yes, I do," the boyish-faced man said quietly. There were still shadows of anxiety moving in his eyes, but he was starting to look a bit more at ease. "But Theo's going to be mad at me if I don't get back soon and start playing. He'll say I'm mooching off him and costing him money. Without Theo, I don't have a place to stay, or any way to support myself."

"You let me worry about Theo. Like I said, in order to help you and my friend, I need to know everything so that I can begin to understand what's going on. I think it may be easier if I just ask questions and you answer them—but if you think of anything to add to an answer, don't hesitate to do so. Don't worry yourself about Theo, or playing chess, or anything else except the conversation that's taking place right now. Okay?"

"Okay."

"Let's start with Rivercliff. Were all of the patients there schizophrenics like you and my friend, or were there also patients there who had been diagnosed with other types of mental illness?"

"I don't know. You'd have to ask Dr. Sharon."

"Where can I find her?"

"I don't know. She just told us to meet her by the Christmas tree on Christmas Eve. How did you know about me, Mongo?"

"I was at the Manhattan Chess Club the night you were playing in the tournament. When I saw my friend's capsules, I realized they were just like the one I saw you take. You say this Dr. Sharon helped you escape from Rivercliff after a patient named Raymond started running amok and killing people. Is that right?"

"Yes."

"Raymond was a patient?"

"Yes."

"What's Raymond's last name?"

"Rogers."

"Michael, why was it necessary to have someone help you to escape in the first place?"

"Because Raymond was—"

"No, I'm asking why you were still there *before* this Raymond started killing people. Whatever else it may do, the medication in these capsules you're taking seems incredibly effective in relieving your symptoms. Both you and my friend seem to be functioning perfectly normally—in your case, *better* than normally. How long have you been able to do this—think, speak, and act like you do now?"

"Oh, I don't know . . . years. Except for the chess, of course."

"*Years?*"

"Uh-huh."

I felt a chill. "Michael, if your symptoms were being controlled by medication, why didn't they just release you and treat you on an outpatient basis? There are thousands of mentally ill people wandering around New York City, some taking medication as outpatients, and they're in nowhere as good shape mentally as you seem to be. Did you do something wrong to get you put there? Were you judged to be criminally insane?"

"I don't think so. I don't remember doing anything wrong."

"What about this Raymond Rogers? Was he diagnosed as criminally insane?"

"I don't know. Nobody was ever released from Rivercliff. Sometimes the doctors would say somebody was going to be released, but they lied. I was there for more than twelve years. I saw new patients brought in, but I never saw anybody released. When a patient died, they just buried him in the cemetery on the grounds. When that happened, they'd bring in a new patient."

I felt another chill, and this time I actually shuddered. "How many patients were there at Rivercliff?"

"I guess maybe forty."

"What about your family? Why didn't they press for your release?

And what about the families of the other patients who died? Didn't anybody want to claim the bodies?"

"None of us had families—in fact, I think that's one of the reasons we were selected to go to Rivercliff. I'd been transferred from a state hospital in Oklahoma. Everyone I ever talked to had been transferred to Rivercliff from some state hospital. And nobody there had families—at least not families that cared about what happened to them. I'd been abandoned when I was a child, but a lot of the patients there had been orphaned."

"Jesus Christ," I mumbled to myself. I'd stumbled into a nightmare. What I'd witnessed the night before with Mama Spit was horrible enough, but the nightmare was just growing darker and deeper. And I was merely hearing about it; the man sitting across the table from me had lived it. It all made me very sad, and very, very angry.

"Mongo, you all right? You look funny."

"Yes, Michael, I'm all right," I replied, looking up at him and forcing a smile. "Just a touch of indigestion. Look, let's assume you're right: one criterion for selecting a patient for transfer to Rivercliff was that the person had nobody on the outside who would be asking questions about him. Why? None of you was ever released, even after your symptoms had been brought under control. Why?"

The questions had been rhetorical, but Michael answered them anyway. "I don't know, Mongo."

"I assume Rivercliff was the only place you were ever given that medication?"

"Yes."

"Well, they had to be up to more than just the testing of a new drug they could never hope to market; they wouldn't even be able to publish papers or data, because they'd end up in prison for illegal and dangerous human experimentation. I think it's safe to assume they weren't acting out of humanitarian impulses. So what did the doctors at Rivercliff want with you? What could they hope to accomplish when they'd broken every canon of medical ethics in the book and could never hope to see the drug they'd developed used in any patient population outside the hospital?"

"I don't know, Mongo."

"All of the patients there took these capsules?"

He nodded.

"Were you or anybody else there ever given any other kind of medication?"

"No. We didn't need any other medication. I remember when I first went there I was on all sorts of different medications, and I was a mess. I was making these uncontrollable movements—"

"Dyskinesia."

"Yeah, I guess that's what they call it. Anyway, the first thing the doctors did when I got there was take away all my other meds and give me one of those capsules. When I woke up the next morning, I felt . . . like I feel now. The voices in my head had stopped, and I could think clearly. And there weren't any of the lousy side effects I used to suffer from with the old meds."

"And they never talked about releasing you?"

"They talked about it, but I knew they wouldn't do it. They never released anybody."

I pointed to the capsule in the center of the table. "What do they call this stuff?"

"They never called it anything; it was just our meds."

"All right, Michael, describe your daily routine for me, if you will. Did you have individual therapy sessions, group counseling, what?"

He shook his head. "Mostly, we could do whatever we wanted all day—there were game rooms, a gym, and a swimming pool. They always had videotapes of the latest movies, and there was a good library. The doctors only seemed interested in asking us questions, and they'd do that, oh, maybe two or three times a week. If they were interested in what you had to say, they'd take you to another part of the hospital and give you some tests. That never happened to me, but I heard about it from others."

"What kinds of questions did the doctors ask?"

"They wanted to know how we were feeling."

"You mean whether you were feeling disoriented, hearing voices, feeling paranoid, that sort of thing?"

"No. They wanted to know if we felt anything, or could do anything, we hadn't felt or done before. You see, people had different reactions to the meds. We all got better mentally, and for the most part we stayed that way. But some people started to change in dif-

ferent ways; sometimes they'd get really good at things. I think this is
what the doctors were interested in. And I know they made changes
in the meds from time to time."

"How could you tell that if the meds always came in the same
black-and-yellow capsules?"

"Aftertaste—sometimes it would change. Also, my stomach could
tell; sometimes the meds made me sick, sometimes not. And I would
feel different; I could still think clearly, but my emotions would be
stronger, or weaker. Sometimes I'd have diarrhea, and other times I'd
be constipated. The meds I have now work pretty good."

"Michael, I'm still not sure I'm following you. What kinds of things
would people get good at? You mean like chess?"

"Yeah, but that's just me. I didn't know I could play chess like I
do now while I was there, because nobody played. They didn't even
have any sets. But there was one guy who suddenly got real good at
music; there was a piano in one of the recreation lounges, and he
taught himself to play. Hum him any tune, and he could sit down at
the piano and play it. He even started writing music."

"Like you, he discovered a talent he hadn't realized he had?"

"Yes—but it wasn't always a talent. There was a woman there—
her name is Greta Wurlitzer, and she was on the bus with us—who
suddenly developed incredible night vision. She could see at night
like a cat. The problem was that the daylight hurt her eyes, so she had
to wear dark glasses during the day. Greta used to joke about it, call
herself 'the night owl.' "

I was immediately reminded of Margaret Dutton and the remarkable senses of taste and smell she had displayed during our Thanksgiving dinner, super-keen faculties I now realized she must have
developed within hours after she had started taking the drug in the
capsules. I said, "The meds obviously relieved the symptoms of
schizophrenia and restored your emotional balance. But you're saying
the doctors at Rivercliff were mainly interested in the *side effects* of the
drug?"

He shrugged, glanced nervously at the clock on the wall to our left.
"I guess so. I really don't know, because we were never told why the
questions were being asked. I'll bet they would have run tests on me
too if they'd known about this chess thing."

"Oh, I think you're absolutely right. Michael, were any of the patients at Rivercliff ever taken off the meds, just to see what would happen?"

"No, at least not that I know of. We were always given our meds."

"Did any of the patients ever *forget* to take their meds?"

He shook his head. "A nurse always brought us our meds in a paper cup every day after lunch, and then would stand over us to make sure we took it."

I sipped at my coffee, which had gone cold, and thought about the many levels of what I could only think of as monstrous evil committed by the doctors at Rivercliff, and whoever was behind them. It was not only that they had imprisoned innocent men and women for life, but they had somehow, in secret, managed to develop what could only be called a wonder drug, the mental health equivalent of a cure for AIDS, and had not bothered to tell anybody about it because they were more interested in the drug's side effects. Then again, they had good reason to keep their activities secret; a drug that changed body chemistry to a point where a patient would spontaneously bleed to death if he stopped taking it wasn't a likely candidate for FDA approval.

"Mongo?" the other man continued anxiously. "Can I go now?"

"I just have a couple more questions, Michael. Dr. Sharon helped you escape from Rivercliff when this Raymond Rogers started running amok. What do you suppose caused Rogers to go wild like that?"

"I don't know. Sometimes things like that just happened."

"Raymond Rogers had gone wild before?"

"Yes. And they'd taken him away."

"Taken him away where?"

"I guess to another part of the hospital. Raymond wasn't the first person to suddenly become violent. When it happened to somebody, big guys would come and take him away. We'd never see them again— except once I saw one of them when I had to go to the infirmary. I think that's where Raymond must have been when he got loose; he must have been sick, and they took him there. That's where he would have found the scalpel and the surgical saw he was using to kill people."

"Did you actually see him kill anybody?"

went in. Emily was huddled on the floor over in a corner. Dr. Sharon grabbed her wrist, pulled her to her feet, and dragged Emily along behind her. She had to do that, because Emily wouldn't have come along with us on her own; she was too scared. Emily was usually like that—too upset to do anything. Emily was the only one Dr. Sharon took with her when we split up."

"Emily who?"

"I never knew Emily's last name."

"Was Emily somebody who had experienced side effects from the meds? Did she do anything special, have some special talent?"

"I don't know."

"You say she was upset most of the time?"

"If she came out of her room to try to mingle with the rest of us, yes. Sooner or later somebody would say something she didn't like, or there'd be an argument, and then she'd just crumple to the floor and cover her head with her hands. Emily was very sensitive, very shy. After the last time they changed the formulation of the meds, she never came out of her room at all. That's why Dr. Sharon had to go in and get her."

"The doctors locked Emily in her room?"

"No. There weren't any locks on the doors—at least not in our part of the hospital. Emily stayed in her room because she wanted to."

"Then the meds didn't work with Emily?"

He thought about it for a few moments, then shook his head. "I'm not sure you can say that. Sometimes she'd open the door and talk to people—as long as they stayed outside. I talked with her a couple of times, and she seemed rational enough. She just wanted to avoid close contact with people. Dr. Sharon was the only person she'd let in her room."

"All right, Michael, so Dr. Sharon was rounding up as many patients as she could to save you from Raymond. And she ended up with twelve."

He nodded. "She opened one of the doors to the outside with a key, and she put us all on one of the buses they'd use to take us on outings—picnics, the zoo, that kind of thing. The key was in the ignition. Dr. Sharon started up the bus, and we drove . . ."

He stopped in mid-sentence, and his face suddenly looked ashen.

His blue eyes again opened very wide, and he nodded in a q
jerky movement. "He almost killed me. I had a cold and a sore th
so I'd been sent to the infirmary. I was sitting on an examination t
while this doctor was looking at my throat. Then Raymond just s
denly stepped into the room and slit the doctor's throat with a so
pel—sprayed blood all over me. Jesus, I was scared. I just sat the
like I was paralyzed, looking into Raymond's crazy eyes. I thought
was going to kill me next, but instead he started to cut up Dr. Sawy
while he played with himself. I came to my senses and ran the hell ou
of there while he was busy with Dr. Sawyer. I saw two dead guard
and a nurse inside another office. There was blood all over the place."
He paused, laughed nervously in a high-pitched giggle. "It scared the
cold and sore throat right out of me."

"I can believe that," I said, nodding slowly. "You say Raymond
was playing with himself while he mutilated the doctor. You mean he
was masturbating, jerking off?"

Michael Stout reddened slightly. "Yeah. It's kind of embarrassing
to talk about."

"There's no reason for you to be embarrassed. It's important that
you tell me everything you can remember, in detail."

He shrugged. "I remember that, all right. Raymond's dong was
already out of his pants when he came in the room. It was poking
straight out of his fly, hard as a rock, and there was jism oozing out
of the tip. He grabbed himself with one hand while he was slashing
Dr. Sawyer's face and sprayed jism all over the floor. That's when I
came to my senses and ran out of the office. But I kind of froze up
again when I got out into the corridor, because I didn't know where I
was going to go where Raymond wouldn't eventually find me, because
now he had the run of the place. That's when Dr. Sharon found me.
She was carrying a black plastic garbage bag. She must have come
from someplace Raymond had already been, because her hands and
face and the front of her smock were covered with blood. She shouted
for me to follow her, and when I couldn't move she grabbed my wrist
and pulled me after her. We ran out of the infirmary and through the
halls of the residence area; Dr. Sharon was banging on doors and
shouting at everyone she saw, telling them to follow her if they wanted
to live. When we got to Emily's room, Dr. Sharon opened the door and

"What is it?" I asked quickly. "What's wrong, Michael? Do you remember something else?"

"I'm . . . I'm not sure. I was sitting near the back. It was all dark outside, so you couldn't see anything, but now I remember I think I heard a kind of thud at the back emergency door just as we were starting up, like something had run into us. Or somebody had jumped on. Oh, wow."

"You're saying the thump you heard could have been Raymond climbing on the back of the bus?"

"Now that I think of it, yes," he said in a voice just above a whisper. "There was a step on the back, and steel rungs he could have grabbed hold of."

"Did you hear anybody climbing up to the top?"

He swallowed hard, shook his head. "No. But I was scared. I wasn't listening for anything; it's only now that I even remember the thump, and I can't even be sure what that was. Everybody was scared and talking a lot—except for Emily, who was sitting on the floor up at the front next to Dr. Sharon. Mongo, I've seen newspaper headlines about how somebody's killing a lot of people here in New York. Do you think it could be Raymond?"

"He'd be my favorite candidate, except I don't see how anybody, even a homicidal maniac, could ride on down the New York Thruway on top of a bus for four hours at this time of year. If he didn't bounce off or freeze to death, he'd attract all kinds of attention up there and have cars honking, especially after the bus got to the city."

Michael licked his lips. His eyes had grown wide. "But there was stuff on top."

"What kind of stuff?"

"There was a railing around the edge, and storage bins bolted to the roof. They held sports equipment, tents, and other stuff we'd use when the staff took us on picnics, or camping. That's why there were rungs on the back. The bins were full of equipment, and not big enough to hide in, but nobody would have seen him if he lay down between them. And he could have wrapped himself in a tent to keep warm."

Ah. "Did Dr. Sharon stop anywhere to discuss what it was she planned to do with all of you?"

He again shook his head. "I don't think she knew then what she was going to do, except get us to New York. She drove right to the Thruway and headed south. She was quiet all the way, and every once in a while she'd reach down to stroke Emily's hair. I think she decided what she was going to do while she was driving, because once we got here she headed right for that place with the skating rink and the big statue."

"Rockefeller Center."

"Yeah. She parked at the curb of a street in the next block. Then she got up and came back through the bus, dividing up the capsules she'd brought with her in the plastic garbage bag. She told us she'd taken as many of the meds as she could find, and she hoped there were enough to get all of us through the next few weeks, at least until Christmas. She said each of us had a decision to make. She said she was afraid that the people who owned the hospital might send men after us to kill us, so we shouldn't help to identify ourselves by talking to anyone about Rivercliff. She said that if men were sent after us, the only way we could be safe was if we went to social workers or the police, told our story, and then asked them for their help and protection. But she also said there was no guarantee anyone would believe us, and she warned us that if we told the police or social workers about our meds, all of our meds might be taken away for testing, and we almost certainly wouldn't get them back in time to take the next day's dose. She said that if that happened, we'd get sick like we used to be, and might never be well again."

"Did she warn you that some or all of you might die if you didn't take your meds?"

"No. She just said we'd get crazy again. That was bad enough. So that's why each of us had to make a choice. She couldn't look after all of us—Emily was the only one she was taking with her. She said she was going to try to get more meds for us, but she wasn't sure she could do it. Any one of us could go to the police or social workers if we were willing to risk having our meds taken away. If any of us chose to take our chances living on the streets, then she would meet us by the Christmas tree next to the skating rink on Christmas Eve. She said she hoped she'd have a fresh supply of meds for us by then, and these would keep us going until she could come up with some kind of a plan for bringing us all in safely, maybe with a guarantee that we could keep taking our meds."

"You'd have had a better chance of being believed by the authorities if your psychiatrist had been with you. Why didn't she offer to go with you to the police?"

"I don't know. Maybe she needed time to come up with a plan. Maybe she was afraid they wouldn't believe her either, or that they'd still take away our meds."

And maybe arrest her, I thought. There had to be some very powerful people behind the operation at Rivercliff, and in the four hours or so it had taken Sharon Stephens to drive to the city they would almost certainly have found out what happened, and taken steps to protect themselves from exposure. They could have put out some kind of cover story to various agencies around the state, including key social welfare and medical authorities, and the police would have been waiting for this shepherdess and her lost flock. The capsules would have been confiscated, and then there wouldn't have been any need to send assassins; all of the patients would have died within forty-eight hours and Sharon Stephens would have been isolated. I wasn't willing to give this keeper at Rivercliff much credit for anything, including her rather belated acquiring of a moral sensibility and her heroics, but she obviously wasn't stupid, and she could think clearly under pressure.

I said, "She probably did the right thing."

"I know all of this sounds kind of weird, Mongo. Do you believe me?"

Nothing in the man's story sounded a bit weirder than what I'd already seen with my own eyes, and I said, "Yes, Michael, I believe you. And your Dr. Sharon knew what she was talking about. I believe people have come here to track you down and kill you, and I believe your meds would have been taken away if you'd gone to the authorities for help. To your knowledge, how many of the other patients made the same decision you did, to take your chances on the street and try to make it until Christmas Eve?"

"All of us did the same thing. It wasn't a hard choice to make, Mongo. Sometimes, even if you've been crazy for years, you can experience little snippets of memory, even if they only come in dreams, of what it was like to be able to think clearly, to be able to act normally and be with normal people, to not hear voices or screaming in your head all the time. Just those little pieces of memory can be so . . . *sweet.* Then, to be able to function normally all of the time is like the most wonderful gift you've ever been given, and it's something you never take for granted. You never forget the torment of the craziness; to call it hell isn't an adequate description. It's worse than hell. All of us had maybe a month or more of sanity in our pockets, and it was worth being cold and hungry—and yes, maybe even dying—to keep that sanity for as long as was possible. To risk having our meds abruptly taken away from us was just . . . unthinkable. I don't think you can understand."

I had a few vivid memories of my own, of the time when my brother's mind had gone over a very high cliff as a result of his being poisoned with "spy dust," a mysterious substance called nitrophenyldienal. I had suffered with him, in a very real way probably more than he did. I remembered him comatose, remembered how his consciousness had been warped when he'd recovered, his loss of "I," and his long, harrowing journey back to sanity. Garth had been changed forever, in many subtle but still distinct ways, but at least he could function again as a rational human being. I never again wanted to lose my brother to madness, didn't want to see anyone lost to madness. So I thought I could indeed understand what his meds meant to Michael Stout, but I didn't contradict him.

I asked, "Any sign of Raymond when you got off the bus?"

"No. Mongo, you're not going to tell anybody about me, are you?"

"No, Michael, I'm not going to tell anybody about you—at least not anybody who would do you harm. Where do you keep your supply of meds? Are the capsules back at Theo's place?"

"No. I never leave them anywhere, because I'm afraid somebody might steal them. I always carry them with me."

"Good. When Dr. Sharon dropped you all off at Rockefeller Center and told you to meet her on Christmas Eve, did she give any indication of just how she planned to get a fresh supply of your meds?"

"No."

"Did she or any of the other doctors ever mention who actually owned the hospital?"

"No."

"Did anyone ever tell you where the meds came from, or what company manufactured them?"

"No."

"When you split up, did Dr. Sharon give even a hint of where she and Emily might be going?"

"No. I've told you everything I know, Mongo. Can I go back now? Theo's really going to be angry at me for staying away so long. He'll call me a freeloader, say I'm costing him money."

"You can stop worrying about what Theo calls you, Michael," I said as I rose, picked up the fifty-dollar bill, and stuffed it into his shirt pocket. "Also, your career as a chess hustler is over, at least for the time being. You're not going back to Theo's place. You're coming to live with me for a while."

CHAPTER 6

With two recovering schizophrenics in residence, the brownstone was beginning to resemble a halfway house. After introducing Michael to Francisco and Margaret Dutton, and leaving instructions for my bemused but sympathetic secretary to bring them anything they wanted, I ensconced myself in my private office on the ground floor and settled in for a good long, hard think. Although I hoped I had put up a cheerful, optimistic front for Francisco and my two guests, the fact of the matter was that I felt shaky, not only made sick to my stomach by what I had witnessed and heard but also not a little overwhelmed by the responsibility I had taken upon myself and the position I had put myself in. I needed time to center myself, and then figure out what I was going to do for my next trick. Of one thing I was certain, and that was the need for extreme caution.

I had entered the lair of monsters, and the ice-pick-wielding man who was dispatching New Yorkers by the dozens was only their mascot. The killings had started at just about the time when Raymond Rogers would have hit town.

I believed every word of Michael Stout's story, for so much of it jibed with what I had already seen and heard from Mama Spit. The horror of the patients' situation was not lost on me, and I was struck dumb by the unimaginable cruelty of the people who had run Rivercliff on a day-to-day basis, physicians who had betrayed their Hippocratic oath and become willing pawns in conducting Nazi-like illegal and immoral research on fellow human beings. And then there was the equally monstrous, inconceivable motives and behavior of some pharmaceutical research team, possibly but not necessarily an arm of the company that manufactured the drug. They had come up with at least a preliminary model, however flawed, of a miracle drug for schizophrenia, one that was generations ahead of any medication currently available. Yet they had then kept it a secret for years because they or their backers were apparently more interested in the flawed drug's side effects than the fact that it might furnish normal lives to untold numbers of men, women, and children who suffered from one of the most debilitating of mental illnesses.

Instead of searching for what might be only a minor reformulation that would produce freedom for the many, they had chosen to imprison and experiment on a few. Monsters; every last one of them, from the maintenance personnel at Rivercliff who had conspired to keep the secret, to the doctors who had conducted the experiments, to the drug company executives who had cooperated, to whoever was behind it all. It made me very angry, and it was this anger as well as my nausea and horror that I had to overcome before I rode off in search of windmills, or started pushing any buttons that could open a trapdoor under me as well as the wandering members of Sharon Stephens's lost flock.

All of which led me to the next mantra in my meditation: pondering who might be pulling the strings. It would take an extremely powerful organization to mount and maintain an operation like Rivercliff. Over the years laws had been broken, state and federal regulatory guidelines and commissions blithely ignored with impunity, detailed and confidential information gathered from state institutions across the country, specific patients without family or friends culled and transferred to Rivercliff. All this, presumably with no follow-up from the bureaucrats who had sent them there, and very likely with no paper trail of records. Accomplishing it with no apparent breach of security was no mean feat. And then there was the question of finances, how Rivercliff could have stayed afloat with an apparently large building or complex of buildings, a professional staff and patient population of half a hundred, all with presumably no revenue from insurance companies or funding from state and federal mental health programs.

It didn't take me long to come up with a favorite candidate for
Culprit, my usual suspect when it came to conspiracies of this mag-
nitude, expense, and lunacy—the beloved, frequently deadly CIA. It
was probably a group of busy beavers in one of the Company's science
research divisions. I was going to need help.

Normally it would be Garth I would turn to, assuming he was not
already involved and running at my side, but my brother and his
wife were on a skiing trip that was scheduled to last through New
Year's, and since I had nothing specific to ask him to do, I saw no
good reason to interrupt their vacation. What I needed most was
information, and I needed it quickly. I had three weeks to take care
of a lot of business. Not the least important was the task of somehow finding a fresh supply of the drug that was keeping the schizophrenics mentally afloat and alive. Accomplishing this would give
me a time cushion of however long it might take, after the survivors
had gathered on Christmas Eve, to negotiate a safe passage for them
through the treacherous shoals of bureaucracy to a haven with some
authority that understood and respected their special need. I knew
these three weeks could slip through my fingers like water; I
couldn't count on Sharon Stephens getting the job done, because I
couldn't be certain I'd find her before the professional assassins on
her trail took her out. Indeed, except for the pressing needs of Margaret and Michael, it was possible that replicating the drug in large
quantities could be a wasted exercise, for all of the remaining ten
patients who were presumably still alive and out on the city streets
could be dead by Christmas Eve; in addition to whatever else I had
to do, I was going to have to start tracking the shepherdess, Ms.
Jekyll and Dr. Hyde, and her lost flock myself.

I needed the NYPD, state police, and FBI playing on my side, and
I was severely limited in the amount of information I could offer up as
enticement to get them to even enter the game; no matter what, I was
not going to offer up Margaret Dutton or Michael Stout, except perhaps as a very last resort if it became clear there was no other way to
save their lives and sanity. Finally it came down to the question of
whom I was going to reach out to first, and I was afraid I already knew
the answer. I might have plenty of contacts, and even a few friends,
at One Police Plaza, in Washington, and other seats of power, but I

was convinced that most of the coming action would take place on the playing field of Manhattan, since I was certain that most of the missing patients, like Michael, had stayed close. Sooner or later I was going to have to deal with Felix MacWhorter, and if he found out he'd been left out of the loop at the beginning, not only could it prove seriously counterproductive but I'd have destroyed any chance I had of building a relationship with him.

Step One.

I picked up the phone and called Midtown North.

"Midtown North. Sergeant Colchen speaking."

"Lou, it's Mongo."

"Mongo, my friend," the police sergeant said, and laughed. "Angel was telling me about the show you and the chief put on earlier. I wish I'd been here. Angel said it was the best stuff he's seen since Abbott and Costello."

"Yeah. We plan to polish it just a little more, and then maybe take it on the road. As a matter of fact, I'd like to speak to the dear man. Is he around?"

"You've got to be kidding. In case you haven't noticed, he doesn't much care for you; his blood pressure goes up when he so much as thinks about you. I've even heard him refer to you in unflattering terms, such as 'fucking dwarf vigilante.' "

"Well, that does it; I'm not going to ask him to marry me. But I'd still like to talk to him."

"Seriously, Mongo," the desk sergeant said, lowering his voice. "I don't think he'll take your call; if he does, all you'll get is a hassle. Why bother? Tell me what you're looking for, and I'll try to accommodate you. You and Garth have always been straight with us, and it's not your fault that a lot of action comes your way. The chief just has some bug up his ass."

"Thanks, Lou; I appreciate that very much. But it's MacWhorter I have to talk to. Tell him I may be able to provide him with some information on the ice-pick killer."

There was a short pause, then: "No shit?"

"No shit. There's been some action coming my way."

"Hang on."

I didn't have to wait long, less than twenty seconds, and then

MacWhorter's sharp, impatient voice came over the line. "What's this business about the ice-pick killer, Frederickson?"

"Chief, I'm involved in a matter where I've happened to come across certain information, and you're the first person I'm calling."

"You told me earlier you weren't on a case."

"I'm still not; I don't have a paying client. It's just something I got mixed up in, and now I think the police should act as quickly as possible. I'm not certain, but I have reason to believe that the name of the ice-pick killer could be Raymond Rogers. One possible way to confirm it is to check the victims' clothing, and even the crime scenes themselves, for any semen stains. There'll probably be a very low sperm count, but if it is Rogers, his prostate seems to be working serious overtime. You can get a detailed description of him by getting the state police to subpoena the records of an upstate New York mental hospital called Rivercliff. While they're at it, the state police might want to scope out that whole operation, because there may be some funny doings up there. Finally, I have reason to believe that if you perform an autopsy on the corpse of the man you found in the Carnegie Hall Dumpster you'll find some kind of toxic substance in the tissue. If that turns out to be the case, and if the police lab can identify the substance, I would appreciate it very much if you'd be kind enough to share that information with me."

There was a rather prolonged silence, during which I could hear MacWhorter's hoarse breathing. When he finally spoke again, his voice sounded odd. "Frederickson?"

"What?"

"I already have a description of Raymond Rogers."

"What?! Who?!"

"You're the third person who's called me about this Rogers. The only difference is that the other two were dead certain the killer is Rogers. One even claimed to be an eyewitness to one of his murders."

"Who were they, Chief?"

"Both women, and neither would give her name. The first sounded cool, matter-of-fact, professional. She just said the killer was Raymond Rogers, and hung up. The other one, the woman who said she'd watched him kill somebody, called herself 'the night owl.' Even described him—tall, rangy, dark hair and eyes."

"Jesus Christ," I breathed. My mouth was dry, my palms moist, and my thoughts were not only racing but stumbling over each other.

"Frederickson?"

"Yes, Chief?"

"You want to tell me now what this is all about?"

"I'm not sure what you're referring to by 'this,' Chief," I said carefully. "I picked up some information, and I passed it on to you. I don't have anything else to tell you."

"Listen to me, you little shit," MacWhorter said. His voice had risen only slightly, but the anger in his tone was naked and shining. "This is the kind of crap you and your brother pull all the time, and it's *exactly* what I was talking about this morning. You're involved in something the police should know about, and you're in it right up to your eyeballs. This time I may just push you under and let you drown. You call me up and give me not only the name of this wacko but the name of the mental hospital he escaped from. Then you tell me what the M.E. is going to find if he does an autopsy on a body found two blocks from your home. Now, you may think you're going to catch this freak all on your own, get some more publicity, and make the police look like fools. If you think you can get away with withholding vital information from me, you're out of your mind. This is a serial killer you're playing with, Frederickson; not leveling with me could get people killed."

"I'm not playing with a serial killer, Chief," I said, leaning back in my swivel chair and rolling my eyes toward the ceiling. I was really sorry I'd made this call—or at least sorry I'd called MacWhorter. "And I'm not withholding any information that could help you. It seems to me you should be thanking me for giving you the information I did. Were you this courteous to the two women who called to give you Rogers's name?"

"We still haven't found Mama Spit."

"I told you that whatever happened to Mama Spit is a complete mystery to me."

"She's a material witness to a murder."

"No kidding? I seem to recall I was the one who told you that."

"I think you know where she is."

"You think what you like, but that's a pretty goofy idea."

"Who's your client?"

"I keep telling you I don't have a—"

"Don't play word games with me, Frederickson. On whose *behalf* are you working? How did you happen to come up with all this information you've been giving me?"

"I'm not going to tell you that."

"The nature of your investigations and what people tell you isn't privileged information."

"I never claimed it was. I just said I wasn't going to tell you. That's what you get for calling me names and hurting my feelings."

"All right, wise guy, I want you to get your ass in here right now."

"Would you, really? Why? I've already told you all I'm going to tell you."

"Then maybe you'll be sharing a cell with the rest of the scumbags we pick up around here. I want a written statement from you describing what matter you're currently investigating, and how you came up with the name of Raymond Rogers."

"I always cooperate with the police, MacWhorter. I'd probably feel better about coming in to chat with you if I hadn't already done that once today and met with a less than friendly and respectful reception. Then you wanted to throw me out, and now you want me to come in. Make up your mind. If I make any written statement, it will be about how you've verbally abused me on two separate occasions when I tried to give you information concerning criminal activities."

"If you're not here within the next two hours, Frederickson, I'm going to issue a warrant for your arrest on the grounds that *you're* a material witness in a murder case and you're withholding evidence. You want to play games with me, I'll have your license pulled."

"MacWhorter," I said in my mildest, friendliest tone, "has anybody ever told you that you're a seriously stupid man? If I wanted any shit from you, I'd squeeze your head and it would come out your ears like toothpaste. Until and unless you do arrest me, this is the last conversation I ever intend to have with you. The next time I come across information I think the police should have, I guarantee I'll take it to a cop who's a lot smarter and more civil than you are, and that leaves me the choice of just about anybody else on the force. Stick your threats up your fat ass."

So much for my public relations efforts with the local constabulary. I hung up the phone while MacWhorter was shouting at me, leaned forward in my chair and drummed the fingers of both hands on the desk. I had personal ties to enough ace attorneys to stock a law firm, so I wasn't going to waste time worrying about being hassled by the police captain when I had more important things to worry about, like winning a race against madness and death before Santa arrived.

Step Two.

If it was the CIA that was behind all the doings at Rivercliff, and I didn't harbor a lot of doubt, I thought it highly likely that the killers they had hired to work New York City were freelancers from a long ways out of town. It was past three in the afternoon, which meant it was well past the dinner hour at Interpol headquarters in Berne. But the man I wanted to speak to, Inspector Gérard Molière, often liked to work late at night in his office, and so I thought calling him now was worth a try. I had met Molière two years before, when Garth and I had been in Switzerland trailing a man by the name of Chant Sinclair, an infamous terrorist who had turned out to be not such a terrorist after all. I hoped the inspector remembered me, and that we were still on good terms. I thumbed through my Rolodex until I found the number I wanted, dialed it.

"*Oui?*"

"It's Robert Frederickson, Inspector. I'm sorry to be calling so late."

"Mongo *le Magnifique!* How are you, my friend?!"

Well. It seemed Gérard Molière did remember me, and we were still on good terms. "I'm fine, Inspector. How about yourself?"

"I am well, my friend. It is so terrible, this thing that is happening in New York. So many people killed."

"Yes, Inspector. It is terrible."

"Garth dropped by last week to say hello. He and his wife are skiing in Zermatt through the holidays."

"He hasn't broken anything yet?"

"Not that I could see. His wife, she is so beautiful."

"Mary is that."

"When are you coming to visit? You will be my houseguest."

"Thanks, Gérard. I appreciate that. Right now I've got some important business to take care of. I hate to impose on you, but I was hoping that you might be able to provide some information that could prove very useful to me."

"Of course, Mongo. I will be happy to help, if I can. What do you wish to know?"

"There are a couple of assassins working New York, professionals. They've already killed one person that I know of, and I suspect they've targeted close to a dozen more. I want to stop them, and it would be a big help if I could find out who they are. Since they do seem to be pros, I figure they may have worked in other countries, or come from another country, and Interpol might have something on them."

"MO?"

"A specially packed, low-velocity twenty-two-caliber bullet to the base of the skull. They've been described as being very young. An eyewitness to the killings says they looked like teenagers—a male and a female."

"Punch and Judy," Gérard Molière replied without hesitation.

"Come again?"

"Punch and Judy are their code names, *noms de guerre*. They are husband and wife whose real names are Henry and Janice Sparsburg. They are rumored to live somewhere near Paris, but the Sûreté appears content to leave them unmolested as long as they limit their business activities to countries outside Europe. Their preferred method of killing is the same as you described."

"How old are these people?"

"They are certainly not teenagers. They are young merely in appearance, and then only if seen from a distance. Dressing and behaving like young people seems to be a fetish with them, and they are rumored to make regular visits to a plastic surgeon. May I ask whom they have killed over there, and why?"

"Just between you and me, I think the CIA hired them, but I can't be certain of that. A dozen patients escaped from a very shady mental hospital where they've been conducting illegal experiments for years. I think Punch and Judy have been sent to kill them before they talk to anybody about it."

"Why don't these people go to the police?"

"They're probably not even aware that they're being hunted; but even if they are, they'll probably still avoid the police. They're on an effective but very dangerous medication I'm sure our FDA has never even heard of, much less approved. Without the medication, they'll slip back into insanity and probably die inside twenty-four hours. They're afraid the drug will be confiscated. They have a limited supply of the medication, so I'm trying to identify the drug and get more of it in order to buy them more time. But it's all going to be a pointless exercise if they're killed before I can find a way to help them."

"I understand."

"Anything else you can tell me about Punch and Judy? Personal habits? Favorite haunts and restaurants?"

"I'm afraid they're too professional to be that predictable, Mongo. I have heard the rumor that they are brother and sister as well as man and wife, but I can't see how that information would help you. They are very . . . how do you say? Kinky?"

"That's as good a way of saying it as any."

"It particularly interests me that you suspect the CIA of having hired these assassins. If it's true, there may be some irony in the situation."

"How so?"

"There are rumors that Punch and Judy were discovered and developed—if that is the proper way to describe the nurturing and training of assassins—by a department of the CIA called the Chill Shop."

"The Chill Shop?"

"Yes. That is what other CIA operatives with whom I have occasional dealings call it. These people I have spoken with don't much care for the operation, or the personnel who run it. That name derives from the acronym BUHR—the Bureau of Unusual Human Resources. I heard it was shut down some time ago because of budget cuts, but that information may not have been accurate."

"This Chill Shop was—is—a school for assassins?"

"No. Punch and Judy represent only one of their products. Chill Shop personnel were tasked to find people with unusual talents, skills, or characteristics—even subjects some of us might describe as 'freaks'—that might prove useful in covert intelligence work. That's all I know about it, Mongo. If you like, I will make discreet inquiries about this matter, and get back to you if I find out anything that I think could be helpful to you."

"Thanks, Gérard. I'd really appreciate that, and I owe you."

"You owe me nothing, Mongo. Speaking to you and possibly being of service is my pleasure."

"Oh, there's one other thing. Since Garth is in the neighborhood, there's a good chance he may drop in again. If he does, I'd appreciate it if you wouldn't mention this conversation to him."

There was a pause, then a hesitant clearing of the throat. "Are you sure, Mongo? Garth would certainly want to know if you're in danger."

"I don't think I'm in any danger at the moment, Gérard, because the bad guys don't know I'm on to them; but even if I were, there's nothing Garth could do about it. I plan to proceed very carefully. If my brother gets wind of this, he'll head right to the airport and fly back here, and I don't see any reason right now to disrupt his and Mary's vacation. If I do need his help, I'll call him myself."

"If the time comes when you need help, my friend, it may be too late to call."

"I've given the matter a lot of thought, Gérard. Right now I can handle things myself."

"I'll do as you ask, Mongo."

"Thanks again, Gérard. *Ciao.*"

"*Ciao,*" the Interpol inspector replied, and hung up.

Step Three.

It was time to mix my metaphors and go trolling for more lost sheep. I had plenty of room in the brownstone.

CHAPTER 7

I *went back upstairs to check on Margaret again. She was sleep-ing, which was to be expected, but her color was returning and her pulsebeat was regular. I went in the other room to ask Michael to write down the names and descriptions of the other* patients who had escaped with him on the bus. When he had done so, I memorized the information and tore up the paper.

Although Sharon Stephens and the patients could be scattered through the five boroughs, and would be if they were acting logi-cally, I still had the feeling that most of the people, if not the psy-chiatrist and her ward, had remained in Manhattan, in close proximity to the site where they hoped to rendezvous and receive salvation on Christmas Eve. So Manhattan was where I would begin my search.

I took the A train to the northern end of the borough, and then slowly walked through the George Washington Bridge bus terminal, searching end to end and top to bottom, looking for anyone who might fit the descriptions Michael had given me. It was no easy task. The patients could have altered their appearance, and it wasn't as if all the homeless people and drifters in the terminal were standing up against a wall and facing me as if they were in a lineup; many were sleeping with their faces to the wall, or were covered with mounds of rags or surrounded by plastic garbage bags stuffed with their meager belong-ings. Finally, it came down to the question of how one could pick out a particular escaped mental patient from all the other mental patients wandering around the streets of the city as though it were some great, labyrinthine outpatient ward.

I didn't see any man or woman who exactly fit any of the descriptions I had been given, but when I saw somebody who came close, or appeared relatively lucid, I would stop, offer the person a dollar or two, show them the black-and-yellow capsule I carried, and then begin asking personal questions about Rivercliff, Dr. Sharon Stephens, and Raymond Rogers. What I was looking for was a reaction, shadows moving in the eyes, a sharp intake of breath, or an attempt to move away. All I got were requests for more money.

When I struck out at the bus terminal, I headed for the nearest homeless shelter, an armory. I slowly walked through the cavernous space, examining the faces of the men and women who had already checked in for the night and were resting on their cots as I discreetly held a handkerchief over my nose and mouth to try to protect myself from the new and virulent strains of tuberculosis that were now spreading rapidly through the city's population of homeless.

As I worked my way downtown through shelters and other havens for the helpless, I developed a list of questions for any of the guards, volunteers, or social workers who would talk to me. Had they noticed anything "unusual" about any one of the people who had first come in during the past two weeks? That question always got a laugh. Had they noticed anyone displaying any unusual talents or traits, like being very skilled at chess, or being able to see particularly well in the dark, or anything at all peculiar? More laughs. I had no trouble getting people to talk to me, only in taking me seriously after I had asked my first few questions. I came to realize that, with the noticeable exception of three or four fresh volunteers who had only been on the job a week or two, few of the employees any longer "saw" much of anything around them at all. They simply could no longer distinguish individual faces in the vast, cruel tapestry of human misery that cloaked them, the tide of suffering that swept in each evening to overwhelm, and then swept out again the next day. Most of the staff, in the interest of self-preservation, had willfully allowed themselves to grow numb, half blind and half deaf. I couldn't say I blamed them in the least.

I found nobody who matched any of the descriptions.

By 10 P.M. I had worked my way south toward my own neighborhood, and I decided to visit the one city shelter and three Salvation Army and church relief centers in the area before calling it a night. I was getting more than a wee bit discouraged. If the patients had seriously gone to ground and were avoiding all relief centers, or were scattered in the other boroughs, I had little real hope of finding them even if I devoted all my time to the search. And that would be counterproductive, since come December 26 or thereabouts they would all be mad or dead or both anyway. The only solace I could take was in the knowledge that if I was having so much difficulty finding the lost flock, then so must the assassins on their trail.

I was coming out of the shelter when I looked across the street and saw something that made me stop so abruptly I almost tripped over my own feet. There, standing at the curb under a streetlight, was a young couple—at least they certainly appeared young from a distance—with their arms around each other's waist, apparently engaged in earnest conversation. From the way they dressed and by their physical mannerisms, their gestures, the man and woman looked to be in their late teens or early twenties. From what I could see of their faces, they certainly appeared youthful—but there was no bus stop where they were standing, and it seemed to me that there were any number of other, more pleasant places where a young couple could go to chat rather than this forlorn, potentially dangerous block, across the street from a shelter for homeless men. I waited for a stream of cars to pass, then headed in their direction.

They saw me coming, turned their heads slightly to regard me for a few moments, then resumed their conversation; as I drew closer, it sounded to me as if they were speaking Dutch, or perhaps some Scandinavian language. I stepped up on the curb next to the couple and waited for them to take notice of me, something which they at least pretended not to do. They were both about the same height, about five eight or nine, and what I saw when I looked into their faces amazed me and made the hairs on the back of my neck rise. While the man and woman had indeed looked like college students from where I had stood across the street, up close I could see that they were no spring chickens. Like an optical illusion gone sour, they had aged twenty years or more in the time it had taken me to cross the street.

The longish, dyed blond hair of both the man and the woman hid the multiple scars I knew they both bore behind their ears from multiple visits to plastic surgeons; their flesh, which had the starched look and translucency of parchment, was stretched like drumheads across their skulls, lending both of them the expression, even when speaking, of a perpetual, faint grimace. The man had brown eyes, and the woman one blue eye and one green; the eyes of both protruded slightly from their sockets, and looked like glass marbles in the mercury glow from the streetlight. I had no idea what the man and woman would have looked like if they had allowed themselves to age normally, but they couldn't look any worse than they did now.

I'd seen enough, and was about to retreat into the shadows when the woman with the mismatched eyes suddenly glanced down at me and asked me a question in what I now thought sounded like a German dialect.

"Uh, excuse me," I said, smiling up into the stretched faces. "Could you tell me how to get to Carnegie Hall?"

They conferred for a few moments in the language that was incomprehensible to me. Finally the woman looked at me and winked her blue eye. "You are perhaps trying to have some fun with tourists?" she asked in heavily accented English. "We have heard that joke. The answer is: Practice, practice, practice."

"Uh, right you are. Well, thanks anyway. Have a nice evening."

I didn't go far, south half a block and around a corner. Then I stopped and peered back around the edge of a building. The man and woman were still standing at the curb, talking. I was certain they were Punch and Judy, trolling the same shelters and relief centers I was, but avoiding the risk of identification by remaining at a distance to watch who went inside and who came out. They would have whole dossiers on the escaped patients, including photographs and behavior profiles. Taking out this decidedly unattractive duo could produce all sorts of dividends. They were unlikely to know anything about Rivercliff, the drug or the company that manufactured it, but they could tell me the names of their employers, people who presumably would know. Their forced retirement would also certainly make the streets a lot safer for the lost flock, and might even bring a faint smile to the thick lips of Captain Felix

MacWhorter, perhaps even raise his level of tolerance for having me live in his precinct.

But I was going to need more than my own conviction and evidence of plastic surgery to remove them from circulation. It was going to cost me valuable time to gather enough evidence for MacWhorter to take them in, but the effort certainly seemed worth it.

Fifteen minutes went by, and upwards of twenty men entered the shelter without the couple giving any one of them so much as a glance. That surprised me, and took a bit of a nick out of my confidence that they were Punch and Judy. In fact, they seemed far more interested in each other than in who was entering the shelter across the street. Then they surprised me a second time by abruptly heading off down the block in the opposite direction. They were definitely not acting like the stalkers and professional killers I wanted them to be, but I followed them anyway.

Since I was the only dwarf in the general vicinity, I had to keep a respectable distance between us or I would immediately be made if one of them happened to glance back. However, they didn't seem to be in a hurry to get anywhere, and they were easy to follow. They went north awhile, then turned east on 76th Street. Three quarters of the way down the block they paused outside an apartment building. They demurely kissed each other on the cheek, the woman disappeared into the building, and the man resumed walking. It seemed unlikely that Punch and Judy would be living in separate quarters, and the behavior of this couple was growing ever more depressingly unsuspicious. Still, I continued to follow the man, who disappeared down the steps into the subway station at Columbus Circle.

I sprinted the rest of the way down the block, across the street, and scurried down the stairs, toward the almost palpable rumble of incoming and outgoing trains, hoping to at least catch a glimpse of him to determine whether he was going towards the uptown or downtown stairs. There was no sign of him. I dug a subway token out of the change in my pocket, dropped it into the turnstile, then hurried down another flight of stairs leading to the platforms for the downtown trains. I knew I was running a considerable risk of being spotted if he was on the platform, but I didn't see him anywhere.

I hurried back upstairs then down another flight to the platform for the uptown trains, but I didn't see any sign of the man there either. I headed home, my thoughts once more turning to the image of a man with an ice pick, taking care to avoid dark areas, and paying close attention to anybody who passed close to me on the sidewalk.

By the time I reached my block I had convinced myself that the couple had not been Punch and Judy, that it had simply been coincidence that both the man and the woman had undergone extensive plastic surgery, and that they had been standing in that particular spot across from the men's shelter. I had been very careful in tailing them, which meant that the woman most likely really did live in that particular apartment house, and the man had simply stepped onto a train that had been in the station and had almost immediately pulled out. In any case, whether or not the couple had been Punch and Judy was a moot question; they were gone now. At least I had gotten some exercise.

As I crossed the street heading for the brownstone, I noticed that the light in the stairwell leading down to the belowground floor Garth and I used as a storage area was out, leaving the stairwell and half the stairs leading up to the main entrance in darkness. That was not good for my own security, or for the safety of my neighbors, and I decided I would replace the bulb before I went to bed.

I was halfway across the street when I saw the figure sitting in the shadows on my stoop, in almost exactly the same spot where I had found Margaret Dutton. But this wasn't Mama Spit. I went a few steps closer, and my mouth went dry when I saw the dyed blond hair and pale sheen of the taut flesh of the woman's face; I'd not only been made but had, but good, by the two professionals. It was the last thought I had before the steel prongs of a stun gun probed into my back on either side of my spinal cord, sending a few thousand volts of electricity coursing through my body. It smarted pretty good; it felt like somebody had poured molten lead into a hole in the top of my skull, burning out my brain and severing every neural connection in my body. I dropped to the pavement like a stone. A powerful hand grabbed the collar of my coat and dragged me the rest of the way across the street; I was bumped up over the curb, hauled across the sidewalk, and unceremoniously bumpety-bumped down the steps into the darkened stairwell. Punch was now joined by Judy, and they used separate, thin ropes to lash my wrists and ankles. When they had accomplished this, Punch tossed the ends of both ropes over the street-level railing above my head. Then he pulled on the ropes and tied them off, leaving me drooping in the air like a hammock. It was an extremely uncomfortable position—which, of course, was precisely what they'd had in mind.

My eyes had grown accustomed to the gloom, and it was useless to struggle, so I just sagged there, trying not to think about the pain that was already nibbling along my spine, and watched while the man, who I now realized was wearing a toupee, pulled a thick leather glove over his right hand. He removed a small glass bottle from his pocket, unscrewed the cap, and poured a small amount of a clear liquid into his gloved palm. Suddenly the air was filled with the fetid odor of feces.

"It won't do you any good to try to cry out, Dr. Frederickson," the parchment-faced man with the blond toupee said in perfect English that no longer carried any trace of an accent. "I will immediately muffle any cries with my glove. Like this."

Having made this pronouncement, Punch proceeded to cover my nose and mouth with the liquid-soaked glove. Whatever was on the glove didn't appear to be the real thing, but it might as well have been, because the smell and taste immediately made my mouth feel like a recently used toilet. After a few moments he took the glove away, and I spat.

"That is really vile stuff," I said in as even a tone as I could manage from my extremely stressed, rather undignified position. "I certainly don't plan to cry out, and I hope you're not planning on doing anything that would make me want to change my mind. How do you know who I am?"

"Don't be so modest," the woman said in English that was as perfect and unaccented as her husband's. "Doesn't everyone know Mongo the Magnificent, the famous ex-circus star, former college professor, karate expert, and renowned private investigator who also just happens to be a dwarf? You and your brother have made headlines all over the world."

Ah, yes, the perils of celebrity. "I can see I'm going to have to tell my public relations people to tone things down a bit."

"I can't believe you could have been so stupid as to approach us like that on the street, and then ask a dumb question about how to get to Carnegie Hall."

I couldn't believe it either. If I lived to New Year's, I was going to make a serious resolution to stop trying to be such a clever little rascal. "I didn't know who you were when I approached you, and I still don't know who you are. I've been looking for a teenage runaway. I came over to ask if you might have seen him, but when I heard you talking I assumed you didn't speak English. The question about Carnegie Hall was just a display of my razor wit employed in an attempt to amuse myself. What the hell do you want?"

"You're lying," Judy said, and Punch indicated that he agreed with her sentiments by poking me in the ribs with the stun gun. I screamed and went into convulsions, and Punch immediately slapped the glove that smelled like feces over my mouth. That stopped the screaming, but not the convulsions. The electricity and repulsive odor comprised a double-barreled bazooka attack on all my senses, pairing the extremes of pain and revulsion, and it was most effective.

I'd been tortured before; I hadn't much cared for it then, and I didn't much care for it now. In fact, I hated being tortured. Just like the times before, I cried and screamed—or tried to—and threw up and most sincerely begged them to stop, and, just like the times before, I knew that if they finally found out what they wanted to know, they would kill me. Just like the times before, I knew I was going to have to somehow summon up the will to look beyond the terrible pain, try to think happy thoughts about the fact that I was still alive, and keep lying in order to keep me that way.

They let me hang around, as it were, twitch and soil myself for what felt like a couple of centuries, but was probably only about five minutes. My back felt like it was about to break, and might have if they hadn't flipped me around into a position that was only slightly less uncomfortable. My whole body had become one huge cramp, but in the new position I was able to breathe—and presumably talk—a little easier. I couldn't decide which was worse, the artificial odor on the glove or the real smell of my own vomit, and I knew I was going to have to endure—survive—one more slam of electricity before they would be ready to believe whatever tale I was going to tell them. It would have to be good enough to satisfy their curiosity yet make them decide not to kill me, and it was a whopper I had yet to come up with. My current situation was seriously interfering with my imaginative flow.

"Untie the ropes and let me lie down on my back," I croaked. "I think I'm rupturing a disc or two. I'll tell you what you want to know."

Punch said, "Tell us what we want to know, and then the pain will stop. How did you know who we are?"

"Hey, pal, if I'd known who you were, I wouldn't have come up to you on the street and made clever remarks. If you're going to torture me for information, at least don't waste time by asking stupid questions. It's my body you're using up. I had a description of two people, and you two looked like you might fit it. That's why I came over to you, to take a closer look."

"Who gave you this description?"

"There was a witness to the killing you pulled off here a week ago."

"Who?"

"How the hell do I know? It was somebody in the neighborhood. The police wouldn't give me a name."

"Was it the woman sitting on the grate, the one dressed in rags?"

"I told you I don't know, but I seriously doubt it was her. I know her. She's not only a loony but half blind and deaf."

"She's not up there now. Where is she?"

"How the fuck would I know? She's probably in some shelter—or maybe she went to Florida for the winter. Jesus H. Christ. Hurry up with the questions, will you? My back is really giving me problems."

"The killing you mentioned is a police matter. Why are you involved?"

"I'm chairman of our neighborhood Crime Watch committee."

That did the trick. This time I got the stun gun in the belly, and my bones rattled as I twisted around in the ropes, convulsed, threw up, and cried. It was now time for Mr. Scheherazade to step through the curtain and go for one more night, this one.

"Interpol," I gasped when I was finally able to speak.

The man and woman looked at each other, obviously surprised. Judy asked, "What about Interpol?"

I spat out vomit and stifled a sob. "You're blown; the whole operation is blown. One of the patients who escaped from Rivercliff walked into a relief center and told her story to a social worker. The social worker called the police, and the police called the Feds because they smelled something very big and fishy about the whole thing. Word about what was going on leaked to a senator who's a friend of mine, and she's planning an investigation into just who's responsible for Rivercliff. In the meantime, her committee has hired me to do some preliminary investigating and search for the rest of the patients, besides the one you killed and the one who came in, who are still hiding out on the streets."

"That's nonsense," the woman said, sounding none too sure of herself. "What you're describing couldn't possibly have happened so quickly."

"What can I tell you, lady? You tell me how I could have become involved if things aren't the way I just told you."

Punch raised the stun gun threateningly. "If your senator doesn't know who Rivercliff belonged to, how could you know we'd been hired, and how could you know that the man we killed was one of the escaped patients?"

"I didn't know that at the time. It was just a hunch. The killing had the signature of professionals. Now, why should professionals take out a homeless vagrant if he wasn't in fact one of the people I was supposed to be looking for? I told you there was a witness. I called Interpol with your description because I thought it possible they might have a line on you. They did. Punch and Judy. They even know your real names, and the fact that you live near Paris. That's it. So untie me. You don't have any reason to kill me, and you have several very good reasons not to. I'm just a hired hand in this case, working for the real heavyweights who are after your asses. Back off now and go home, and maybe those heavyweights will let you continue to enjoy your lifestyle. Kill me, and they'll know you did it. Then things could get real nasty for you. If you know about me, then you must know about my brother; he will definitely track you down, and he will most definitely kill you both. Cut me loose, and you cut your losses."

I squinted in the gloom at their shiny faces, trying to gauge how I was doing, hoping I could remember whatever story I had just told them in case I had to repeat it. Both Punch and Judy looked singularly unimpressed with the threat of my brother tracking them down, my argument, or both.

The woman said, "You've been looking for the patients."

"That's right. Just like you."

"Have you found any?"

"No. Have you killed any others?"

I didn't expect an answer, and I didn't get one. Punch and Judy looked at each other for some time without speaking, as if they could communicate telepathically. Finally the man looked back at me, said, "Your story doesn't make any sense. If the police know about Rivercliff and the patients, why aren't there more cops out on the streets looking for them?"

"I don't know how many cops, maybe some in plainclothes, are looking for them, and neither do you. Sometimes the truth is kind of crazy. Hey, could anybody make up a story like I just told you while he's dangling here being electrocuted? I don't want you to hurt me anymore. Believe it, and let me go."

He raised the stun gun for me to see. "I want to hear about this business with senators and congressional committees and Interpol one more time. But first—"

He had brought the electric fangs of the stun gun to within a fraction of an inch of my neck, but he suddenly froze at the sound of brakes squealing as a car pulled up to the curb and stopped. The car's engine was turned off, a door opened and closed, and then footsteps clicked on the sidewalk, coming closer, going up the steps to my front door. I heard the doorbell ring from deep inside the brownstone, and I was glad I had given Margaret and Michael strict instructions to stay away from windows, and never to answer the door. The doorbell rang again, and then my visitor pounded on the door. Finally I heard a familiar voice shout, "Hey, Mongo! You up there?! If you are, you'd better stop playing games and get down here! The chief says I got to bring you in! Mongo?!"

It was Lou Colchen. Never again would I complain that there was never a cop around when you needed one—but then, I might never again get the chance to complain about anything. Punch had clapped the foul-smelling glove over my mouth the moment the car door had opened, and now I watched as he and his wife exchanged glances.

"Mongo?! You hear me?! I see lights on up there! If you are in there, you may as well come down now, because my orders are to wait right here until you show up! Come on, now! There's no sense in making me wake up the whole neighborhood!"

My captors continued to stare at each other, their expressions mirroring uncertainty. My heart was already pounding, but it began to beat even faster when a knife suddenly appeared in Judy's hand. She started to press the blade to my throat, but Punch, bless his dark heart, abruptly grabbed her wrist and pulled her hand away, shaking his head. He nodded toward the steps, and she nodded back. He took his hand away from my mouth, and then they bounded in unison up the stairwell and sprinted away down the sidewalk, their sneakered feet making hardly any sound.

"Hey, you two! What the hell?!"

I tried to spit, but there was no saliva left in my mouth. I smacked my lips and swallowed until I could work up a little moisture, then croaked, "I'm down here, Lou."

"Mongo? Where . . . ? I can hear you, but I can't . . ."

"Under your feet. In the stairwell."

I heard him skip down the steps over my head, then come along the railing until he was a dark outline at the top of the stairwell. A bright light came on, shining full in my face. I closed my eyes and turned my head away as pain shot through my skull.

"Holy shit," the gray-haired policeman said, then quickly climbed down the stairwell to the landing. He set his flashlight down, then used a pocketknife to cut the ropes that bound my wrists and ankles while he supported me under the back with one strong arm. He caught me as I fell, then started to lay me down.

"I don't want to lie down, Lou," I rasped. "Lift me up so that I can grab the railing."

"What?"

"Just do it, Lou."

He did, grabbing me by the seat of the pants and hoisting me into the air so that I could grab the bottom brace on the steel railing over my head. I hung there, breathing deep sighs of relief as my weight served to stretch out the muscles and ligaments in my body, every one of which was cramped, knotted, twitching, and screaming in pain.

Being stretched out felt absolutely divine. As far as I could tell, I hadn't broken any bones during the convulsions, or suffered any serious back injury, which I considered delightfully surprising considering the way I'd been trussed up, worked over, and had thrashed around.

"Mongo . . . ?"

"I'll be with you in a couple of minutes, Lou. I just need to hang out here a little while longer."

"What the hell happened to you?"

". . . Mugged."

"Muggers are going to the trouble of tying up their victims these days?"

"These were kinky muggers. Lou, I'm really happy to see you. I mean, I'm really, *seriously* happy to see you."

"Jesus, Mongo, you smell like shit and puke."

"You should get a whiff of me from where I am."

I was actually starting to feel better. I released my grip on the railing and dropped to the landing of the stairwell. That turned out to be an overly optimistic estimate of my recuperative powers. Normally, such a drop would have been no problem at all, but now my legs wouldn't support me, and I collapsed in a heap on the cold concrete. Lou lifted me up by the armpits, then sat me down on the steps next to his flashlight. My muscles were already starting to twitch and cramp again, and I arched my neck and back.

"Hey, buddy, I think I'd better get you to a hospital."

I shook my head. "I don't need to go to the hospital. I'll be all right. I just need to do a few more stretching exercises."

"That's up to you. But if you're not going to let me take you to the hospital, you're going to have to come with me anyway. The captain wants to talk to you. Now."

I sighed. "Give me a break, will you, Lou? I just got the shit kicked out of me. I'm still alive, thanks to you, but I really don't feel like chatting with MacWhorter, or anybody else right now. Tell him I'll be there in the morning, but not to expect me too early."

The policeman shook his head. "I can't do that, Mongo. Sorry. The captain's been calling you all afternoon and night. First your secretary says you're out and he doesn't know where you are or when you'll be back, and then he starts getting your machine. My assignment was to find you, no matter how long it took, and I'm not supposed to show my face at the station house unless I've got you in tow; otherwise, I'm going to be walking a beat on Staten Island. He means it, Mongo. You know how he gets. I can see you're hurting, but that's the way it's got to be."

I dredged up another sigh, this one even deeper, louder, and more heartfelt than the first. "You mind if I clean up first? I don't want to stink up the station house."

"You're not going to skip out on me, are you, Mongo?"

"Skip? You've got to be kidding me, Lou. I might try to crawl out on you, but skip? No way."

"Make it snappy, will you?"

"Snap this," I grumbled to myself as I got to my feet and stumbled up the stairs.

Naturally, I was in no hurry whatsoever to get back downstairs, because I was certainly in no hurry to go another round with MacWhorter while trying to keep my wits about me as I figured out what I was going to tell *him*, which was probably going to be only a slightly less fantastic *bubbameister* than whatever it was I had told Punch and Judy.

I stripped off my soiled clothes, sealed them in a plastic bag, which I set down by the kitchen door to take out with the garbage. Then I stepped into the shower, turned the water on as hot as I could stand it, then lay facedown in the tub and let the needle spray wash over me as I reflected on how very close I had come to being dead. Very sore was preferable to very dead, I concluded, and started to feel better about life in general.

After twenty minutes or so of stretching out and soaking under the hot water, I got to my feet, soaped up, rinsed off, and got out of the shower. I was moving easier, and it at least felt as if I might be able to get about without looking and feeling like a palsy victim. I dressed in jeans, a sweatshirt, and sneakers, then checked on Margaret and Michael, who were both sound asleep. I considered calling in some outside help to stand guard while I was gone, but then decided that it was unlikely that Punch and Judy would return to the brownstone, at least not so soon. I went to the bar in Garth's apartment, whacked my brain and body with a quarter of a tumbler of scotch, then went back downstairs, double-locking the front door behind me. The policeman was leaning against the hood of his cruiser, sipping at a carton of coffee he'd gotten from the deli up the block.

"You took your own sweet time."

"You'd better cuff me," I said, going across the sidewalk to him and holding out my wrists. "It's procedure, and you know how MacWhorter is about procedure."

He looked at me in an odd way, then crumpled up his empty coffee carton and threw it into a wire trash container a few feet away. "You've got a really strange sense of humor, Mongo. Get in the car, will you?"

CHAPTER 8

"*T*his is bullshit, MacWhorter, dragging me down here in the middle of the night!*" I shouted as I marched into the police captain's office. "Don't you sleep?! You're wasting your time, and mine! The first thing I want to do is call my lawyer, and then you and I can sit and stare at each other until she gets here!"

The burly policeman looked up from the stack of papers on his desk. In the harsh light thrown from his desk lamp he looked as if he had indeed not slept in some time, or even bothered to change his uniform. There were sweat stains around his collar and under his arms, and he would certainly not have passed one of his infamously rigorous inspections. He was unshaven, his beard a dark shadow cupping his face, and the large rings under his eyes were the color of bruises. "You don't need a lawyer, Frederickson," he said in a hoarse voice, "because you're not under arrest."

I stopped in front of the desk. "I'm not?"

"You're just here for a friendly chat. Sorry if Lou dragged you away from something you were doing."

"Actually, I was in the middle of being tortured, but it's all right. I was getting tired of it anyway."

He studied my face, blinked slowly. "If that's a joke, I don't get it."

"Didn't Lou call in a report?"

"He said you'd been mugged by a couple of guys in front of your house, and he was giving you time to clean up."

"That sounds about right. Before you bother to ask, I didn't get a good look at them."

"Two guys beat you up, and you didn't get a good look at them?"

"They were wearing ski masks."

MacWhorter grunted, then leaned back in his chair and smiled thinly. "Actually, I'm surprised they survived the encounter, much less got away. You're a pretty tough little bugger."

"Yeah, but I'm getting old. I can't mix it up like I used to."

"Now that you mention it, you look like shit, Frederickson."

"You don't look so hot yourself, Captain."

"How long have you had that twitch?"

"Not long. Why don't we both go home and get some sleep?"

MacWhorter sat up straight, pulled his chair closer to his desk. Color had risen in his cheeks, but his tone was even, and he seemed to be making some effort to control his temper. "I'll tell you why I can't go home, Frederickson, and why you're not going home either until I get some straight answers from you. Because more than two dozen people are dead, their hearts or spinal cords punctured, and eleven of those deaths occurred in my precinct. Guaranteed, there'll be more by morning. It's hard to nab somebody who has no apparent motive and who seems to have nothing better to do than wander around the city jabbing people with an ice pick. The reason I can't sleep is because I know more people will be dying while I do. I want to catch that crazy son of a bitch, and I just happen to have living in my precinct a civilian who seems to know more about what's going on than the whole NYPD put together. It's nothing short of amazing to me how this kind of weird shit always seems to stick to you and your brother; if there's something really bizarre going down, one or both of you are odds-on favorites to be somewhere right in the middle of it."

"I've often thought the same thing myself, Captain," I replied carefully.

"You were right about the stiff we found in the Dumpster. I kicked some ass and got an emergency autopsy performed. All of his tissues, and especially his brain, were saturated with some kind of drug."

"Will you tell me what it is?"

"Actually, there appear to be a number of drugs involved. There were traces of psychoactive drugs they use for nut cases, and don't ask

me to try to pronounce the names. The bulk of the stuff they found
can't be identified, at least not by our people. Forensics has sent
tissue samples to the FBI labs in Quantico, and we're waiting for the
results. As for that upstate mental hospital—"

"Rivercliff."

"Yeah, Rivercliff. The whole place burned to the ground better
than two weeks ago. The Smokies suspect arson, but they aren't sure.
Nobody who was inside survived—not patients, not staff. More than
sixty people dead. And all of the hospital records were destroyed. The
Smokies and the Feds are looking into it, but I'm not holding my
breath waiting for them to tell me anything. In the meantime, I've got
Dr. Death, identified by you and two anonymous sources as Raymond
Rogers and who you say came from Rivercliff, running around the city
stabbing people to death. It's the kind of thing that makes it hard for
me to sleep, Frederickson. You know what I mean?"

"Jesus Christ," I breathed, thinking of the sixty people who had
been murdered to cover up somebody else's crime.

"That's all you've got to say to me?"

"I have to be very careful what I say to you, Captain. Every time
I open my mouth, it only makes you angrier."

"That's because every time you open your mouth you say too much,
or not enough, or you give me bullshit. You want something?"

"What?"

"You want some coffee?"

"I want a drink."

He rubbed a hand across his grizzled chin, sniffed. "It smells to me
like you've already had a drink."

"What are you, president of your local temperance union? I want
another one."

"I don't drink."

"It's not for you, Captain, it's for me."

"There's no liquor on the premises. It's against regulations."

"What about that bottle you keep in your desk for emergency
situations like this one? I know it's there, because I've seen it in all
the cop movies."

"They've never shot any movie in here. I don't have any bottle in
my desk."

"In that case, I guess I'll have coffee."

"You know where it is. Go help yourself."

MacWhorter was in a decidedly strange mood, I thought as I shuffled out of his office, down a grimy corridor, and through a swinging door into the squad room, where I poured myself a cup of coffee from a pot sitting on a hot plate. I exchanged a little friendly banter with some of the cops going off duty or coming on, then went back to MacWhorter's office. He was sitting in almost the same exact position as when I had left him, but he had pushed the desk lamp off to the corner of his desk, so that now his face was half hidden in shadow. I doubted that his sudden change in mood, the shift to good cop from bad, was due to lack of sleep, so I wondered just what he thought being civil to me was going to accomplish. His first question surprised me.

"Where's Garth? I don't often see one of you without the other, even since he moved to Cairn. It's like the two of you are joined at the hip."

"He's off with his wife on a skiing vacation in Switzerland."

"Garth skis?"

"He's taking lessons. As far as I've heard, he hasn't broken anything yet."

"He ever talk about me?"

I sipped at my coffee, said, "Nope."

"I'm a good cop, Frederickson."

"I've never heard anybody claim otherwise."

Now he leaned forward in his chair, so that his whole face was caught in the bright cone of light cast by the desk lamp. Something in his green eyes had changed, but I couldn't tell what I was seeing there. He somehow seemed more vulnerable to me. "I wouldn't be a cop at all if it wasn't for your brother, Frederickson," he said in a voice that had grown hoarse. "I owe him big-time."

"I see. That explains why you always have such nice things to say about the two of us."

Anger flashed in his eyes, but it was almost instantly gone, supplanted by something that looked very close to shame. It occurred to me that it was costing Felix MacWhorter something to say whatever it was he was trying to say to me, so I decided to keep my smart-ass remarks to myself, at least for a time, and listen.

He stared at me for a few moments, then said, "Your brother and I were partners a whole lot of years ago. It was right after he came on the force. We were the same age, but he had more experience in law enforcement than I did."

I nodded. "He was a county sheriff in Nebraska, where we come from. He did a hitch as an MP in Vietnam, then heard how much fun I was having in New York and decided to join me."

MacWhorter shrugged, then glanced over my head at the wall behind me—or something else, perhaps his past. "We worked out of Fort Apache up in the Bronx. At the time the precinct was . . . a little dirty. There were a lot of cops on the pad. Most of it was small-time stuff—free meals, a couple of drinks, maybe a Christmas turkey. That kind of thing. But there was also some serious shakedown action going down, money changing hands, a little cash in envelopes that eventually became more cash in envelopes offered to cops for 'extra services,' maybe keeping a closer eye on some store that had been robbed a few times. Anyway, I was having money problems, so I started taking some of the envelopes that were offered to me. One day Garth caught me at it, and he told me to stop. I told him to fuck off and mind his own business, because I needed the extra money, and because I was really earning it by keeping an eye on the stores when I was off duty. He said that was a protection racket, not police work, and that he'd have to fight me if I didn't stop. Hell, I had fifty pounds on him, and I'd won the division boxing championship the year before; no country hick was going to tell *me* what to do. So I fought him."

"What happened?"

"He beat the shit out of me."

"Yeah, well, Garth was always pretty good with his fists. Fast hands."

"He dogged me after the fight, stuck to me like flypaper when we were on duty to make sure I didn't take any more money from shopkeepers. I knew that if I tried to, Garth would kick my ass again."

"And?"

"And it turns out your brother was working for Internal Affairs— mind you, he'd *volunteered* to work for IA, to help clean up the precinct. Who ever heard of such a thing?"

"It doesn't surprise me. Besides being good with his fists, Garth has always had a strong sense of justice. He took being a cop very seriously."

"Better than a third of the cops in that precinct got canned or transferred because of your brother, Frederickson. A few lost their pensions. I'd tried to go on the pad, but I got off scot-free because your brother decided that since I was his partner I was a problem he'd solve personally. He saved my career."

"And so you show your thanks by spending the rest of your career bad-mouthing him. I don't understand you, MacWhorter, and I don't understand why you dragged me down here in the middle of the night to tell me this."

He flushed, shifted in his chair, and looked away. "I'm trying to explain something to you, Frederickson, and it isn't easy for me. So cut me some slack. Garth had saved my ass, and I hated him for it; he'd shown himself to be a better man than I was, and I hated him for that. I felt ashamed, and I couldn't stand it. All I could allow myself to think about was the fact that your brother had ratted on his fellow officers. Most cops hate Internal Affairs, and Garth had volunteered to do their dirty work for them. He'd hurt people who were friends of mine, cops who'd thought Garth was their friend. He was a rat and a traitor, and just because he'd saved me from myself didn't alter that fact. That's the way I had to look at it in order to live with myself. Hell, I knew he resigned because the department screwed him over, betrayed him, and almost got both of you killed. But I still had my head up my ass. I couldn't forgive him for being a better man and cop than I was, for dropping the dime on my friends and saving me, and so I chose to keep trying to convince myself that he'd left and teamed up with you because he wanted to cash in on your fame. Then I started moving up in the ranks, and I started to see things differently—especially when I was given command of this precinct. I damn well wished I had a Garth Frederickson working for me. But I didn't behave differently. I'm a proud man, Frederickson, stubborn, and maybe even a little bit stupid at times. For a man like me, old attitudes die hard. Somewhere along the line all the mixed feelings I had about this thing turned into confusion. I'm not a man who enjoys spending much time looking into my own head, Frederickson, and the confusion I felt only made me more resentful of your brother. Somewhere along that same line I guess I started to take it out on you."

I paused with my cup of coffee halfway to my mouth, and I wondered if the astonishment I felt showed on my face. "My God, this is an *apology*."

The heavyset man smiled thinly. "Let's not get too carried away. I still think the two of you mess way more than you should in police business, just like I damn well know you're doing now. Let's say I'm calling for a truce. You know more about this Raymond Rogers than you're telling me. I want to catch a mass murderer, and I'm asking you to help me, if you can. You get no more threats and disrespect from me, and I want no more bullshit from you. Tell me what's going on. Deal?"

"Deal," I said, pulling the wooden chair I was sitting in closer to his desk. "The people who were working me over a little while earlier when Lou so conveniently showed are a fun couple by the name of Henry and Janice Sparsburg, nationality unknown but I believe American. They're professional assassins who go by the *noms de mort* of Punch and Judy. You can probably get more on them from Interpol, which is where I got my information. Their most distinguishing characteristic is that they've both had about a half dozen face lifts too many—plastic surgery is part of their thing. From a distance they look twenty years younger than they are, but the illusion fades rapidly the closer you get. Up close, they look grotesque. Think Dorian Gray. You could send out a call to post extra plainclothes cops at all the shelters in the city, because that's where Punch and Judy have been hunting up to now, but it's probably a waste of time. Now that I've made them and know what they're up to, they'll probably change their strategy. They're the people who killed the man you found in the Dumpster. They're working for the people who ran Rivercliff, and I have a hunch—only a hunch—that's the CIA. The good doctors at Rivercliff were conducting illegal experiments on human beings for years, and Rogers, who has to be our ice-pick killer, is only one of a dozen patients who escaped from the place after he went ballistic and started slicing and dicing his keepers. Besides Rogers, there are still eleven patients and a Rivercliff shrink by the name of Sharon Stephens out on the streets—that's assuming Punch and Judy haven't whacked any others. Stephens is probably one of the women who called you to identify Rogers, and 'the night owl' is Greta Wurlitzer. The stuff you found in the corpse's tissues is some kind of very powerful psychotropic drug that was used in the experiments at Rivercliff. Punch and Judy's job is to clean up the mess, kill Stephens and all the patients so that the truth about Rivercliff will never come out."

MacWhorter did amazed very well; he blinked rapidly while his mouth opened and closed a few times. Finally he said, "And just when were you thinking about getting around to telling me all this?"

"I was getting around to it when I walked in here, but then you launched into your True Confessions, and I didn't want to interrupt your soliloquy. Besides, I wasn't too happy about being busted, which is what I thought was happening. Your being so pleasant to me helped to jog my memory and organize my thoughts."

MacWhorter grunted and rolled his eyes toward the ceiling, then rose from behind his desk and walked out of the office. I watched through the glass as he talked to the desk sergeant and two detectives he'd summoned. The detectives hurried away, and MacWhorter came back into the office, closing the door behind him.

"You're probably right about these creeps who worked you over changing their MO, but at least now there'll be cops all over the city looking for them. If we come up with any likely suspects, you'll be available to identify them?"

"Day or night."

"Like I said, you look like shit, and you've got that tic, but at least you're still walking around. What'd they do to you?"

"They gave me a massage with a stun gun. If you think my face is twitching, you should feel my insides. It'll pass."

MacWhorter winced. "Jesus."

"My thought at the time, exactly."

"What'd they want?"

"I approached them on the street because I thought they looked like they might fit the description I'd been given by Interpol. This turned out not to be one of my cleverest ploys, because, as it turns out, they knew who I was. I followed them, but they gave me the slip, turned the tables, and ambushed me when I got home. I presume they looked up my address in the phone book. They wanted to know how

I'd made them, and how I'd gotten involved in their business in the first place."

"How *did* you get involved in the first place?"

"I met one of the escaped patients—he just kind of fell into my lap by accident. It was also by accident that I found out about his situation, and that of the other patients. I'd like to think that what I've told you will help you catch Raymond Rogers, but I don't think it will; his behavior is too random. I don't know anything else that would be of help to you. I'm aware that catching Rogers, and Punch and Judy if you can, is the job of the police. I'm not interested in anything but trying to find a way to help the patients, and that's been my only concern from the beginning. I just suspected that the guy in the Dumpster might be one of the escaped patients, and you confirmed it when you told me the results of the autopsy."

"Slow down, Frederickson; you're going just a little too fast for me. You say these escaped patients are being hunted by this Punch and Judy team?"

"Correct."

"Are the patients aware of this?"

"Not about Punch and Judy specifically. They're aware they could be in danger."

"Why don't they just go to the police? They'd not only get protection, but a roof over their heads and some food in their bellies. And then you'd have some proof to corroborate what you're telling me."

"They're afraid to go to the police, or identify themselves to anybody else in authority. They had that option before, and they still have it. Every single one of them is choosing not to exercise it. Nobody but Rogers has broken any laws, so the rest of them really aren't your concern. They understand the risk they're taking, the possibility that people could be sent to kill them. What they don't know is that the killers are here now, or who they are. That's why I'm looking for them; I want to warn them about Punch and Judy, and bring them in to some safe place if I can."

"And just why haven't they exercised their option of seeking police protection?"

"I'm not going to tell you that, Captain."

"Why the hell not?"

"Because it can't help you catch Rogers, and the information might put you into a very difficult position you don't want to be in. Your job's tough enough as it is. Again; with the very large exception of Raymond Rogers, they haven't broken any laws."

I thought MacWhorter might turn ugly on me again, but he didn't. He stared at me for some time, then grunted and abruptly strode out of his office a second time. He was gone for a couple of minutes, and when he returned he was carrying a mug of coffee for himself and a second mug for me. He sat back down behind his desk, sipped at his coffee while he mulled things over some more, then set the mug down on his desk and smacked his lips.

"They're afraid of being sent back to a mental hospital."

I nodded reluctantly. "Something very close to that, Captain. You're getting warm."

"Maybe they should be back in a mental hospital."

"Maybe."

"From what you tell me, Rivercliff wasn't exactly Club Med."

"It was Club Med all right, but not in the way you mean it."

"Even if it was a hellhole, that doesn't mean they shouldn't be getting proper care in some other place. Christ knows, we've already got more than enough crazy people wandering around out there. Besides, who's to say one of them might not flip out like Rogers did and start randomly killing people? Can you guarantee that's not going to happen?"

"I'm not in a position to guarantee anything, but I can assure you, on the basis of my observation of the one patient I've met, that it's highly unlikely. They don't need to go back to an institution, and their medical needs are being met at the moment. Being sent anywhere isn't what they're most afraid of."

MacWhorter again sipped at his coffee, had himself another good think. Finally he said, "Their medical needs are being met?"

"That's what I said." And wished I hadn't.

"They're on some kind of shit they took with them, right? It must be the same stuff we found in the stiff's tissues, the stuff you're so anxious to have me identify for you. So I assume Rogers is on the same shit, and maybe it's that shit that caused him to go over the edge when he discovered he could get his rocks off by sticking ice picks in people. How am I doing now, Frederickson? Am I getting any warmer?"

"Is he getting his rocks off by sticking ice picks in people?"

"Yep. You were right about that too. Semen traces on all of the victims' clothing we've been able to reexamine properly, and even at a couple of sites on the pavement. You were also right about the low sperm count. The guy is a walking cum factory. What does he do, walk around with his dick out?"

"I don't know. It's possible, but I think it's more likely that his pants are soaked with semen, and some of it rubs off when he makes contact with his victims."

"I believe we were discussing the shit these people are taking, and whether it could be responsible for making Rogers the way he is. I asked you if I was getting warmer, and you haven't given me an answer."

"I think it's time we changed the subject. I told you there are things you don't want to know because I know you care about what happens to these people. Let's suppose, for the sake of argument, that you're absolutely right, that they're on a medication that enables them to function normally, but it's also the same drug that turned Rogers totally dysfunctional and caused him to start killing people. I really don't know what's making him kill, but I'll bet you real money that the drug these people are taking, *if* they're taking any drug, was never submitted for FDA approval by the CIA or the company that manufactured it. It won't be listed anywhere. So what are you going to do if one of them shows up and you know he's carrying some of this strange dope? Are you going to let him keep it? How could you, considering the risk involved? But if you did take it away, then maybe this person would go nuts again—or worse. Maybe this person dies on you. I don't think you want that responsibility. You should worry about catching Rogers, who's a criminal."

"And you insist this drug is only hypothetical?"

"I'm asking you to listen very carefully to what I'm saying. In the hypothetical situation I've just outlined, for your own future peace of mind you would not want to have probable cause for search and seizure with any escaped patient who voluntarily came to you for protection."

"In this hypothetical situation, maybe there's some substitute medication they could take that's safe and approved."

"Maybe, maybe not. They obviously don't think so. Neither does the shrink who helped them escape, and she's in the best position to know. It could very well be that they know this hypothetical uncontrolled is the only thing that can keep them alive and truckin', and they don't want to ask the police for help for fear it will be confiscated."

MacWhorter grunted, then narrowed his eyes as he studied my face. "I don't suppose you're trying to get more of this hypothetical uncontrolled for these people, are you? That would be pretty stupid."

"I told you what I'm trying to do; I want to find them before Punch and Judy put a bullet in their skulls. But I also need a place to bring them, someplace where their needs will be understood and they'll be guaranteed safety."

"You could be looking for some big trouble that wouldn't be at all hypothetical."

"Captain, every time I open my mouth to you, you want to close it by lopping my head off."

The burly policeman shook his head. "You're wrong, Frederickson," he said evenly. "That's not what's happening here. I very much appreciate this little chat, and I'm inviting you to take me completely into your confidence. It isn't for you to decide whether or not laws are being broken, and telling me everything you know now could protect you in the future if things go sour. Man, if you're trying to obtain and distribute shit that has the potential of turning people into homicidal sex maniacs, you are sticking your neck out a long, long way. It doesn't matter what your motives are. Can't you see that? I'm not threatening you; I'm trying to give you a warning. You want to be looked on as an accomplice if one of these people you're trying to help turns into another Raymond Rogers? I can imagine hypothetical scenarios where you could wind up in prison for a very long time."

"Change the subject, Captain, or I walk. What else do you want to know? Is there anything that isn't clear to you?"

I waited, meeting his gaze while he considered the question. Appearances and occasional behavior notwithstanding, there wasn't any moss growing on Felix MacWhorter, and giving him free license to keep firing at me until his gun was empty was risky business. But I thought it was worth the risk. For the most part, what I was telling him was the truth, and a mollified, relatively informed Felix MacWhorter could prove to be a valuable ally to Margaret Dutton, Michael Stout, and the others when they did turn to the authorities for help, which they would eventually have to do.

He began to tap the fingers of his right hand on his desk, an indication to me that he'd reloaded. "How did Punch and Judy manage to keep you from beating the shit out of them?"

"They got the drop on me, and they had me trussed up like a pig."

"And they were torturing you until Lou came along."

"Right."

"It wouldn't have taken them a second to slit your throat, or put a bullet in your brain."

"And then off Lou, for that matter."

"So why didn't they? You knew all about them, so why didn't they kill you?"

"An excellent question, one I've been asking myself. I don't have the answer."

"Maybe not, but I'll bet you have a theory."

"A couple of them, actually. First, they may have believed a bullshit story I told them, and—"

"They're buzzing you with a stun gun, and you told them a bullshit story?"

"What else was I going to do? They'd have killed me on the spot if I'd told them the truth. Knowing that you're going to die if you don't come up with just the right tall tale does wonders for focusing the mind."

"What was the story?"

"I told them that the cops, FBI, Daughters of the American Revolution, and every character on Sesame Street knew all about them and Rivercliff and the escaped patients, and that it was only a matter of time before they were caught if they didn't get out of the country. They weren't quite sure they believed me, but it set them to thinking. They were getting ready to buzz me again when Lou came calling."

"I still don't understand why they didn't kill you—and Lou."

"They probably would have if they'd been convinced it wasn't true, because then nobody could have pinned the murders on them. But if it was true that the whole operation was blown, then killing me could have serious consequences, and killing Lou would most definitely have serious consequences. The NYPD would have shut down the entire city until they were found, if you did know who they were. Kill me, and they might not have been safe even back on their home turf. They had a pretty good line on me, so they must know something about Garth and his reputation for tenacity. It's possible they were more worried about him than about the authorities, because he wouldn't be in the least concerned with jurisdiction or legal niceties. It's possible they didn't kill me because they didn't want him on their trail. My brother can get pretty furry."

"You mean like a squirrel?"

"I mean like a werewolf—although he can get pretty squirrelly before he tears your throat out. Lately, he's been doing John Wayne imitations when he's mad at somebody; if you hear the Duke talking to you, then it's time to get out of the vicinity. Garth can be very dangerous if you're a bad guy, and he takes no prisoners. They may not have wanted to take a chance on messing with him if my murder could be pinned on them. Like I said, I'm guessing. At the time, they didn't seem all that impressed by anything I was saying."

"You're probably right on one or both counts. Of course, by letting you live, they guaranteed they'd be blown."

"That's true—but now they know exactly where they stand, which has to be in the shadows. They'll try to use me as a stalking horse, a Judas goat. They know I'm looking for the patients, so they'll keep a close watch on me and hope I do their job for them. Most likely, they'll bring in a team of fresh faces to follow me around. Punch and Judy still have their assignment, which is to wipe out all the living evidence of what happened at Rivercliff, and money is no object to their employers. What their employers won't accept is failure. They'll plan to come around later, when they've done what they were paid to do, and kill me at their leisure, make it look like an accident."

"So you'd better watch your ass."

"I always do."

"You'd best start doing a better job of it than you did tonight."

"Your point is well taken."

"With luck, we'll find them before they kill anybody else. May I assume you'll be in touch right away if you come up with any more information that could help us catch Rogers?"

"You may definitely assume so."

"You want a ride home?"

"No, thanks," I said, rising and arching my back, which still hurt. "I need to stretch my muscles. See you."

He waited until I got to the door of the office, then said, "Frederickson."

I looked back over my shoulder. "What?"

"I'll fill you in—unofficially—if the FBI can identify the substance found in the Dumpster body. You've earned that much. What you do with the information is up to you. You know the risks involved in trying to obtain more of the stuff, and you've been warned."

"Thanks, Captain. I appreciate it."

"One other thing, Frederickson."

"What's that?"

His thick lips curled back into just the slightest trace of a smile. "I still think you're an arrogant, publicity-seeking, interfering dwarf prick."

I favored him with my own slightest trace of a smile. "The onset of a relationship like ours is always the sweetest part, Captain. I love you too."

CHAPTER 9

I slept fitfully, awakening often with painful muscle spasms and cramps, my dreams haunted by the pasty white faces of deadly puppets coming at me with cattle prods. I awoke in midmorning twisted like a pretzel. Drinking up all that voltage pumped into me by Punch and Judy had definitely not been welcomed by my muscles, joints, nerves, and acetylcholine, and my body was telling me to go on about my business if I liked, but it would take its own sweet time recuperating, thank you very much.

After a half hour of stretching exercises, calisthenics, and a hot shower, I could move more easily. I dressed, then went downstairs to check on my charges. Margaret was stronger, able to sit up now, and I found Michael in her room. Apparently they enjoyed each other's company, and had been talking all morning, swapping stories. Margaret had been telling the man about her former existence—what she could remember—as Mama Spit, and Michael had been telling her about life at Rivercliff. From Margaret's description of the murdered man who had given her the plastic bag of black-and-yellow capsules, Michael had given the patient a name—Philip Mayepoles. I duly noted the information so as to pass it on to MacWhorter.

It occurred to me that it might be very useful at some time in the future to have the reminiscences of the two schizophrenics on tape, and so I retrieved a tape recorder from my apartment, gave it to them along with several blank cassettes. When I left them, Michael was speaking into the microphone, talking about Rivercliff.

When I went downstairs to my office, I found Francisco in a foul mood. Precisely those qualities that made him such an excellent administrator and assistant also made him an occasional pain in the ass. He was obsessive about having clean desks—mine as well as his; he considered it his sworn duty to see that all business—mine as well as his—was taken care of promptly, and in the past week I had certainly let things slide. He knew nothing about what I was involved in, but he did as he was told and never asked questions, in this case not even about the miraculous transformation of the woman who, until a week before, had sat in rags on a grate and cursed and spat at him every time he passed by. Francisco had no objections whatsoever to playing butler for my two mysterious guests and monitoring their movements to make sure they stayed out of sight; what he did object to was the small mountain of unsigned documents, unfinished reports, and unanswered messages that were piling up on the desk in my office, which was behind his. When he began to mutter darkly about how he was going to have to look for new employment after Frederickson and Frederickson lost all its clients and could no longer afford to pay him, I saluted, then dutifully marched on my cramping legs into my office and closed the door behind me.

The first call I made was to Veil Kendry, a friend who, along with my brother and Chant Sinclair, was one of the three most dangerous men I knew. In addition to being a world-class painter, a creator of eerily beautiful murals that could be divided up into segments, he was a consummate martial artist, my personal *sensei*, who had, on more than a few occasions, taught me more than a few things about wreaking havoc on people who were trying to wreak havoc on me. Veil had other students, men and women from whom he accepted no payment and whom Veil chose through a selection process I did not understand; Veil, something of a mystic, would say only that they had been "sent" to him, as I had been "sent" to him. I didn't care how he selected them, but at the moment these were the kinds of people I needed sent to me.

I trusted Veil completely, and so I told him the whole story about Mama Spit, Michael Stout, Rivercliff, Raymond Rogers, the drug, the shepherdess and her lost flock, Punch and Judy. He immediately understood the nature of my problem; Punch and Judy knew where I lived, and I had to worry about a return visit, if not by them personally, then by other assassins who might be in the employ of the people responsible for Rivercliff. I had to worry not only about myself but also about Francisco, if they came during the day, and Margaret Dutton and Michael Stout were a surprise package the assassins would be most delighted to find and dispatch. Whoever was sent was certain to be highly skillful at breaking and entering as well as killing, and it was possible everyone in the brownstone could be murdered in their sleep unless precautions were taken. We needed protection.

Veil told me he would assume responsibility for the security of everyone in the brownstone, around the clock; two-person teams would be assigned to eight-hour shifts, with one guard on the ground floor and one on the top. He would take the midnight-to-eight shift himself, since that was the time he usually painted and he would use the hours to work. I declined his offer to have somebody follow me around when I left the house. I insisted on paying him and his students, but he only laughed, reminding me that he would be dead if not for me. I reminded him that I would be dead if not for him, and argued that at least his students should be paid. He explained that his students were not allowed to take money for the use of the skills he taught them, and that the people he chose to guard the brownstone would be only too happy to have the opportunity to practice something he called "vigilance technique." I thanked him profusely, and hung up.

I spent some time returning what I considered to be the most important calls, canceled some appointments and rescheduled others in order to provide myself with blocks of time to do whatever it was I was going to have to do to prevent the tragedy that was going to take place in less than three weeks if I couldn't find a fresh supply of the drug the escaped patients were taking. A half hour later the first team of bodyguards arrived, a black man named Ted, who appeared to be in his mid-twenties, and a slight, fresh-faced Asian woman named Kim, who looked as if she could be bowled over by a good sneeze, which I knew was not the case. I showed them around the brownstone, introduced them to Margaret and Michael and Francisco, then left them to their own devices.

Punch and Judy, or anybody else who tried to enter the brownstone uninvited, were going to get the surprise—maybe the last—of their lives.

Step Four.

I did some paperwork, hid the rest of the stack behind a filing cabinet when Francisco wasn't looking, and at eleven-thirty sneaked out past Francisco and walked the few blocks to Frank Lemengello's lab. His was a report I wanted to hear in person.

"The reason the capsule is so big is because there's so much stuff in it," the husky, bushy-haired chemist said as he ushered me into his office. "There isn't just one component, but a whole slew. It's like a soup—a cocktail, if you will. There's a mixture of different drugs, and I wouldn't be surprised if some of them didn't actually counteract each other. Here's the breakdown."

He handed me a computer printout listing the chemicals by name and molecular structure. I noticed one long line of letters and numbers with a big question mark beside it. I didn't much like what I was hearing, which sounded very complex, or the sight of the big, hand-drawn question mark on the printout, which was worse than complex, and did not bode well. "Can you be a little more specific, Frank? How many ingredients can you identify?"

"I can put a name to five. There's lithium, Thorazine, Ritalin, a chemical analog of Prozac, and even what appears to be an analog for Roxian, a Swedish medication for schizophrenics used for a while in Europe, until a couple of patients died. Most are heavy-duty psychotropics, used for treating the seriously mentally ill."

"By 'analogs' you mean they're not the actual drugs, but close to it?"

"That's right. It's all noted on the printout, along with the relative proportions found in the capsule. I've never heard of mixing those drugs together like that. Most of them can have some pretty unpleasant side effects."

"Like what?"

Frank shrugged his broad shoulders. "The side effects can range from simple things like dry mouth and constipation to serious depression and dyskinesia—uncontrollable muscle contractions and rigidity. Lithium, for example, is actually toxic. It's almost never given in the same dose to different patients. Usually the physician takes into account the body weight of a patient before prescribing a particular dosage, and then the blood is closely monitored for levels of toxicity."

"I know about the side effects you mentioned. What about others?"

"They'd all be listed in the literature, or on the labels or in the pamphlets given out by the various companies that manufacture the drugs. You can look them up in a pharmaceuticals manual."

"What about side effects that aren't listed on labels or in the literature?"

"Like what?"

"I don't know—anything."

"All side effects that have been observed in human testing have to be described in the written materials put out by the pharmaceuticals companies licensed to manufacture the various drugs. It's the law. If you can tell me what it is you're rooting around for, maybe I can be more helpful. The things I mentioned are the major side effects associated with those drugs—that I know of. But then, I'm not a physician."

"Frank, I don't know what I'm rooting around for. Tell me about the drug you can't identify."

"Now there's a puzzler. As you can see from the printout, more than half of the compound in the capsule was this stuff, more than all of the other drugs combined. But it's new, with a molecular structure not described in any of the pharmaceuticals or chemical manuals. It doesn't have a name. All I can tell you is that it's a large molecule, a really big mother. It's very complex, and almost certainly man-made."

"What's your best guess as to what this big mother molecule does?"

"It could be a kind of binder to help the other drugs work together more effectively, or it could be a whole new type of psychotropic. My best guess is that it's both."

"And?"

"I can't tell you any more than that from just looking at the molecular structure. Psychotropics act on the brain in ways that aren't completely understood. For example, nobody knows why lithium works so effectively for some manic-depressives. Give Ritalin to a hyperactive kid, and it calms him down; give it to a normal adult, and he'll start climbing the walls. I'd say this new stuff is definitely toxic. I wouldn't want any of it in my bloodstream or brain."

"Is it possible that this drug magnifies side effects, or even creates new ones?"

"Why the hell would any manufacturer want to create a drug to treat mental illness that would amplify side effects? That's a crazy idea—if you'll pardon the expression."

"Forgive the stupid questions of a naive layman. I'm not concerned with the manufacturer's motives, only in whether you think it's possible this drug might act in that way."

"I can't tell from the data I have. Where the hell did you get this stuff, Mongo?"

I considered my answer carefully. I hated to lie to Frank, but I couldn't afford to provide him with information that he didn't need to know and that could prove dangerous for both of us. I needed his help, if I could get it, and he had to remain almost totally ignorant of what I was up to if I didn't want to make him a witting accomplice. I finally decided on a reply that was at least partially true. "It's floating around on the street."

"You mean dope dealers are offering this stuff for sale and people are actually buying it?"

"Well, not exactly. It's just out there on the street."

"The drugs I can identify in that capsule you gave me wouldn't give a healthy person anything but grief."

"It's a little complicated, Frank. I just need to know all I can about that combination of drugs."

"There isn't much more to tell you, except that I don't see how this compound could have any value as a street drug. Except for the Ritalin, which is actually methylphenidate hydrochloride, and granted that I don't know what that new drug does, there's nothing in the compound I can identify that would give anybody a *high*. Ritalin is nothing more than a mild stimulant, and the other drugs are used to treat schizophrenia and other psychoses. You'd get a lot more bang for your buck with the amphetamines or cocaine for sale out there. An emotionally stable person wouldn't get any jolt out of taking this stuff, would still experience the nasty side effects, and might be in big trouble if he or she suddenly stopped taking it cold turkey without medical supervision."

"Why, Frank? What might happen to a person who'd been on this stuff for a time and then suddenly stopped taking it?"

"I'd just be guessing. An MD could give you a better picture."

"Please. Guess away."

"The known psychotropics in this compound alter blood chemistry, in some cases dramatically, and I have to assume the unidentified drug does the same thing—maybe in an even bigger way. So your blood and all of your organs kind of become adapted to that alteration. My guess is that once you start taking this stuff you have to keep taking it, or be weaned off it very carefully to allow the blood chemistry to return back to normal. Abrupt withdrawal could cause trauma. An analogy would be an alcoholic getting the shakes and DTs if he doesn't get his booze. Except that I suspect being suddenly deprived of this stuff could kill you. Why can't you bring me nice, simple things, like those samples of Hudson River water you lugged in here a couple of years ago?"

"You think medical people, maybe a psychiatrist or some kind of researcher, could tell me what that unidentified drug is?"

Frank shook his head. "I strongly doubt it; they'd consult the same references I did. You'd have to find the manufacturer. They're the people who researched and developed this compound, in house, and exactly how they did that is most likely a closely guarded trade secret. They're probably running computer models and doing animal testing, hoping to eventually get FDA approval for human trials. That could take years, because they've got a lot of rough spots to smooth out. They could never get approval for this formulation—too toxic. This stuff is dangerous."

"Frank, let me ask you a question. Could a good chemist—you, for example—make up a batch of this compound using the ingredients in the capsule as a model?"

He studied me for a few moments, and when he replied his voice had a slight edge to it. "Why would any respectable chemist want to do such a thing?"

"I'm just curious. Could it be done?"

"Highly unlikely. The five drugs I mentioned are off the shelf, available by prescription or DEA license. But that last drug, which makes up the bulk of the compound, is another matter. Researchers for pharmaceuticals companies use supercomputers to design and manufacture new drugs like that. It's not like processing heroin or cocaine, where the method is known. I couldn't replicate the stuff, and I wouldn't if I could. There would be no purpose. God knows how long the company that made this compound has been working on formulation, and what they have is still useless, dangerous to humans. Trying to replicate it without proper licensing is probably illegal, and the fact that there are capsules out on the street represents a serious breach of security by the manufacturer. Do the police know about this?"

"I've been reporting to the local precinct commander personally," I said, rolling up the computer printout and putting it under my arm. "Thanks, Frank. Send me a bill."

"Will do. Always a pleasure doing business with you, Mongo. I hope you and the cops nail whoever is responsible for letting that stuff escape from the lab, and I hope they get put away."

I hoped for the same thing. But I didn't want them put away just yet—not until their current victims were out of harm's way, and that necessitated getting another batch of the compound, possibly a big one, before those victims went away permanently.

Step Five.

An unplanned improvisation.

I'd hoped to persuade Frank Lemengello, once he'd identified what was in the capsule, to make up some for me after he'd been told the reason I needed it. But he'd made it clear to me that he couldn't, and wouldn't, no matter what the reason, and I couldn't say I blamed him. But if Frank couldn't do it, I had to find somebody else with the appropriate expertise who might be willing to at least take a stab at it, and I knew only one other candidate—a highly unlikely one, since I wasn't sure he would even talk to me.

I waited across the street from the lab, next to a newsstand, for twenty minutes. At 12:45, Bailey Kramer, wearing a sheepskin coat, emerged from the lab and headed in the opposite direction, presumably to have lunch. I hurried across the street and ran after him, catching up with the defrocked professor as he waited for the light to change at the end of the block.

"Let me buy you a hot dog, Bailey," I said as the light turned green and I fell into step beside him.

He glanced down, and if he was surprised to see me he didn't show it. His face didn't reveal any emotion, and he simply said, "No, thank you."

"All right, then, a real lunch."

"No, thank you," he repeated, and quickened his pace.

"This is important to me, Bailey. It could also be important to you."

"What do you want from me?"

"I can't talk and jog like this at the same time."

Kramer abruptly stopped walking and turned to face me, studying me with his soulful dark eyes. "What do you want?"

"What do you want to eat?"

"A hot dog will be fine."

I bought us hot dogs and sodas at a Sabrett stand in the next block, and we sat on the concrete lip of a fountain and reflecting pool outside a bank. The tall black man ate his hot dog and sipped at his soda in silence as he stared down at the sidewalk. I wondered if he was thinking of the future Garth and I had helped take from him. I finished my dog and soda, got up to throw our wrappers and cans in a trash basket, came back, and again sat down beside him.

"I have a job for you, Dr. Kramer."

"If you want to talk to me, Frederickson, don't call me Dr. Kramer. I already have a job that you got for me."

"I have another job for you, Bailey, in addition to the one you have now."

"Mr. Kramer."

"I have another job for Mr. Kramer, if he wants it. It's not an easy job; in fact, it's so difficult that I'm not sure it can be done by one man, even you, in the time I need it done—which is by Christmas Eve, two and a half weeks. I can't pay you even a small fraction of what this work is worth, assuming it is possible for you to do it. Also, you will most likely end up in prison for a long time if you get caught doing it, because it's essentially the same kind of work you got busted for."

He slowly turned his head to look at me, and for the first time his face and eyes registered emotion—in this case surprise bordering on astonishment. "You want me to design a narcotic?"

"Not exactly. I want you to replicate a compound. Most of the ingredients are off-the-shelf prescription drugs, but one ingredient hasn't been identified, and there's where the hard work begins. What you'll end up with isn't a narcotic, but it's highly toxic. To make this compound would almost certainly be deemed illegal, at the least, and in your case a parole violation, which amounts to the same thing."

Bailey Kramer slowly shook his head. His initial look of astonishment had mellowed to mere amusement, and there was a thin smile tugging at the corners of his mouth. "You sure are one terrific salesman, Frederickson. Let me see if I've got this straight. *You*, of all people, want me to do something illegal for you, essentially the same thing you and your brother got me busted for, and you can't even begin to pay me what the job is worth."

"Yeah. That's about it."

"Would you like me to distribute the product for you too?"

"No distribution. I'm your sole customer."

"What, am I supposed to take a commission?"

"No commission. What you make won't be for sale."

"It sounds to me like you're going to make an even worse dope dealer than a salesman. Why the hell do you want to joke with me, Frederickson?"

"I'm not joking, Mr. Kramer."

"Stop calling me Mr. Kramer. It sounds silly coming from someone with whom I have such an intimate relationship."

"I didn't want to make my main pitch and then have to temporize with a lot of ohs, ands, buts, and the like. I figured it was best to give you the bad news up front."

"Devilishly clever of you, Frederickson. What's the good news?"

"I'm not sure there is any for you; that's for you to decide. Can I give you the rest of my spiel now?"

Kramer shrugged, and once again there was the slightest trace of a smile on his face. "After that teaser about the possibility of going to prison for doing this thing, how can I resist?"

I took another one of the black-and-yellow capsules I had borrowed from Margaret Dutton's supply out of my pocket, used it to tap on the rolled-up computer printout I had taken from under my arm and placed between us on the stone ledge. "This printout is a chemical analysis of the ingredients contained in a capsule just like this one. Like I said, most of the ingredients are prescription drugs—but the main ingredient, the stuff that makes it work the way it does, hasn't been identified. It's something new that's been carefully designed for its purpose, and it will probably have to be synthesized from scratch. I don't know how I'm going to get hold of the prescription drugs to add to it, but I'll think of something. I'll supply you with all the equipment, materials, space—whatever you need. I don't know how I'll do that either, but I will. You just sit down and make me a list of what you require. What I need for you to do is come up with a way to replicate that unidentified substance. I need a lot of it, enough for an indefinite number of doses in the ratio you'll find in this capsule, and on the printout. And I need it by Christmas Eve—a day or two before, if you can manage it, because I'll need time to package the doses."

"Frank did this analysis?"

"Yep."

"Did you ask him to make this stuff for you?"

"Not directly. He clearly indicated that he wouldn't even if he could, and he said he couldn't."

"So now you want me to make it for you."

"Yep."

"You going into the drug-dealing business, Frederickson?"

"If you want to look at it that way, yes. Except this dope isn't a narcotic; it's an extremely powerful psychotropic."

Kramer picked up the printout, unrolled it, and gave the contents barely a glance before saying, "It's a number of psychotropics, and one amphetamine."

"All working in concert with the unidentified substance to provide one hell of a jerk back to reality—that is, if you're psychotic."

"It looks very toxic."

"It is very toxic. I said so."

"Frank told you he couldn't replicate this. You think I can?"

"You tell me. Better yet, show me. You're the hotshot chemist.
Will you do it?"

"What the hell do you want this stuff for, Frederickson? This drug
compound can't be much good for anything. Normal people wouldn't
get anything out of taking it but a puckered mouth and a sour stomach. Half of these drugs are already available, in carefully monitored
dosages, to the people who need them if they're under a doctor's care.
I don't need to know a great deal about the unidentified drug on the
printout to recognize that this formulation could kill you. Any psychiatrist who prescribed this should be locked up."

"It's a long story, Bailey, so I'm going to give you the Classics
Illustrated version. Right now there are about a dozen very seriously
mentally ill people here in the city."

"This is a news flash? I would have thought there were more than
that not far from where we're sitting."

"Not like these people, Bailey. I'm talking serious psychotic.
These people are chronic schizophrenics who have been institution-
alized most of their lives. But they're able to function normally,
thanks to the compound in this capsule. It's true that the drug is
highly toxic, but it seems to be its own antidote—probably one of
many functions of that unidentified component. The problem is that
you can't stop taking it once you start. It's been manufactured il-
legally, and used exclusively for illegal experiments on the people
I mentioned. There probably isn't any way of getting a fresh supply
of this stuff through any kind of normal, legal channel. All of these
people are going to run out of the supply they have by Christmas
Eve. When that happens, they'll first plunge back into madness,
and within a few hours they'll die—quickly and badly, from massive
internal hemorrhaging. The supply I want you to replicate represents an insurance policy that will buy them the time I need to try
to find a way to solve their medical problem through more accept-
able channels. Without a new supply of this specific compound,
they're outta here come Christmas."

Bailey put the printout back down on the ledge, looked away.
"Shit," he said quietly.

"This is a heavy-duty job with heavy-duty risks, Bailey. What else can I say? If I could think of any other way to get it done, I wouldn't be coming to you."

Now he turned back, and his soulful eyes searched my face. He no longer seemed amused. "So you're helping these people."

"I'm giving it my best shot. I'm not sure how much good it would do if things don't work out and we get caught at this, but I'll give you a letter detailing this conversation and specifying that you're acting only at my urgent request. Maybe we can come up with some scam that makes it look like I'm blackmailing you. If you go down, I go down along with you, and you can plead extenuating circumstances. I'll back you up. I give you my word on that, and you'll have the letter to corroborate your story."

"Stuff your letter," he said softly, and narrowed his eyes. "It cost you something to come to me like this, didn't it?"

"Not really. After Frank turned me down, I couldn't think of any other option. These people, and particularly one of them, are important to me. Even if I did feel a little uncomfortable and humbled coming to you, that would be pretty petty stuff compared to what's going to happen to those ex-patients if I don't get more of their medication."

"Why you, Frederickson?"

"Why me what?"

"Why should you do this? I don't need any silly, self-incriminating letter from you to know that your ass is on the line right now, regardless of what I do or don't do for you. Before I give you an answer, I want you to explain to me why you'd risk so much for these people."

"What, are you bucking for psychiatrist? You're starting to piss me off, Mr. Kramer, and this may be the last time I buy you lunch. I don't have any explanation. I'm doing it because the situation fell into my lap, it has to be done, and I didn't see anyone else waiting in line to do it. Maybe I'm doing it because being around and talking to some of these people makes me a little more appreciative of what a marvelous gift it is to have my own brain in reasonable working order when I wake up each morning. Give me a break."

Now Bailey Kramer laughed; but it was a gentle, warm sound, with no trace of mockery. "You really are a goddamn professional do-gooder, aren't you? You're unreal, dude. You rescue fallen molecular

chemists from their jobs as hack drivers and find them meaningful
work, and you spend your own time and money, and maybe risk
getting into big-time trouble with the law, to help a bunch of loonies,
most of whom—if I'm reading correctly between the lines—don't even
know who you are."

"Yeah, yeah, I'm a regular Mother Teresa."

"And now you're making this totally absurd request, trying to drop
this particular little job in my lap because it has to be done, and you
can't think of anybody else who can do it."

"Yep."

"Give me the capsule," Kramer said, picking up the printout with
one hand and holding out the other. "I'll see what I can do. I should
know within a day or two if I have any chance of success, and I'll let
you know if the answer is negative. I won't keep you in suspense."

I handed him the capsule, resisting the strong impulse to throw my
arms around his shoulders and kiss him. "People who accede to my
totally absurd requests are granted permission to call me Mongo."

"I'll think on it, Frederickson."

"I haven't told you about the potential payoff—assuming, that is,
you don't end up in prison."

"You said you couldn't pay me."

"I said I couldn't pay you a fraction of what the work is worth. If
you're successful, I think the work could be worth millions. In addition to being very wealthy, you just might get back your career and
reputation."

He stared at me for some time, then said quietly, "Explain how I
might get back my career and reputation."

I smiled. "You mean as opposed to the millions I mentioned? You
don't need that kind of spare change?"

"Obviously, Frederickson, you've never been totally humiliated
and virtually destroyed because of your own stupidity. I don't need
millions of dollars; I need a chance to take off the dunce's cap I put
on myself. I need not to be a fool."

"I've been humiliated, Bailey, and I've been a fool on more than a
few occasions. I hear what you're saying."

"Tell me."

"There are probably generic equivalents to all of the prescription drugs in this compound, so patents aren't a problem. But the un-identified drug is the engine that really drives this witch's brew. The people who designed, manufactured, and tested it weren't interested in helping schizophrenics to function normally; their only interest was in some bizarre side effects caused by the medication. Right now, your only concern is replicating the drug exactly as it is within the next two and a half weeks to allow the patients to live long enough for some researcher to come up with a safe substitute. That's in the future, and I could be looking at that researcher. The point is that, even with its toxicity and deadly side effects, to call the medication inside that capsule a wonder drug would be a gross understatement. I've seen how quickly and powerfully it works, and I think it's nothing short of downright stone miraculous. People who were hopelessly mad become sane and able to function normally. It's far and away more effective than anything on the market, and for all we know it may be useful in treating other kinds of psychoses. But it will have to be reformulated to make it safer before it can be submitted for FDA approval and human testing. Get me a batch of the original replicated, and then you can work on that reformulation at your leisure. Believe me, the people who designed that drug have never been in any patent office, and they're not going to follow you into one. They won't be looking to take any credit, and if I have my way they'll be spending the rest of their lives in prison."

"Interesting," Kramer said in a mild tone.

"I'm glad I've piqued your curiosity."

"This drug sounds like something the CIA would dream up."

He'd surprised me. "Why do you say that?"

"The CIA is always nosing around academia. They like to keep up with the latest research in chemistry, pharmacology, psychology—all sorts of areas. You'd be amazed at how much academic research is totally funded by the CIA, although they're almost never up front about it."

"I wouldn't be amazed at all."

"You're in danger, aren't you?"

There didn't seem to be much sense in denying it. "Ah, well, you know how it goes, Bailey. Mongo's the name, danger's my game."

"I'm serious. I've had dealings with these people, probably turned down close to two dozen research grants for odd jobs they wanted me to do. They're very strange."

"Tell me about it. My safety isn't your concern, Bailey. And you should be safe as long as you lie low while you're working on this, and don't talk to anybody else about what you're doing."

"You don't have to worry about that." He paused, lowered his gaze, then added softly, "Thanks."

"For what? Giving you the chance to get sent to prison?"

He looked back into my face, said, "For having the chutzpah to come to me with this totally absurd request."

"You can do it, Bailey."

"I don't need a pep talk, Frederickson," he said with a wry smile as he put the capsule in his pocket, picked up the computer printout, and rose to his feet.

"When will I hear from you?"

"When I have something to say. I told you I'd let you know in a day or two if I won't be able to do it."

"Call or fax me with a list of everything you need—amount of lab space, equipment, materials, general expenses, whatever. The phone and fax numbers are on the printout."

"Sure. I'm not doing this for the potential payoff, Frederickson— not the potential profits from marketing a safe version of the drug, and not even for the chance to get my old life back. At least, those aren't the major reasons."

"I don't care why you're doing it, Bailey. I'm grateful to you."

"Maybe your reasons are good enough for me; I'd like to save these people's lives."

"It wouldn't surprise me at all."

"I'll be in touch," he said, then turned and walked away.

CHAPTER 10

S *tep Six.*
With MacWhorter on Punch and Judy's case, Veil and his students safeguarding my charges, and Bailey Kramer at work trying to replicate the drug, I had breathing room to go off on another tack. As a result of our recent work on an industrial espionage case in the prescription drug business, Garth and I had made a lot of contacts in the pharmaceuticals industry. I figured it couldn't hurt to do a little poking around in a few executive suites to see if I might not be able to get a lead on what company had been playing Igor to the CIA's Dr. Frankenstein.

Since there were upwards of a hundred drug companies that had corporate headquarters or major branch offices in New York, and since my time was severely limited, to say the least, I decided to start at the top with Lorminix, the biggest drug and chemical company of them all, a giant cartel with corporate headquarters in Berne and its largest distribution outlet and branch office in New York. In addition to the logic of starting with the largest researcher, designer, and manufacturer of pharmaceuticals in the world, with sensitive, up-to-date information on just about everything that was going on in the business, I had another reason for going first to Lorminix; I had a personal relationship with the vice president for North American Operations, Peter Southworth. Not only had I worked with Southworth on the industrial espionage investigation, but we had served together on the board of directors of the Bronx

Zoo, which housed a certain animal in which I had an intense personal interest.

I considered Peter an interesting man—not exceptionally bright, but good-hearted, and with the strength of character to fend off the bitterness that I was certain he must feel, and which could have twisted his life if he had allowed it. His grandfather had founded Lorminix, and his family had run it up until the time of his father's death, when control had passed to Peter. Peter had simply lacked the vision, marketing skills, toughness, or whatever it was that was needed to run such a gigantic enterprise. Whatever the reason, in a relatively short time he had just about run the company into the ground before it had been acquired by a team of European businessmen in a leveraged buyout that had brought Peter millions of dollars and a lifetime sinecure, but on the payroll of a company that was no longer his. He had immediately been shunted off to New York, and it was widely known in the industry that he was nothing more than a figurehead, even in his own office. The fact that he had so much money, a great deal of which he gave away through various philanthropic foundations he had set up, could not erase the fact that he had lost the family business, and been branded an incompetent. Unless there was something about his personal situation or contract I didn't know about, I frankly couldn't understand why he remained where he was. A very wealthy man like Peter Southworth can find a lot of better things to do with his time and money than sit around a plush office on sufferance. Like start another business, or, through investment capital, buy his way to an executive position of real power with another company. Maybe he was just gun-shy, or possibly gutted. The long knives of big-time capitalism will do that to a man. In any case, it was none of my business. I liked the guy, and felt sorry for him. I hoped he could be useful.

I'd made an appointment, and I was immediately ushered into his palatial office by his secretary the moment I arrived. The secretary left, but reappeared with coffee and croissants before I'd barely had time to shake Peter's hand and settle down on the plush, butter-soft brown leather sofa he'd motioned me onto, and which stretched along the entire length of one of the walls in his office.

"Mongo the Magnificent!" the lanky executive exclaimed, slapping me on the back as he sat down next to me on the sofa. He was wearing a thousand-dollar Armani suit and three-hundred-dollar wing-tip shoes, a wardrobe that clashed somewhat with the gold hoop earring he wore in his left earlobe and his long, graying brown hair which he wore in a ponytail, probably some kind of statement he was trying to make that had nothing to do with fashion. "It's good to see you, my friend. How the hell are you?"

"It's good to see you, Peter, and I'm doing fine. You look well."

"I am. We miss you at the zoo's board meetings. They just aren't the same without you. Too damn stuffy; not zooey enough, in a manner of speaking. Why did you resign?"

"I just didn't have the time to spare any longer."

I also didn't have the time to sit around all afternoon chatting with Peter Southworth, something I was quite certain he would be happy to do, since there was very little real work or decision making his bosses in Berne let him handle. In order to expedite the point of my visit, I took the last of the black-and-yellow capsules I had appropriated from Margaret's supply, one I would at least be able to return, and set it down in the center of the glass-topped coffee table in front of us. "Peter," I continued, "I was hoping you might be able to help me on a very important matter I'm working on. Have you ever seen a capsule that looks like this? It looks larger than average to me, and I don't recall ever seeing a medication that was packaged in black-and-yellow. I thought a pharmaceuticals man might have. Is there anything you can tell me about this? I'm looking for the manufacturer."

He stared at the capsule on the glass for what seemed to me an inordinate length of time, almost as if he couldn't quite manage to focus on it. It seemed an odd reaction; the capsule was unusual enough so that it seemed to me he would recognize what it was immediately, or not. Finally he looked back at me, said quietly, "I don't think I can help you, Mongo."

And that seemed an odd choice of words. I couldn't help but notice two things: he hadn't really answered my question, and a furrow had appeared on his brow. Peter Southworth was a naturally cheerful and open man whose emotions were transparent, and at the moment he definitely looked worried. "Well, I guess you'd certainly know if it had been manufactured by Lorminix, wouldn't you?" I said carefully, watching his face. "I was just hoping you could steer me to the company that did make it. This is very important, Peter. Otherwise, I wouldn't be taking up your time."

He abruptly rose from the sofa, went across the room, and sat down behind his enormous desk, turning his back to me. I could hear his fingers nervously drumming on the oak desktop. "How important is very important?" he asked in a tone that had suddenly become curt and distant.

My heartbeat began to race, and I felt a tightening in my stomach and the muscles across my back that had nothing to do with the treatment Punch and Judy had recently entertained me with. "As important as anything ever gets, Peter. Life and death important. That is not an exaggeration. People are going to die if I can't get more of this stuff, soon, and its main component is known only to the people who make it. It's a very powerful psychotropic, an experimental drug that was being tested on schizophrenics. The researchers who were doing the work dropped the ball on the project. They abandoned their test subjects, and these people have only a very limited supply of the medication left. The drug changes blood chemistry. Once a person goes on it, he can't go off. To do so causes a severe allergic reaction that includes cellular collapse and imminent death. There is no known substitute. It's a complicated story, but the bottom line is that all records have been lost, and nobody seems to know who made the stuff. The patients whose lives depend on this medication don't have much time left, and I have to contact the manufacturer in order to get a fresh supply. That's how important it is. Now, can you help me?"

The man whose back was turned to me drummed his fingers some more, then said, "The sons of bitches. Fuck them."

Feeling a little light-headed, I rose from the sofa, walked around the coffee table and over to his desk. "Uh, Peter . . . just what sons of bitches would we be fucking here?"

"Those pinstriped pricks in Switzerland!" he snapped as he abruptly swung around in his chair to look at me. There was a grim expression on his face. "There was a woman in here earlier talking about a capsule just like that one. Actually, there were two women, but one did all the talking."

I stiffened and swallowed hard. My mouth had suddenly gone very dry. "Earlier today like when, Peter?"

He glanced at his elegant and very expensive watch. "About three hours ago, just before lunch. They'd left just before you called."

"What was the name of the woman who did all the talking?"

"She said her name was Dr. Jane Knowlton, or Nolte, or something like that. She didn't show me a business card, so I can't remember exactly."

"What did she look like?"

"Very attractive—pretty short, great legs. Blond hair cut short, green eyes, great teeth. She'd called in the morning, told my secretary she was a psychiatrist involved in a research project studying psychotropic drugs. She wanted to know if I would agree to talk to her for a few minutes. I said I'd see her at eleven-thirty. But the minute she walked in here, I knew there was something not quite right about the situation."

"Like what?"

"For one thing, the woman she brought with her. She wasn't much more than a kid, maybe in her early twenties. She had long black hair and these really big brown eyes she kept staring at me with. The shrink introduced her as Roberta something, her research assistant. She was real skinny, downright anorexic. I don't think she was any research assistant."

"Why do you say that?"

"For openers, she didn't take any notes—didn't even have anything to write on. She just didn't have the air about her of a professional. She never said a word, just kept staring at me with those spooky eyes. She was real skittish, looked like she was ready to jump out of her skin at any moment. Every once in a while she'd squint and shake her head a little, like she might have some kind of nervous disorder. The blonde did all the talking, asked all the questions, and every now and then she'd glance over at the one with the big eyes, and the kid would nod. Then the blonde would start asking questions again. It was kind of bizarre, and to tell you the truth, I was sorry I'd let them into my office without having my secretary first make some calls to check on the shrink's credentials. You had to have been there. They both made me nervous right off the bat. I'm kind of an easygoing guy, but I think I'm going to have to start being more careful about salesmen, or anybody else, I let just walk in here. Sometimes I forget what I'm worth, and one day I'm liable to find a gun in my face."

"What kinds of questions did the blonde ask?"

"Well, she began by changing her story right off the bat. She showed me a capsule just like that one over on the table, and she asked me the same question you did—if I knew who'd made it. She said it came from a bad batch of drugs the manufacturer had supplied to some mental health clinic in the city. People were getting sick from the drug. Records had been misplaced, and nobody could identify the supplier, so she was working with one of the city's mental health agencies to track down the manufacturer. Well, the story was preposterous. The city keeps multiple records of all its pharmaceuticals suppliers, and if there really had been some kind of emergency involving a tainted drug, I would have been visited by somebody with a badge who wouldn't have had to lie his or her way into my office."

"Did you tell her you didn't believe her story?"

"Nope. I wasn't about to confront two strange women who might turn out to be drug addicts or loonies. Besides, I could see she was afraid—both of them looked scared. And I did believe her when she said it was very important, at least to her, that she find the manufacturer. She said it was a matter of life and death, just like you did. She also said she didn't have much time. By now she was almost pleading, and she actually had tears in her eyes. She said she'd already made inquiries at a couple of dozen other companies, and nobody had been able to help her. Anyway, I'd never seen a capsule like that one, with no markings whatsoever, and I was kind of curious myself. I told her Lorminix didn't make the drug, whatever it was, which was the truth; or at least I thought so at the time. Then she asked—virtually begged—for my help, asked if I would make inquiries for her. She said she couldn't give me the capsule itself, but she'd made enlarged color photographs of it, and she wanted to leave one with me. By that time all I wanted was to get the two of them out of my office, so I took the photograph and told her I'd look into it."

"How were you supposed to contact her if you found out anything?"

"I was supposed to call her. She wrote down a phone number on the back of the photograph."

"Peter, I need to contact those women. Do you still have the photograph?"

"Sure," he said, frowning slightly and looking around him. "Let's see now, where did I put it?"

"Think hard, Peter. It would be most useful to me."

He bent down out of sight behind his desk, and I heard him open a drawer and begin to rummage through it. Then I heard that drawer close, another open. I stood in front of the desk, a frozen smile on my face, fighting my impatience.

"I was so happy to see them leave, I wasn't really thinking when I put away the photo," Peter said, his voice slightly muffled by the mass of oak between us. "I know it's around here someplace. Just give me a minute."

"When I asked you before what sons of bitches you were referring to, you said it was the pinstriped pricks in Switzerland."

"That's right," the muffled voice replied. "Those arrogant bastards treat me like I was a piece of shit."

"Your people in Berne know about this?"

Now he surfaced, empty-handed, looked around the cavernous office and scratched his head, absently tugged on his hoop earring. "Yeah. Sure, I was glad to get rid of them. But I was still curious, and I'd been struck by how desperate they'd seemed. It occurred to me that some of the woman's story, the part about people being in danger from the drug, might be on the level. There are a number of pharmaceuticals companies in Europe who don't do a lot of business in the United States and don't have offices here, so I figured it couldn't hurt to check with the pricks in Berne to see if they recognized the capsule, could tell me what kind of medication it contained, and might know who made the stuff. I faxed them a message about my little meeting along with a copy of the photograph. Usually it takes them about a week to respond to anything I send them, but this time I got a return fax in under five minutes. I was ordered to destroy the photograph, and fax them the phone number I'd been given, along with any other information I had on the women. Then I was supposed to forget about the whole thing; I was ordered not to discuss the matter

with anyone. Like I said, fuck them. If there are people in trouble
because of this stuff, I want to help."

"Peter," I said, gripping the edge of the desk. "I know you dis-
obeyed the order to destroy the photograph, because you said it's still
around the office someplace. Did you fax them the telephone number
the woman gave you?"

There must have been considerable tension in my voice, because
he looked at me with a puzzled, somewhat defensive expression on his
face, then averted his gaze. "Yeah. I've gotten kind of used to doing
most of what I'm asked."

I reached across the desk and snatched the telephone virtually
from under his nose, picked up the receiver, and started to dial my
office number. "I need to use your phone, Peter. Just keep looking for
the photograph. Take your time; concentrate on trying to remember
where you might have put it."

My secretary answered in the middle of the third ring. "Frederickson and Frederickson."

"Francisco," I said, watching Peter Southworth as he suddenly
snapped his fingers, rose from his desk, turned, and opened the top
drawer of a metal filing cabinet that stood against the wall behind his
desk, "go into my office and get out my New York City reverse
directories. They're in the bottom right-hand drawer of my desk."

I waited, sighed with relief when Peter, with a satisfied look of
triumph, pulled the photograph from the file drawer. He handed it to
me just as Francisco came back on the line.

"I've got them, sir."

"It's Manhattan. Give me an address on this."

I read off the telephone number written on the back of the photograph, waited thirty seconds, and then Francisco gave me an address
on Warren Street, downtown in the financial district. I thanked him,
broke the connection, then quickly dialed the number. I got a busy
signal. I waited a couple of minutes, tried again. It was still busy.

Right. I wasn't going to bother to ask an operator to cut in, because
I was certain I'd only be told the receiver was off the hook.

"Thanks, Peter!" I called over my shoulder as I rushed for the
door, snatching up the capsule off the coffee table. "You've been a big
help! Gotta run! I'll get back to you!"

I caught a cab down on the street, hopped in, gave the driver the address, and asked him to hurry because it was an emergency. The tall Rastafarian with shoulder-length dreadlocks merely looked at me as if I was crazy, then gradually eased his clunky taxi out into the clogged traffic.

As we slowly rumbled down Seventh Avenue, I absently patted first my left armpit, then my right ankle—futile, somewhat bittersweet gestures that only served to remind me that I was unarmed, my Beretta and trusty little Seecamp—constant companions in the bad old days, before Garth and I wound up spending most of our time working for Fortune 500 companies—back in the safe in my apartment, which is where they now remained most of the time, except for occasional outings for target practice or semiannual cleaning and oiling.

There was always the slim possibility that three hours wasn't enough time for the Lorminix executives in Berne to have contacted Punch and Judy, and for Punch and Judy to have found and gone to the address—but, of course, in an age of direct overseas dialing, faxes, cellular phones, and beepers, there had been plenty of time. If Punch and Judy, or some other assassins, weren't already there, they were certainly on the way. I could only hope there was some reason why Sharon Stephens and her frail charge wouldn't be summarily executed like Philip Mayepoles, who had ended up in the Carnegie Hall Dumpster.

We finally made it downtown. I paid the driver, got out, and looked up at the four-story building on Warren Street. There was a camera and electronics store on the ground floor, and another door next to the store entrance, presumably the one I wanted. I went into a deli down the block and bought myself a forty-ounce bottle of Colt .45 malt liquor as a beer-poor substitute for its namesake. Back out on the street I poured the beer into the gutter, then, gripping the empty bottle by the neck, I approached the door next to the camera-store entrance. It was open, and when I looked at the lock I could see that it had been jimmied. Not a good sign, but no less than I had expected.

The door opened into a narrow hallway, with a steep wooden stairway at the end. On the wall to the right were three mailboxes, two of them labeled with company names. The third mailbox, for what I assumed was a loft on the top floor, had no nameplate or company logo. That looked to be where I wanted to go.

I cautiously made my way up the ancient stairway, staying near the inside wall so as to avoid making the stairs creak, and peering around every corner before proceeding upward. As I made my ascent, I found myself growing increasingly depressed and anxious at the thought of what I was likely to find at the top—namely, the corpses of two women with neat, bloodless little bullet holes at the base of their skulls.

At the top of the stairway, beyond a short, narrow landing, there was a sliding steel door that was open perhaps an inch. Gripping the neck of the beer bottle even tighter, I stepped up on the landing, hooked the fingertips of my left hand around the edge of the steel door, sucked in a deep breath, and gave a little tug. The door made only a slight scraping sound as it slid open wider. I peered around the edge of the door and found myself looking across an expanse of raw, open, unfinished loft space. A maze of beams, wires, and pipes crisscrossed the ceiling. There were only two hanging bare lightbulbs to light the place, and the atmosphere was decidedly dim and gloomy. Near the opposite wall were two mattresses covered with sheets and blankets, one chair, and a small coffee table, all of which looked like they had been scavenged off the street. There was a telephone on the floor, and its receiver was off the hook.

When I cautiously poked my head in and glanced to the right, I found myself looking into the startled faces of two women—one a leggy blonde with green eyes, the other a very thin young woman with long black hair and the largest, most expressive eyes I had ever seen. Both were bound by the wrists and ankles with rope, and they had duct tape strapped over their mouths.

I put a finger to my lips, then gestured to indicate that I needed to know where their captors were. The psychiatrist motioned with her head and leaned over slightly to indicate that I should look the other way. I turned to my left, where there was a sink and toilet stall, and when I moved a few more inches into the loft, I could see that beyond the toilet stall there was an open doorway leading into a section of the loft that had been partitioned off. Through the doorway I could see kitchen cabinets and part of another sink. I nodded reassuringly to the women, then removed my shoes, straightened up, and, clutching my glass Colt .45 firmly in my right hand, shuffled past the sink and toilet stall to the entranceway. I could smell the aroma of fresh-brewed coffee, and I heard Punch and Judy talking; from the direction of their voices, I could tell that they were sitting, probably at a table, right around the corner, against the partition.

"Shazam," I said as I stepped through the doorway.

Judy was sitting closest to me, so she was the one who would need more, and extensive, plastic surgery after I gave her the beer bottle full in the face. As Punch knocked over his coffee mug clawing for the gun in his shoulder holster, I upended the table on him, sending him toppling backward in his chair. I pushed the table aside with my foot, then crouched down and cracked him in the jaw with the heel of my hand, a blow carefully calculated to knock him unconscious and perhaps remove a few teeth, but not break his jaw so that he wouldn't be able to talk.

The initial reunion festivities over, I went back into the loft proper, put my shoes back on. I walked over to the women, removed the duct tape from their mouths, then began to untie the ropes from their wrists and ankles.

"My God," Sharon Stephens gasped in a high-pitched, breathy voice. "Who are you?"

"Well, Doctor, you know I'm not from the CIA, so I must be your fairy godmother." Without waiting for a reply from the psychiatrist, I turned to the frail woman with terror still swimming in her eyes, said, "Emily, my name's Mongo. I'm not going to hurt you, and neither is anyone else. You're safe now. Okay?"

I watched as the fear in her incredibly expressive eyes was replaced by trust and relief, and she nodded tentatively.

Sharon Stephens said, "Mongo? I think I've heard of you. Aren't you—?"

"I've heard of you too, lady. To you, I'm Dr. Frederickson, or Mr. Frederickson, or just Frederickson."

She smiled thinly as I finished removing the rope from her ankles, then started on her wrists. "I take it what you've heard isn't so good."

"I'm trying not to be judgmental. Anybody who helped a dozen people escape from Rivercliff can't be all bad. Look, I don't want to spend a lot of time up here; our friends resting in the kitchen might have backup, and I don't know how long it may be before their friends show up. Why aren't the two of you dead?"

The blond woman swallowed hard, replied, "They want Emily, and Emily doesn't function well without me. How did you know . . . ?"

"Let me ask the questions for now," I said, removing the last length of rope. There looked to be enough of it for my purposes. "Why do they want Emily?"

The woman rubbed her wrists and ankles to restore circulation, got to her feet, then helped the younger woman, whom I had freed first, get to hers. They stood for a few moments staring at me, their arms around each other. They looked at one another, then back at me. "She's an empath," Sharon Stephens replied at last.

"An empath?"

"Emily is extremely sensitive to what other people are feeling."

"You mean she's like a mind reader, a telepath?"

"No. Simply what I said."

"Just what the CIA needs, somebody who's sensitive to other people's feelings," I replied curtly. "You can tell me all about it later. Right now, you can both give me a hand dragging those two hotshots in here. I want them under that low-hanging beam over there by your beds. Let's move fast."

The women did as they were asked, each of them taking one of the bleeding, unconscious Judy's ankles and dragging her out of the kitchen, while I performed the same service for Punch. I tied their wrists separately with the ropes they had used to truss the psychiatrist and Emily. Then I tossed the ends of the ropes over the low-hanging beam above my head, pulled both assassins up until only their toes were touching the floor, tying off the ends of the ropes to an exposed pipe in the wall. Then I went back into the kitchen, retrieved Punch's .22 pistol, brought it back, and handed it to the blond woman.

"Did your former employers teach you how to use a gun?"

"No."

"Well, it isn't rocket science. It's loaded. Just point it at the chest of anybody who comes through that door who doesn't look like me, and then pull the trigger. Don't hesitate, don't ask questions, and don't threaten. Just aim and shoot. Use both hands."

"I'm not sure I can do that."

"Then the chances are pretty good that both of you will be gone if friends of this couple show up before I get back. They'll be professional killers."

"Where are you going?"

"Not far. The electronics store downstairs. I need a tape recorder."

"I have a small one in my purse."

"Ah. That should save me a trip."

Sharon Stephens retrieved her purse from the space between the mattresses. She took out a small, voice-activated tape recorder and handed it to me, along with the gun. I stuck the gun in my waistband, pointed to the small spool of tape inside the recorder, continued, "What's on here?"

"Just conversations I had with various drug company executives. There's nothing on the tape worth keeping."

"You've got that right," I said as I punched the rewind button. "Lorminix, the last place you visited, is the company that manufactured your little wonder drug."

Her jaw dropped slightly, and she put a hand to her mouth. "How did you find that out?"

"Not now, Doctor," I said, striding over to the steel door, which I closed and locked. "I don't know how much time we've got before somebody tries to contact these two, or comes looking for them, and I don't want to be interrupted. You two might want to excuse yourselves into the kitchen for a few minutes, maybe turn on the water if it gets too noisy in here. You're not going to like what I'm about to do."

The women stayed where they were. Both Punch and Judy had regained consciousness, and were beginning to moan in pain. I quickly searched through Punch's pockets until I found what I was looking for, his stun gun. Both grimaced and looked away, obviously not liking what they saw.

I continued, "I guarantee the two of you are going to get a charge out of seeing me again."

"Don't," the woman whispered weakly, blood dribbling out of her broken mouth.

I pressed the voice activation on the tape recorder, set it down on the floor at their feet. Then I held up the stun gun. "Now, let's see if

I can get the hang of how this thing works," I said, and jabbed the steel prongs into Punch's exposed belly. I held it there for a second or two while he screamed and thrashed, then took it away and let him hang and twitch while I turned my attention to Judy. One of the woman's eyes was swollen shut, but the other was open wide, glittering with terror as I held the stun gun up in front of her. "You know the drill, madam," I continued. "I need the answers to a few questions, and I'm going to use the interrogation technique you taught me. First, I get your attention—"

"Stop it!" Sharon Stephens shouted as I started to extend the stun gun toward Judy's rib cage. "You don't have to torture them!"

"I appreciate your fine sensibilities, Doctor," I said over my shoulder. "I'm sure they were honed at Rivercliff. I told you to excuse yourself. Information these two have might be able to save the lives of the rest of your patients, and I don't have time to fool around with lies."

"You don't need to torture them. Emily can tell you what they're feeling."

"Believe me, lady, I already know from personal experience how they're feeling. They feel downright rotten."

"That isn't what I mean. She'll know if they're telling the truth."

"Explain," I said, turning around to face the psychiatrist.

The woman shrugged, then glanced at the frail girl, who was still clinging to her. "Emily's just very sensitive to people's feelings—their reactions, body language, tone of voice. She can tell if people are lying or telling the truth. She just senses it."

Well, well. An empath. Emily was beginning to sound remarkably like my brother, and some things I'd only suspected about the CIA's motives were becoming clearer to me. "How reliable is she?"

"I told you she's the reason we're both still alive. She's more reliable than any polygraph. I'm not just saying that; she's been thoroughly tested."

I nodded. "And that's the reason the Chill Shop wants her."

Sharon Stephens frowned. "I don't understand what you mean. What's the 'chill shop'?"

"The Company's BUHR—Bureau of Unusual Human Resources."

"I worked for the CIA, yes, but I've never heard of this BUHR."

"Well, Doctor, my guess is that they're the people who paid for the work you did at Rivercliff. Listen up, and you may learn something." I paused, extended my hand toward the frail younger woman. "Emily, will you help me? I need to know if these two people who came for you answer my questions truthfully."

Emily looked at Sharon Stephens, who nodded. Then the dark-haired woman took my hand, and I led her over to where Punch and Judy were strung up to the ceiling beam. She sat down on the floor at their feet, next to the tape recorder, crossed her legs, and stared up into their faces. Punch and Judy, looking decidedly unhappy, stared back at her.

"What about you two?" I asked, looking back and forth between the two assassins. "You ever heard of the Chill Shop?"

Neither answered. I clucked my tongue in disapproval, waggled the stun gun at them, then stepped toward Punch.

"Yes!" the man said quickly. "We . . . work for them. It's like you said."

I glanced down at Emily, who looked up at me and nodded her head.

"Excellent," I said, and crouched down close to the recorder. "Hello, Captain. This is the arrogant, publicity-seeking, interfering dwarf prick speaking. I trust I have your attention. I have here for you a couple of early Christmas presents, along with their taped confessions—inadmissible as evidence, of course, but they should help you get your very own confessions. Now you'll know everything I know, and I'm sure you'll put the information to good use. I'm leaving Punch's gun here next to the tape recorder, and I'll bet you a dinner that ballistics tests will match it to the bullet found in the skull of the corpse in the Dumpster. Ho-ho-ho on you."

Judy moaned, whispered, "They'll pay you . . . a great deal of money if you . . . let us go."

"Sorry, lady," I replied, straightening up. "I'm incorruptible in my quest for truth, justice, and the American way. Now, I think you get the picture. I'm going to ask you some questions, and the two of you are going to answer them. Answer them truthfully, and you get to go on to the next set of questions. Simple. But if my friend Emily tells me you're fibbing, then I will ask the ladies to step out of the room, I tickle you with your own little toy, and you do the electric boogaloo. Frankly, I'd enjoy that. It doesn't matter which one of you lies; you both get zapped. So, for your sakes, I hope you're fond of each other."

I started with a few simple questions about Lorminix, the Chill Shop, and Rivercliff that I already knew the answers to—a test for Emily as well as the two assassins. Punch and Judy got the answers right, and after each one Emily looked at me and slowly nodded her head. My human lie detector seemed to be in good working order, and my subjects reasonably cooperative, so I got serious.

When I asked for the names of the personnel at BUHR, Judy told me they didn't know, that they'd been hired by a middleman. Emily looked at me, shook her head. I clucked my tongue, then asked the psychiatrist and Emily to go into the kitchen. That was all it took. Judy started giving names, from the director of the operation right down to the various secretaries. Emily just kept nodding.

Twenty-five minutes later I had exhausted my repertoire of questions. I not only had the goods on BUHR and key people at Lorminix, but also the names of virtually every outfit and government agency Punch and Judy had ever worked for, as well as the identities of their victims. The information on the tape was going to keep a lot of law enforcement agencies in a number of countries busy for some time, but it was of only limited use to me at the moment. I was happy to hear that Philip Mayepoles had been the only patient the assassins had found, less pleased that nothing they had told me was going to help me solve the problem of obtaining a fresh supply of the patients' medication in the time I had left. Punch and Judy knew the names of a lot of players, because they'd been plying their trade for some time, but they knew almost nothing about the technical details of Rivercliff, nor did they know if any more of the drug could be found in the United States—or anywhere else, for that matter.

I turned off the recorder, set Punch's gun down next to it, then called Felix MacWhorter to tell him what he could have if he cared to send some of his people downtown. I also suggested he send a paramedic or two. Then I hung up and turned to the two women. "Let's get out of here."

"Where are we going?" the psychiatrist asked.

"To a safe place."

CHAPTER 11

At first Michael was speechless when he saw Emily and their psychiatrist, but then he let out a whoop of joy and rushed over to them. There were lots of hugs and kisses, and a few tears, and then it was time to get down to the business of organization.

The brownstone was getting crowded. After introducing the new tenants to the old, the guards, and Francisco, I left it to Margaret and Michael, who enjoyed seniority, to work out sleeping arrangements. I explained the house rules about staying away from open windows, not answering telephones or the door, and then I took Sharon Stephens with me down to my office, closing the door after me. I sat down behind my desk, and she sat stiffly, her knees close together and her hands in her lap, in a chair by the wall to my left. Her green eyes at once mirrored both relief and anxiety.

"Thank you for rescuing us, Dr. Frederickson," she said with a quick, nervous smile that showed the fine white teeth Peter Southworth had mentioned.

"You're welcome, I'm sure," I replied evenly.

"I . . . have so many questions."

"I know the feeling."

She clasped and unclasped her hands, looked down at them. "You don't think much of me, do you?"

"I don't know what to think of you. You saved those people's lives, and you've been going to a lot of trouble and risking your own life to try to keep them alive. On the other hand, if it hadn't been for you, and people like you, they wouldn't have been prisoners in danger in the first place. What was a nice girl like you doing in a purgatory like Rivercliff?"

"I didn't know what kind of work I was going to be doing when I was assigned there, Dr. Frederickson—and I'd only worked there a short time. I answered an ad in one of the medical journals; it said the CIA was looking for physicians, especially psychiatrists. I wrote them a letter, filled out an application, and went for an interview. I'm sure thousands of government employees have done the same thing. Psychiatry is a very difficult branch of medicine to make a living in these days. I assumed I would be treating CIA personnel and their families. I was never told anything about this BUHR, this 'chill shop.' To me, the CIA was just the CIA, with everybody focused on the same mission, which was to protect the nation's security. I was excited, thinking I was actually going to be doing important and worthwhile work for the government."

"The CIA is a whole other country unto itself, lady. They have some very strange customs and notions there."

"I was naive. By the time I realized what was going on, and what I was expected to do, it was too late. I was already in place at Rivercliff. I'd signed what seemed like dozens of security pledges, and I assumed they had me. I felt like a prisoner myself. I was afraid. A number of times I thought of quitting, and even mentioned it to my supervisor once, but he made implied threats that the CIA would make a great deal of trouble for me if I quit, and that I would have difficulty going back into private practice. Somebody else I talked to about quitting said there could be legal consequences because of the papers I'd signed."

"That was absurd. They were the ones committing illegal acts. You were recruited by a particular department at the CIA, and if I have my way they're definitely going to be put out of business when this is all over. Michael told me you warned him and the other patients that people might be sent to kill you. I have to ask how, if you hadn't realized by then just how rotten and ruthless your employers really were, you guessed that they might go so far as to kill all of you in order to cover up the Rivercliff operation."

She shrugged her shoulders. "I guess I did realize it by then—especially after what they did with a man named Raymond Rogers."

"I know about Raymond. What did they do with him?"

Her emerald-colored eyes clouded, and she averted her gaze. "When I first started working there, I *did* feel that I was doing something very worthwhile, working on the cutting edge of research that could radically change the lives of so many sick people for the better. But I was just a junior staff member. I didn't know for some time that nobody was ever released, and it wasn't until a month and a half ago that I realized the real purpose of Rivercliff."

"Studying the side effects of the medication supplied to you that was given to them."

She looked back into my face, slowly nodded. "That's correct. How did you learn so much in such a short time?"

"You have to be a chess player who's kind to street people."

"I don't understand."

"Never mind; it's not important how I know what I know. I need to know more. Is there a name for the drug you gave the patients?"

"If there is, I never heard it. We all just called it 'meds,' like the patients. If the senior staff members who ran Rivercliff had a name for it, they never told me."

"You were willing to medicate patients with a drug you didn't even know the name of?"

Sharon Stephens flushed slightly. "It wasn't exactly like working at General Hospital, Dr. Frederickson."

"I can believe that. You never asked what this drug was?"

"Of course I asked. I was simply told I had no need to know. There were no labels on the bottles that came up to the infirmary."

"What about the shipping cases the bottles came in?"

"If the bottles came in shipping cases, I never saw them. For the past week and a half I've been talking to drug company people, trying to find out the name of the manufacturer. We have to get more of the medication."

"I'm aware of that."

"When you questioned that man and woman, you asked if Lorminix made the drug, and they said yes."

"Knowing that isn't necessarily going to help us get a fresh supply

of the drug in the time we have. Lorminix is going to stonewall and
deny any knowledge of the drug—for years, if they have to. Clandes-
tinely supplying dangerous drugs to the CIA for illegal human experimentation is the kind of secret corporations pay lawyers and PR
agents millions to safeguard. Lorminix has manufacturing plants and
distribution centers all over the world. Making that stuff for the CIA
was a relatively tiny operation, and probably done at one site, say in
Brazil. By now they've probably shut down that operation, shredded
records, and maybe even destroyed whatever supply of the drug they
might have had on hand."

Tears glistened in the psychiatrist's eyes. "Are you saying it's
hopeless? All of the patients are going to die?"

"I'm saying Lorminix is going to be less than cooperative."

"We only have two and a half weeks left."

"Less than that. My friend Margaret upstairs only has thirteen
capsules left, counting the dose she has to take tonight."

Sharon Stephens frowned. "Margaret is schizophrenic?"

I nodded.

"How did she get the capsules?"

"Philip Mayepoles slipped them to her just before he was killed by
Punch and Judy. He may have dropped a few while he was handing
them to her, or maybe he didn't have that many to begin with. Also,
I had to take a few to use for my own purposes. The point is that
Margaret isn't going to make it to Christmas Eve. It would really have
helped if you'd seen a label on a shipping carton, so we'd at least
know where to look to find out if there is any more of the drug left."

"I'm sorry."

"So am I, but it can't be helped."

"What are we going to do?"

"I'm working on the problem. Tell me more about the operation at
Rivercliff. Besides handing out meds once a day, what were your
duties? Did you test the patients?"

"No. All the testing was done by senior staff doctors, people who'd
worked for the Company for years. Junior staff members were only to
observe patient behavior, looking for side effects, and write daily
reports on a certain number of patients we were assigned to track. The
side effects could be broken down into three broad categories. Some

patients experienced a marked amplification of some natural sense—
like smell, taste, hearing, or eyesight."

"That would be my friend Margaret. She's got the nose of a bloodhound and the palate of a gourmet chef."

The woman nodded. "Emily also falls into that first category. We
all know that some people are naturally hypersensitive to other people's feelings, empathic. The medication pushed Emily's hypersensitivity way beyond the range of anything that could be considered
natural empathy. She's like a sponge, soaking up what other people
are feeling from the way they speak, the tension in their voices or
bodies, body language, facial expressions; she picks up on the slightest cues. That's what makes her potentially so valuable to the CIA—
she can tell when people are lying, apparently even sociopaths and
psychopaths, people who can sometimes beat polygraph tests."

"The CIA trains its own agents how to beat the polygraph. So do
other intelligence agencies. Sometimes all it takes is a little Miltown
or Valium."

"I don't think they could fool Emily. She would be invaluable in
certain types of situations, like negotiations, or interrogations of enemy prisoners. It's why I took her with me when I went to question the
drug company executives. It's what Rivercliff was all about—trying to
develop people with very specialized skills that could be exploited by
the Company. There weren't many of these; Emily was one of the
few."

"I thought you said nobody ever told you anything."

"Emily and some of my other patients told me about the tests they
were put through, I saw what went on around there, and I guessed
what they wanted. You have to give me credit for a bit of intelligence,
Dr. Frederickson. If all I was supposed to do was observe the side
effects of a single medication, then that must have been all they were
interested in. My guess that they found very few patients of use to
them is simply based on observation. Just because somebody suddenly can learn to play the piano and begins composing music doesn't
mean he or she is going to be of any use as a spy, does it? Also, I have
to assume they would have taken out anybody they thought could
prove useful to them, and none of the patients I worked with were ever
released."

"What about other patients? Were any of them ever released—harvested?"

"I have to assume so, if the particular side effects they were exhibiting were deemed useful. My point is that there couldn't have been many."

"Michael was there for years, and he told me nobody was ever released."

"He wouldn't necessarily know if a patient had been harvested, as you put it. There were different groups of patients in separate sections of the complex, and each group was kept totally segregated from the others. Also, even if a patient in his group had been harvested, Michael might have been told that the person had died. Like I said, I'm just guessing. I doubt the agency would have kept spending all that money over the years if they didn't occasionally get *somebody* they could use. Like Emily."

"You're probably right. If BUHR had deemed Emily useful to the Company, why wasn't she harvested?"

"Probably because she can't cope with other people's negative feelings; in case you haven't noticed, there's a lot of negativity in the world."

"I've noticed."

"The medication treated Emily's symptoms of schizophrenia, but she was—is—always on the edge of a different kind of breakdown. Imagine constantly experiencing not only your own fears and pain and anger but those of everybody else in your immediate vicinity as well. All those things enter Emily's mind and tear at her. She can't tolerate, at least for long, being around other people who are stressed, or angry, or sad, and since there was always the risk that she would run into those feelings if she mingled with the others, she preferred to spend all her time in her room. They—we—couldn't put her on tranquilizers, because that would dull her hypersensitivity, the one thing that might make her useful to the Company in the first place. She became my sole responsibility. I was supposed to develop some kind of nonchemical therapeutic program that would stabilize her emotionally. If I'd been able to do that, I believe she would have been taken out."

I nodded. "The second category of side effects is the amplification of natural talents?"

"Yes," she replied with a faint smile. "Observing that was the most satisfying part of the job. To see people who had been hopelessly mentally ill and delusional most of their lives suddenly not only be able to function but also discover they had some extraordinary talent was wonderful. People who'd only talked to trees were suddenly able to do remarkable things, assuming the natural talent had always been there, buried under the schizophrenia, in the first place. We had mathematicians, musicians, painters, poets."

"And at least one budding chess master."

"It was kind of magical, watching these people. It could also be very funny. We had ourselves quite an assortment of jugglers, comedians, ham actors, you name it. We could have mounted our own Broadway show."

Considering the fact that Dr. Sharon Stephens's show folk had been prisoners, kept sane and alive, like all the others, only so that they might one day serve as indentured servants for the CIA, I wasn't amused. I asked, "What was the third category?"

Her smile vanished. "Monsters," she replied in a voice that cracked.

"Like Raymond Rogers?"

She hesitated, frowned slightly. "Yes and no."

"Let's do the yes part first. Rogers was turned into a killer, a homicidal maniac totally out of control. Did that happen a lot?"

"Not a lot. There were only a few cases like Raymond's that I observed while I was there. It would happen suddenly; a patient would appear to be a category one or two—sometimes for weeks, or even months—and then one day go berserk. It was totally unpredictable. There was always at least one male nurse on duty at all times who was armed with a tranquilizer gun in case that happened."

"That danger exists for the patients who are out there on the streets now? And the people upstairs?"

Again she hesitated, then slowly, reluctantly, nodded. "Yes. Percentagewise, the risk is minimal, but it exists. Raymond exists. They have to be monitored constantly. I'll have to talk to the guards you introduced me to, tell them what signs to look for. They must watch out for your friend and the patients as well as intruders."

Terrific. Felix MacWhorter had been dead-on, much more so than either of us could have realized about the risks I was undertaking when he had warned me against trying to obtain more of the drug for the patients. It was risky even shielding these people. My neck was stretched a long way out on the chopping block, along with the necks of more than seven million other people in the city. My particular good deed could conceivably set an all-time record for tragic consequences. My mouth had suddenly gone dry, and I swallowed in an attempt to work up some moisture. I felt a crush of responsibility, and for a fleeting moment I wished I had less time to deal with the problems of Margaret and the patients, not more. "What happened to the people who went homicidal?" I asked.

"They were tranquilized and taken to a secure lockup facility in a separate wing."

"And?"

"Raymond was the only one of them I ever saw again. I don't know what happened to the others."

"And that's why you say Raymond is different?"

"Yes," she replied in a voice that was becoming increasingly stressed and halting. "As part of my training, I was allowed to observe a couple of his training sessions. I think he was . . . the only one they could . . . control. Or whom they thought they could control."

"Tell me about Raymond's training sessions."

She stared at the floor, clasping and unclasping her hands. "Dr. Frederickson, I . . . I . . . ."

"Come on, Doctor," I said impatiently. "Time's a-wasting. This isn't Nuremberg, and it isn't the time for soul-searching. You did the right thing when the chips were down. We've got a very big mess to try to clean up, so just tell me what they did with Rogers. How did they control him?"

"I think . . . One of the senior doctors explained that all of the patients who had gone berserk had bloodlust, but it was generalized. They were all males. I got the impression some of them finally managed to kill themselves. With Raymond, there was a specific link between killing and his sex drive."

"An off-the-shelf serial killer."

"Exactly," the woman said in a voice barely above a whisper. "After he'd killed, there was a period of reversion. He would become calmer. I was told you could even talk and reason with him for a while, until the bloodlust began to mount again, but I never witnessed that, and I never spoke to him. I was . . . very frightened."

"I'm sure Raymond and his keepers had some interesting conversations. So when they wanted to calm him down, they gave him things to kill?"

She nodded. "It was what he needed, along with his medication, to remain functional."

"Other patients?"

"No," she replied, still staring intently at the floor. "Animals— mostly dogs and cats."

"Well, he's certainly graduated from dogs and cats, and he isn't exactly treating his bloodlust with moderation. He's insatiable. The death count as of noon today was thirty-three. What was he doing up in the infirmary on the day he got loose?"

"I don't know. I'm not sure."

"Which is it? Was it standard procedure to treat these homicidals in the infirmary?"

"No. When they needed medical attention, they were usually treated in their own wing, after they'd been tranquilized. At least that's what I was told. Maybe . . ."

"Maybe what, Doctor?"

Now she looked back up at me and met my gaze. She had gone very pale, but her voice was steady. "I've given this a lot of thought, Dr. Frederickson. There was no reason to bring Raymond up to the main infirmary, not unless they wanted to use some of the specialized testing equipment we kept there. He certainly wasn't tranquilized, and he wasn't even wearing physical restraints. There were only two guards with him, and he killed those. They must have thought they had him under control. I think it's possible they planned to run some final, sophisticated tests on him before . . ."

"Before harvesting him for possible use as a terror weapon?"

"Yes. It's one explanation. It's possible they were going to send him out on a trial run, perhaps put him in a situation like the one he's in now. They must have thought they had him under control, could just send him out and reel him back in when they wanted. They were wrong."

"Indeed. Maybe BUHR didn't even care about reeling him back in, just in seeing what would happen. He's probably not coherent, and he'd die anyway if he were taken alive and his pills taken away from him. They might figure there were other Raymonds to be shaped."

"I'm just speculating."

I didn't care what she was doing, didn't care whether she was right or wrong. I'd heard quite enough about Raymond Rogers, and whether or not his handlers had intended to set him loose in some foreign country, for whatever insane reason, was beside the point; he was loose in New York City. The more I heard, the angrier I got; it was also enough to make me increasingly nervous, and I was in no position, had already gone too far, to have my resolve weakened.

I said, "You escaped with twelve patients. One is dead, and two are upstairs. That leaves nine. Four of them are males. You have any idea at all where I can find them? Not only are they in danger, but they could become killers themselves. One Raymond Rogers is enough."

She slowly shook her head. "I explained their options to them, and they all decided to go into hiding. I assume they're scattered around the city. They're supposed to meet me by the tree at Rockefeller Center on Christmas Eve. I was hoping I could find the company that manufactured the drug, somehow find a way to force them to give me more of it. I talked to dozens of people, and I wasn't getting anywhere. I was feeling so hopeless. Then those two people found me. And then you came along, out of nowhere. I don't know how to thank you."

"Thanks are premature, Doctor. I'm not exactly riding a tidal wave of optimism, and I'm very ambivalent about what both of us are trying to do right now."

"None of this is the patients' fault, Dr. Frederickson. They didn't ask to be mentally ill, nor to be sent to Rivercliff, nor to be experimented on with a drug that just happens to let them think in a way most of us take for granted but to them is a miracle."

"Thank you, Dr. Schweitzer. I'll try to keep bearing those things in mind."

"Sorry. I didn't mean to sound . . . What can I do to help?"

"Does Michael know that he could go the way of Raymond Rogers?"

"No. Those kinds of emotional meltdowns were rare, and to my knowledge neither he nor Emily ever witnessed one."

"Okay, what you can do to help is go back upstairs and brief the guards, and then check out the living arrangements to make sure we can all kind of keep an eye on each other. If Michael and Emily don't know about this latest twist, I don't see any reason why they should be told. It wouldn't serve any purpose, and they've got enough to worry about."

"Who are those people?"

"Friends of a friend. We'll be safe as long as they're here." At least from outsiders, I thought, but didn't say so.

Tears sprang to the psychiatrist's eyes. "I . . . still don't know how to thank you for all you've done—what you're doing."

"I'll share all my neuroses with you when this matter is resolved. That should be enough for a research paper or two."

She smiled. "Promise?"

"Promise."

I waited until she'd left the office, closing the door behind her, then picked up the phone and called Felix MacWhorter to see if he'd picked up the package I'd left him. He had, and the DA's office was already busy building a case against Punch and Judy. Interpol had been notified, and the information on the tape recording had been passed along to a variety of government offices in Washington. I was betting the Chill Shop had been shut down five minutes after the CIA had found out Punch and Judy had been caught, and they would already be busy preparing denials that BUHR had ever existed. It was even possible any more Company or Lorminix hunting patrols left in the city would be called back, but I wasn't going to count on it. The police captain wanted me to come in for another chat, but I said I had other, more pressing things to do at the moment. He didn't argue with me.

Step Seven.

It was time to get my brother into the act. It was almost midnight in Switzerland, and Garth and Mary had probably been asleep for hours after a day on the slopes, but I figured Garth wouldn't mind being awakened when he heard what I had to tell him and what I wanted him to try to do. I dialed the number of his hotel, thought about what I was doing while the phone rang, then abruptly hung up when somebody answered.

Cancel Step Seven.

I no longer had any qualms about disrupting my brother and sister-in-law's holiday, for the circumstances now certainly warranted it, and they would be the first to agree. Indeed, Garth was going to be more than a little upset with me when he found out I hadn't brought him into the situation immediately, and heard about what I'd been up to while he was gone. It wasn't disrupted vacation plans, but Garth himself I was worried about. My brother was absolutely fearless, and a bullet between the eyes was the only thing that would stop him once he had committed himself to a certain course of action. He was a quiet warrior whose actions spoke very loudly, and who took no prisoners if he thought his cause was just; and I had no doubt that he would think getting more medication for the patients from Rivercliff was the right thing to do. If I involved Garth, I was going to have a lot of explaining to do; once he found out about the drug a certain company with headquarters in Switzerland had been manufacturing for the CIA, and once I told him that somebody in said headquarters might be able to provide information that could save the lives of a dozen people who were otherwise going to die in a few days, he was going to be out the door and on his way to Berne. The one thing predictable about Garth was that he could be unpredictable, and very dangerous to anybody he considered a bad guy. He was in a foreign country, one that went to great pains to protect the privacy and interests of the corporations that were headquartered there. If I told him about Lorminix and asked for his help, he would be working alone and blind, without any franchise or weapons, in what could quickly turn into a very hostile environment. His wife wasn't going to be too pleased with me if Garth ended up in a Swiss prison, or dead, and I wouldn't be too happy myself.

Besides, I might not need Garth. Thanks to my very informative chat with Punch and Judy, I could probably take care of the business I wanted done with Lorminix myself, or at least accomplish as much as my brother could in person.

*   *   *

My alarm woke me at four in the morning. I got up and put on my thick terry-cloth robe. Stepping over the figure of Michael Stout, who was in a sleeping bag in the middle of the floor in the living room, I went into the kitchen to make myself a cup of coffee. Then, wanting to make sure that Michael didn't overhear any of my conversation, I padded downstairs to my office, taking along with me the notebook in which I had jotted down the salient details of Punch and Judy's story. I consulted my notes, then dialed the office number of one Heinrich Muller at Lorminix headquarters in Berne.

"*Ja?*"

"You speak English, Herr Muller?"

"Who is this?" the man on the other end of the line asked in English that had a thick German accent. "How did you get this number?"

"My name's Robert Frederickson, and since this is my nickel, I'll do most of the talking."

"I'm not interested in anything you have to say. Goodbye, Herr Frederickson."

"I got your name and this number from Punch and Judy, Muller. They also let slip the fact that Lorminix occasionally acts as a CIA asset, and that you're the liaison. You're also the cutout. Those two assassins are paid through a Swiss account that belongs to Lorminix. Right now your two hired hands are sitting in a New York City jail cell spilling their guts out. Now do I have your attention?"

The silence on the other end was broken only by the sound of heavy breathing; Heinrich Muller even breathed with a German accent.

I let some more time pass, then continued, "This is your lucky day, Herr Muller. I suspect you've already received a report on me, maybe even have it in front of you right now, so I won't bore you with all my credentials. I'm a private investigator, somewhat to the left of center politically, but I have a special place in my heart for big companies like yours, and I tend to be very sensitive to their needs. Very shortly, the needs of Lorminix will be great. I can not only directly link your company to the CIA, which isn't going to please a lot of your other customers around the world, but I can also prove that you developed and manufactured a very dangerous drug to CIA specifications, and then shipped it to them for illegal experiments on humans. Shades of Nazi Germany, Herr Muller. I can prove that your company bears at least some responsibility for producing a serial killer who's loose on the streets of New York City and probably killing somebody even as we speak. I know all about Rivercliff, Punch and Judy, BUHR—all of it. Your company's ass and your personal ass are fried anyway; if the courts in this country don't kill you with criminal charges and civil suits, the bad publicity will. Luckily for you, I'm here to offer you a measure of corporate and personal redemption. You can help save the lives of some of the people whose heads and bodies you've been helping the CIA mess with. Cooperating in that way could prove advantageous to you, providing a bit of an umbrella in the shit storm that's about to come down on your head. If you help me, I'll do what I can to help you contain the damage, including offering testimony in any court about the way in which you cooperated. If you don't help me, Herr Muller, I'm going to start banging the publicity drums the minute I hang up this telephone, and I'll make sure that you get personal credit for the deaths that are going to occur if you don't help. Now, here's the deal. It's very simple. I want a case—a big case, all you've got—of that mystery drug in the black-and-yellow capsules delivered to my doorstep within the next forty-eight hours. I don't care how you do it, just get it done. If it arrives, you get a friend in court; if it doesn't, I use this same phone to call a friend of mine at *The New York Times*. Now, I want to hear you tell me that you understand."

The response was more guttural breathing.

"Muller? Let me hear it. If I don't, I hang up and call my reporter friend. She'd kill for a story like this."

"*Ja*. I understand."

"Good," I said, and hung up.

I sat for a few minutes, sipping at my coffee, which had gone cold, thinking. I finally decided to give my performance a favorable review, reasoning that my move on Muller had been as good as anything that Garth could have done—and a lot better than a few things he might have done. The next two days would tell whether I had been able to shake loose a supply of the drug, but I wasn't going to count on it. For one thing, there was always the possibility that Lorminix had destroyed any existing supply of the drug after the patients escaped from

Rivercliff. Also, Herr Muller might not panic as easily as I hoped he would; he could confer with his colleagues, who might conclude that, in fact, I probably couldn't prove anything. Then they would take the defensive posture of complete stonewalling, denying everything, letting matters drag on in court, if it ever came to that, for years.

There was nothing left to do at 4:30 in the morning, so I went back to bed.

I awoke again at 6:45. I made more coffee for Michael and myself, then went down to my office. I was very anxious to talk to Bailey Kramer to get at least a preliminary indication of whether or not he could do the job I wanted him to do, and so I called his apartment on the Lower East Side at 7:50. There was no answer, which surprised me; he didn't go in to work until nine, and at that hour of the morning he should have been up and eating breakfast, maybe reading the newspaper. Thinking that he might be in the shower, I waited twenty minutes, called again. There was still no answer.

Now I was getting nervous. I didn't want to call him at work, because I didn't want Frank Lemengello to know anything about the private little arrangement between Bailey and myself. At the same time I wanted to know where we stood, and I didn't want to have to sit around all day biting my fingernails while waiting for Bailey to call me. I presumed it would take some time to find suitable lab space and equipment and anything else Bailey might need if it was possible for him to replicate the drug, and I wanted to get started as soon as possible. I tried Bailey's apartment once more, with the same result, then, at 9:15, I called the lab, thinking that if Frank answered I would simply hang up.

I needn't have worried. What I got was a recorded message informing me that Frank was on vacation and the lab would be closed until after New Year's. Frank hadn't told me he was going away on vacation, but then there was no reason why he should have; we had concluded our business. But with the lab closed, that left the very loud question of just where Bailey Kramer might be.

I worked in the office through the morning, trying to concentrate on contracts and reports while I waited for the phone to ring. At noon a deliveryman arrived with pizza, apparently my guests' choice for their midday meal. Francisco had given Chico Velasquez, one of the day's guards, money to pay, but I waved him off, paid the deliveryman, then took the two pies upstairs myself. I gathered Margaret, Michael, Emily, and Sharon Stephens in my kitchen, and I shared their meal with them. When we had finished, I said, "We have to talk."

Margaret, who was sitting next to me at the table, touched my arm. "Mongo, what's wrong?"

"What's wrong is that you don't have enough capsules to make it to Christmas Eve," I said, turning toward her, glancing at Michael and Emily. "I assume everybody's supply is going to be running out by then. There'll be no safety margin."

Michael ran a hand back through his hair, and his blue eyes glowed with intensity. "Margaret can have some of my capsules. I have twenty-one."

"I'll share mine too," Emily said quietly.

"No," Margaret declared in a firm voice. "I can't accept your offers. But thank you."

"Look," I said, once more glancing in turn at the others around the table, "in a way, it doesn't make any difference. You'll only be postponing the problem of what will happen to all of you when you run out. There may not be any of the drug left in existence; all supplies of it, in this country or anywhere else, could have been destroyed after Raymond Rogers ran amok and you people escaped from Rivercliff. Even the formula itself may have been destroyed. There's a very good chance that's exactly what happened. There are a whole lot of individuals, and one very large corporation, that stand to lose a great deal if any of you survive to tell your stories, and a whole lot to gain if you all end up dead or insane once again."

"Mongo," Sharon Stephens said quietly, "is there any hope at all?"

"Yes, there's hope—but absolutely no guarantees. I've taken steps to try to force Lorminix to supply us with more of the drug, and I've got a very good chemist trying to make more of it. The problem is that I'm not sure Lorminix will come through, even if they do have more of the drug to send, and the chemist seems to have disappeared. There's nothing we can do now about the others, because we have no

way to contact them. We just have to hope that I can come up with
more of the stuff by the time we rendezvous with them on Christmas
Eve. But you're not in that position. You know what will happen to
you if you run out of the medication. Right now is the time, while you
still have a few days' supply left, for you to check yourselves into a
hospital and tell your story. Dr. Stephens and I will be with you to
back you up. If the three of you lapse back into insanity, and maybe
die, then all of this will have been a wasted exercise. So that's my
recommendation; the three of you go to a hospital now, while there's
still time for the doctors to study your conditions and treat you."

There was a prolonged silence, which was finally broken by the
psychiatrist. "I think Mongo's right," Sharon Stephens said softly. "If
you run out, you'll first lose your rationality, and then you'll die.
Maybe it is possible for the doctors to come up with at least an interim
treatment to prevent the cellular collapse that occurs when you stop
taking the drug. Turning yourselves in now for treatment may be the
wisest thing to do."

Margaret, Michael, and Emily all looked at one another, and finally Michael turned to Sharon Stephens. "Does what you just said
mean you think they'll let us keep taking our meds as long as we have
them while they work on us?"

"I don't know," the psychiatrist said in a small voice, looking
away.

I said, "Michael asked what you thought. Give us your best guess."

"I . . . think not," the woman replied. There was anguish in her
voice and expressive green eyes as her gaze swept around the table.
"You have to understand the thinking of the medical establishment,
which is conservative by nature to begin with. You have to look at
things from their perspective. They'd see five people walking into an
emergency room. Three of these people announce that they're schizophrenics, but they display absolutely no signs of mental illness, nor
do they exhibit any of the side effects normally associated with any of
the drugs used to treat mental illness. They talk about being patients
at a mental hospital called Rivercliff, which these doctors have never
heard of. Their records, of course, no longer exist anywhere. Then
these people start talking about illegal experiments that were conducted at this place the doctors can't find listed anywhere. They also

claim that the ice-pick killer on the streets also came from Rivercliff. So now the doctors start thinking that maybe these three people really are crazy, but they're going to be extremely cautious in diagnosing and treating them. It won't matter what Dr. Stephens or the highly respected Dr. Frederickson have to say on the matter. Doctors and hospitals are being sued all the time. Finally, these three people who claim to be schizophrenic pull out bags of capsules, supposed medication that doesn't have a name, and ask that they be allowed to continue taking one a day while the doctors check them out. I ask you, Mongo, if you were a hospital administrator, would you allow the people I've just described to self-medicate after you'd admitted them into your hospital?"

"But you're an MD yourself, a psychiatrist. You'd be there along with me to back up their story."

"My best guess that you asked for is that they're not going to take my word for anything—or yours. How long will it take them to check my credentials? And how do you know what kinds of trash stories my former employer may have already put out about me? Considering the legal consequences of what could happen to them if they make a bad decision, do you think the physicians at any hospital we go to will be able to check our stories and test that medication within twenty-four hours? I said I agreed with your recommendation because we're running out of time and it looks like that may be our best hope, our only choice. You know what's at stake as well as I do. I'm just not optimistic about our chances."

I nodded. "You make some good points, Doctor."

Michael said, "What you're saying is that if we go to a hospital now in order to save time while we still have almost a couple of weeks left, we risk ending up with only one more day to be well and alive."

Sharon Stephens and I glanced at each other, nodded in agreement. I said, "That's about right, Michael."

"Then I'm going to stay out and take my chances that you'll get us more meds, Mongo."

"Me too," Emily said in a voice just above a whisper.

I turned in my chair to face Margaret. She stared back at me, her expression filled with anxiety. "Michael and Emily are Dr. Stephens's patients, Margaret, so I'm not going to say anything more to try to influence them. But you're not anybody's patient; you're just my friend. I feel responsible for you. Time is running out—even more so for you than the others. I want you to listen to me and take my advice. I'll arrange for my own doctor to admit you to the hospital, and I guarantee you *he'll*, at least, listen to me and be on your side. I'll keep your meds with me, and if it looks like you'll be denied permission to keep taking them while they figure out how to treat you, I'll take you right back out of there. Okay?"

"Things may not be that simple, Mongo," Sharon Stephens said in a firm voice. "It's possible the Company has spread disinformation about all of us to hospital personnel throughout the country, just in case we did try to turn ourselves in for treatment; I don't know if that's the case, but it would have been the logical thing to do after we escaped from Rivercliff. Hospital administrators could have been asked to alert their staffs to be on the lookout for people who come in and tell a certain kind of story. If that's how it is, then the police could show up to take Margaret into protective custody. I still concur with your recommendation, for the reasons you mentioned, but I think everybody sitting at this table should be aware of the risks involved. If you do take Margaret into a hospital, you may not have the option of taking her out again."

"It doesn't make any difference, Dr. Stephens," the middle-aged woman with the worn, leathery features said, still looking at me. "I'm not going to the hospital."

I shook my head in frustration. "Margaret, I'll test the waters first. I'll—"

"I know you're thinking of my best interests, Mongo," the woman interrupted. "But even if it was guaranteed that they would let me keep taking my medication, I would still have to answer all sorts of questions that could jeopardize Michael and Emily and the others out there who didn't come in with me. I can't do that. And if they took away my medication, and you couldn't take me out, then I'd end up . . . crazy again, like I used to be."

"Margaret," I said in a slow, measured tone, "that's a risk you may just have to take. If you'll let me, I'll try to negotiate with the medical authorities, or the police, before I take you in with me. If Dr. Stephens and Emily agree, I'll take Emily with me when I talk to them to make sure they don't lie. I know a lot of people. I can try to get a guarantee that you'll be allowed to continue to take the medication you have now while they examine you and search for another way to treat you. But we have to use what little time we have left to the best advantage. If you run out of your meds before another way to treat you can be found, you'll die. That's what the blood on your bed the morning you woke up and found me sitting next to you was all about. With no meds or other treatment, your cells will rupture; your circulatory system will collapse, and you'll bleed to death. Do you understand?"

"Yes, Mongo. But it's not death I'm afraid of. I've been kind of dead most of my life. I'd rather be really dead than the way I was before. Maybe you can't understand that because you've never been insane; you've never heard a lot of voices in your head, never had to live in the cold on the street, never really been hungry and not been able to remember how to ask for help, never been hurt in a shelter. Your mind has never turned on you the way mine has. You know how to take care of yourself. You only understand what it's like to work with your mind, not to have it working against you like an enemy. You can think clearly, recognize your friends, have your mind tell you when it's time to go to the bathroom, and then help you get there. Your mind knows how to shut down so that it can sleep properly when you need rest. These are all things I wasn't able to do when I lived on the street. Mama Spit was what you and other people called me. You're saying that *maybe* the doctors can help me if I go to them now, with you. But maybe they can't. Maybe the police will take me and separate us. Maybe all I have left is ten days. Well, so be it. I'll take those ten days, and I'll die when I become Mama Spit again. But the only way I can be assured of spending those ten days as *me* is to stay here, with my friends—if you'll let me. That's what I'm going to do, Mongo, if it's all right with you. Ten days is a whole lifetime to me."

For some reason I wanted to cry, but I didn't. Instead I rose, smiled, and nodded to Margaret and the others. "Of course you can stay here with your friends, Margaret. And I do understand, folks. I'm not sure I wouldn't make the same decision myself if I were in your position. I just wanted to make sure you all knew you had another option."

"Finding more meds," Michael said in a low voice that trembled slightly. "You'll keep trying, Mongo?"

I sighed. "Of course I'll keep trying. Thanks for letting me share your pizza."

The first thing I kept trying, for the rest of the day, was Bailey Kramer's home phone number. There was still no answer. I kept trying until well past midnight, then finally went to bed.

As I lay awake staring at the ceiling it occurred to me that I had been too impatient and careless in openly approaching Bailey on the street; anyone who might be following and watching me would have seen us talking, possibly guessed what the conversation was about, and what I was asking him to do. Because of me, Bailey Kramer might be dead.

I did not sleep well.

CHAPTER 12

*eil was waiting for me in the hallway outside my apartment when I came out in the morning of the second day after I'd made my call to Heinrich Muller. The man with the shoulder-length blond hair, sea-blue eyes, easy smile, catlike movements, and deadly fighting skills was sitting on the landing, cross-legged and his back to the wall, sipping at a carton of coffee. He nodded and rose to his feet when I came out the door.

"What are you doing here at this hour?" I asked, glancing at my watch. It was 8:30. "Your shift was over a half hour ago. I'd think you'd be home in bed by now. I hope you don't think I'm going to pay you overtime."

Veil smiled thinly. "We had a little incident last night. I wanted you to be aware of it."

I quickly glanced behind me to make sure my apartment door was closed so that Michael, who was busy in the kitchen washing up our breakfast dishes, couldn't hear us. "Are my guests downstairs all right?"

"I presume so. I haven't looked in on them. I don't think they heard anything."

"I didn't hear anything either."

"We had two visitors about three o'clock this morning. They came in through the attic, jimmied the window off the fire escape. They were experts, heavily armed, no identification. They were also well

equipped, and it looked like they were prepared to firebomb the whole
building if they found what they were looking for."

"My guests."

Veil nodded. "And, presumably, you. I didn't have a chance to
interrogate them. I was patrolling the bottom two floors, and Jerry was
up here. He confronted them on the landing just below the attic,
judged the situation was too dangerous to risk failure if he tried to
disable them, so he just killed them both. It was the right decision."

"Ah," I said, thinking that it did not bode well that a brace of
assassins had arrived in the middle of the night, instead of a crate of
capsules in the morning.

"I got rid of the bodies and the equipment they were carrying."

"Where'd you put them?"

"In the Dumpster down the street by Carnegie Hall."

I smiled grimly. "That Dumpster is becoming quite the in place for
corpses."

"The cops are sure to be around the neighborhood asking questions.
I considered not telling you, so that you wouldn't have to lie, but then
figured that wasn't such a good idea. I figured you should know."

I nodded absently, my mind racing. "No, I'm glad you told me. The
police aren't going to bother to canvass the neighborhood; they'll come
right here. The precinct captain is going to have a pretty good idea
where the corpses came from, if not exactly who made them corpses,
but I don't think he'll press it. I'll make sure Francisco understands
that I'm the only one who does any talking to the police, and I'll keep
your people out of sight. What concerns me more than the police is
the fact that I think I just received a very negative message."

"Indeed. When those two don't report in, we're likely to get more
visitors."

"The message is the fact that anybody showed up here at all. I
managed to tag the outfit that manufactured the drug for the agency,
a company called Lorminix with headquarters in Switzerland. I called
over there to the guy who was apparently in charge of the program. I
tried to pressure him into sending me more of the drug so that I'd have
an emergency supply for the three people we've got here, and the nine
others we're supposed to rendezvous with on Christmas Eve at Rockefeller Center."

Veil shook his head. "It doesn't look like he's planning to send you the drug, Mongo."

"Nope—and, in a way, I can't say I blame the son of a bitch. I told him I'd try to help him and his company out if he cooperated, but there's no way anybody can help them if the whole story comes out. The man and his company share responsibility for the serial killer who's loose on the streets out there now; he got that way because of the drug. He's a product of the Company's tests of the drug, and an analysis of his blood, and the blood of the other patients, will prove it."

"Forty-six deaths as of this morning, Mongo."

"Jesus," I sighed. "Lorminix is finished if the truth ever comes out. Every single executive who isn't in prison will be fighting personal and corporate lawsuits until there isn't a penny left in the coffers. They don't know I have patients here, but both the CIA and Lorminix know *I'm* here. The Company and Mr. Heinrich Muller must figure they have no choice but to take me out, destroy any evidence I might have gathered, and then keep hunting for the patients. They will definitely send others."

Now it was Veil's turn to smile without humor. "Well, I hope they clean out that Dumpster on a regular basis, because it may be getting a lot of use. I'm going to double the guard."

I nodded my thanks, and we started down the stairs together, passing yet another one of Veil's students, an attractive redhead in her mid-thirties, who was on her way up. "Where the hell are all these people coming from?" I asked my friend. "I didn't think you took on that many pupils."

"I have enough," Veil replied evenly. "You let me worry about security. Oh, one other thing. Some guy by the name of Theo Barnes was around the other day looking for you and asking questions about Michael. He obviously knows both of you."

"Ah yes, good old Theo. Michael was his meal ticket."

"Problem?"

"I don't think so."

"He was told there was no Michael here, and advised not to call you, you'd call him."

"Advised?"

"Very strongly."

"Good."

"What are you going to do now?"

"First, I'm going to call that prick in Switzerland to let him know I'm alive and very disappointed in him sending me goons instead of the drug. Maybe it will shake him up. If he finds out I'm not so easy to get rid of, thanks to you, he may reconsider his options and send me more of the medication—assuming there's any of it left. After that . . ."

"What?"

I was thinking of Bailey Kramer, whom I hadn't heard from and couldn't reach. There didn't seem to be any sense in going out to search for him, because I didn't know where to start looking. By now I was almost certain he'd been killed or captured and put on ice for the duration as a result of our little chat on the street. I felt very bad, and I didn't want to talk about it. "I don't know," I replied at last. "I don't know what else I can do, and the clock is ticking."

We paused at the entrance to my office on the first floor, and Veil said, "You should have somebody with you when you go out."

I shook my head. "There's nothing any of your people could do about a sniper if somebody wants to take a shot at me, and I can take care of a tail myself. In fact, I'd like to find somebody following me, and whoever it is better have either answers or disability insurance. You're already doing way more than your share by securing the brownstone. But thanks anyway. I appreciate the offer."

"You sure?"

"I'm sure. Go home and get some sleep."

Veil gave me a rather reluctant nod, then poked me on the shoulder and left. I walked into the reception area, said good morning to a rather concerned-looking Francisco, then went into my private office at the rear of the suite, closed the door behind me, then sat down at my desk. I tried Bailey's home again, but there was still no answer. I desperately wanted to find him, rescue him if he was in trouble, but there was nothing to go on. I knew nothing of his habits or friends. The only places where I knew how to reach him were his apartment, where the phone wasn't being answered at any hour of the day or night, and his place of work, which was closed for the holidays. I spent the better part of an hour calling hospitals and morgues in all

five boroughs, but there was no record of any patient or corpse identified as Bailey Kramer, and his general description would have fit
thousands of New Yorkers. There was always the possibility that he
had been arrested for something and was languishing in jail, but I
couldn't risk using any of my police contacts to try to trace him.

It was time for another talk with Herr Heinrich Muller, if he hadn't
yet left the office. When I called his private number I heard a recorded message telling me it was no longer in use. Cute. I found out
the number of the main office, dialed it, got a receptionist who claimed
to speak no English. In my own laborious French I asked to speak to
Heinrich Muller. I was informed not only that there was no Heinrich
Muller working there now, but that Lorminix had never employed
anybody by that name. Even cuter. No, I could not speak with any
other executive, unless I knew that executive's name and submitted a
written request for a telephone interview; no, it didn't make any
difference if I wanted to talk about the CIA, a place called Rivercliff,
or two people named Punch and Judy.

Outrageous.

I slammed down the receiver, leaned back in my chair, and ground
my knuckles into my eyes in frustration. So Heinrich Muller was on
an extended leave of absence—or perhaps even dead. And the giant
drug company, perhaps after consultations with the CIA, was going to
stonewall right to the end. I couldn't see how they could successfully
deny that a Heinrich Muller had ever worked there—but then again,
maybe they could; Lorminix wasn't exactly governed by the laws of
New York State. There was no way I could disprove their story in the
short time I had left, and no point in even trying—at least not over the
telephone. With Bailey Kramer missing, getting the help, however
grudgingly, of Lorminix executives was my last hope of avoiding a
Christmas Eve deadline that was probably hopeless anyway, since I
expected most of the patients would be dead soon afterward. A more
personal approach to the people at Lorminix was needed. It was time
for the approach Garth would undoubtedly have taken, but it was my
job to do, not his.

"Mongo?"

I took my knuckles out of my eyes, saw Francisco standing in the
doorway looking very anxious. "What is it, Francisco?"

"I . . . saw you through the glass. Are you all right?"

"Yeah," I answered, rising from my chair. "Call SwissAir and book me on the first available flight to Switzerland. Also, get me a hotel reservation somewhere in or near Berne, and then call me a cab."

"Yes, sir."

I went up to my apartment, hurriedly pocketed my passport, and packed a bag, evading Michael's tentative, anxious questions about where I was going. I did not want to get his hopes up. This trip to Switzerland was sure to cost me a minimum of two days, assuming I was successful and didn't run afoul of any Swiss police, and by the time I got back, Margaret's supply of capsules would be almost gone. I dearly wished I had made a copy of the Punch and Judy tape to take along with me, but I hadn't. I doubted MacWhorter would authorize releasing a copy when he found out why I wanted it, and there was nothing to be done about it now. On the other hand, key Lorminix executives already knew what I knew, and undoubtedly knew that I knew it; the problem wasn't in getting their attention, but getting them to cooperate.

Francisco was on the phone as I passed the glass wall of the office on my way out. I tapped on the glass to wave goodbye. He saw me and started, then urgently motioned for me to come in. I opened the door and leaned in as he covered the receiver with his palm. "Have I got a flight?"

"Yes. Your plane leaves in fifty-five minutes, and SwissAir will arrange for your hotel reservation. You have—"

"Jesus," I said, glancing at my watch. If I was blessed, I just might make it to JFK in time.

Francisco, a worried expression on his face, held out the telephone. "You have a call, Mongo."

"Is it from or concerning Bailey Kramer?"

"No, but—"

"Then tell them I'll get back to them. I'll call you here or at home when I get in."

Without waiting for his reply, I went out the door, bounded down the steps and across the sidewalk to the cab waiting at the curb. I hurled my bag into the back seat, got in after it, and slammed the door. "JFK," I said to the husky woman driver who was wearing a

Rangers cap backward. "I know you may find this surprising, coming from a New Yorker, but I'm in a hurry. I'll pay for any tickets, and there's a fifty-buck tip if you can get me to the SwissAir terminal in forty minutes."

"Yo," she said, and slammed the car into gear.

As the cab pulled away from the curb, I glanced out the side window and saw Francisco standing outside the entrance to the brownstone, waving his arms and shouting at me. I couldn't hear him through the glass, but when he pointed to his lips and slowly mouthed the word, I could make it out.

In-ter-pol.

"Stop."

"Hey, mister, you want to get to JFK in forty minutes at this time of day, we don't have a second to spare."

"It's all right. Just pull over to the curb and wait for me."

The woman pulled the car over, braked to a stop. I got out, walked quickly back to the brownstone to where Francisco, who had now managed to look even more worried, waited. "Interpol?" I asked.

My office manager nodded. "An Inspector something—a French name. He says it's extremely urgent."

I went into the office, picked up the receiver. "Gérard? What's up? I was just on my way to catch a plane to come over there."

"No, no, Mongo!" the Swiss man said quickly. "You must not come here! My friend, what have you done?!"

"Actually, Gérard," I said, tapping my fingers impatiently on the desk, "I've been up to quite a few things lately. Why don't you tell me what I've done that prompted this phone call."

"Mongo, this call is unofficial, from a friend. This is not an Interpol matter, but I've heard from local sources that you've been accused of a serious violation of Swiss law. If you try to enter the country, you will be arrested and detained. You must not come to Switzerland!"

CHAPTER 13

*T**here seemed nothing left to do but wait, and waiting wasn't* something I did well. As the hours passed, turning into days, I grew ever more tense and irritable, but I tried not to take it out on Francisco, and I made an effort to appear cheerful and upbeat whenever I was around Margaret, Michael, and Emily. I had once more implored them to come with me to a hospital while there was still a safety margin of time, and they had once again insisted that they wanted to wait until they had rendezvoused with the others on Christmas Eve, a date which seemed to be approaching with the speed of an express train. Margaret had finally agreed to share Michael's and Emily's capsules, and when they had finished dividing them up they each had just enough medication to get them through Christmas Day. There had been one capsule left over, and Sharon Stephens was holding it for them. I assumed the other members of the missing flock were in the same situation, and I didn't think one or two days was nearly enough time for the doctors to do whatever work had to be done.

An optimistic attitude had always formed the spine of my life, but I had to admit to myself that I did not believe Margaret or any of the other schizophrenics was going to survive.

There were no more night visitors. The CIA and Lorminix executives had apparently reached the same conclusion I had; all evidence of their wrongdoing would soon be gone.

I had stopped by the lab, just to make certain it was shuttered and locked, which it was. I had also gone to Bailey's Lower East Side apartment, which I'd found the same way. I'd picked the lock on the door and gone in, just to make sure Bailey wasn't lying dead on the floor, but there was no corpse, and everything had seemed in order. The thermostat had even been turned down, as if Bailey himself had simply gone off on vacation—something I couldn't imagine him doing under the circumstances, unless I had totally misread the man, and this was his idea of a joke on me, payback. Bailey Kramer wasn't dead in his apartment, and I just hoped he wasn't dead anywhere else.

I kept calling Bailey's apartment, day and night, out of habit more than hope, but the phone continued to ring unanswered. To keep myself busy I plunged into my work, clearing up all the paperwork around the office, rescheduling appointments I'd had Francisco cancel, lining up new business for the New Year.

And I started to make arrangements for Christmas Eve.

We would go to Rockefeller Center in the late afternoon, wait a certain length of time that had not been agreed upon yet for the others to show up, and then depart, en masse, to walk the few blocks to the nearest hospital, where I was working, calling in every IOU and using every contact I had, to ensure that a small army of specialists—endocrinologists, cell specialists, internists, and neurologists—would be waiting to try to prevent all these people from bleeding to death in the eye of this brainstorm.

My feelings about Bailey Kramer ranged from sorrow and guilt at the thought that I might have been responsible for his abduction and death at the hands of kidnappers, to outrage before the possibility that he might have decided the job was too much for him—or he had second thoughts about becoming involved, or he had wanted to get even with me—and had simply walked away from it all without telling me. Yet the cool temperature—an even 55 degrees—in his apartment kept bothering me; it was highly unlikely that any kidnappers intending to kill him would have allowed Bailey to turn down the thermostat so that he could save on fuel bills. It didn't make any sense.

It wasn't until early morning on the last day, 6:30 A.M. on December 24, as I stared at the dark ceiling above my bed, that a third possibility of what might have happened to him—or, more precisely, where he might have gone—occurred to me. I sat bolt upright in bed, and then, feeling like a fool for not considering this possibility before, I leaped out of bed, quickly pulled on jeans, a hooded sweatshirt, and sneakers. I ran out of the apartment, grabbing my parka on the way out, bounded down the stairs past an astonished Veil and another guard, who were conferring on the second-floor landing, to the front door and out to the street. There was no time for talk or explanations.

The early-morning traffic on Christmas Eve was light, and I knew that cabs at this hour would be scarce; I didn't feel like waiting around for one. Bursting with energy fueled by crazy, desperate renewed hope, I sprinted the several blocks to Frank Lemengello's lab. I arrived at the brick-and-glass one-story building on the corner of 62nd Street thoroughly winded, and I doubled up at the curb, gasping for air until I had caught my breath. As when I had checked before, there were no lights on in the locked building—but that didn't necessarily mean he wasn't there; he could be asleep, or had taken precautions to make sure he didn't announce his presence to police or other passersby with lights on in a laboratory whose sole proprietor was away on vacation.

I tried the front door, as I had done before, and found it still securely locked with what I assumed was a double, or even triple, dead bolt. Before I went to work on that, I thought I would take a little tour of the perimeter to look for signs of life. I went back down the steps, stepped off the sidewalk to the lawn, and slowly walked on the grass along the north side of the building, looking at all the windows. They were dark. I reached the gravel service driveway at the rear, slowly walked down it, again inspecting each window; all I could see was darkness inside, and the pale, ghostly reflection of the rising winter sun. And then, in the window next to the delivery entrance at the back, I saw what I had hoped to find, something nobody would have seen unless they were looking very closely.

At the very corner of the window, escaping through a sliver of the alarm-rigged plate glass where the blanket covering the window had slipped loose, was a pencil line of light.

I bounded up the three steps to the delivery door, used both fists to pound on the steel plate. "Bailey, open up! It's me! Bailey, open the fucking door!"

After about thirty seconds of more pounding and shouting, the door abruptly swung open, and Bailey Kramer, wearing a surgical cap and mask along with safety goggles and latex gloves, stood in the doorway looking down at me. The flesh of his face that I could see was a study in black on black, with inky, swollen bulges under his soulful eyes, whose whites were streaked with blood-red crimson. I wondered when he had last slept.

"Put these on and follow me," he said brusquely, handing me a paper cap and mask, latex gloves, and safety goggles. "And don't get in my way."

I followed him, my heart pounding with excitement and hope, into a large storage and testing room at the back of the building that had been transformed into something that looked like a hybrid of my high school chemistry lab, Dr. Frankenstein's basement, and a moonshiner's still. All of the sophisticated electronic equipment on three long, worn marble-topped worktables had been pushed back and draped, the machines apparently having done their job. The exposed surface of two of the tables was covered with a tangle of Pyrex retorts and beakers of various sizes, all connected to one another by lengths of clear plastic tubing; inside the containers, liquids of different colors and viscosity merrily bubbled away over Bunsen burners. There was a strange, pungent smell in the air that reminded me of a cross between a bakery and a sewage disposal plant. The end result of all this double bubble toil and trouble was something oozing out of a tube connected to a condensation apparatus at the end of one of the tables; viscous pale green gunk was dripping in clots out of the tube onto a ceramic plate, where it almost immediately congealed into a thick paste that had the look and consistency of used bubble gum.

The third stone-topped table, stretching across the front of the room at a right angle to the others, was being used for what appeared to be a mixing operation. There were a number of different drugs or chemicals in shallow plastic bins separated from one another by partitions of plastic stripping. There was an array of tiny measuring spoons and spatulas, and three finely calibrated electronic scales with digital readouts. At the far end of the table was a small mound of powder that was the same color as the compound inside the capsules. This mound had been further separated into several even smaller mounds of uniform size that were arrayed over a sheet of brown butcher's paper.

Meds for Margaret and the lost flock.

One corner of the room had been transformed into a kind of cockroach heaven, a pile of empty pizza boxes, soup cans, paper and plastic takeout food containers, McDonald's and Burger King wrappers, and various other sorts of litter. In the middle of the floor was a folding cot with two army blankets and a pillow without a pillowcase, but it didn't look like it had been used much.

"Bailey, you've done it?!"

The chemist grunted and nodded his head. His back was to me as he stood before an autoclave, impatiently drumming his fingers on the side of a ceramic tray containing a mound of the pale green paste. The red warning light on the autoclave was glowing, and I could see from the dial on the front that the autoclave had been set at its lowest temperature; something was cooking inside. "I'm missing one small chain of the molecule, but I don't think it will make a noticeable difference. This stuff should do the trick."

I donned my cap, mask, gloves, and goggles. "How can I help?"

"It will be easier for me to show you than try to explain. I'll have a new batch of the key ingredient coming out of the oven in a minute or two. It has to be mixed with the other drugs in a very precise ratio to produce the compound we need. Find paper and a pencil somewhere. I'll give you the precise weights we need of each ingredient as we go along the mixing table together. Those are the final dosages there at the end."

I went to the front of the building, into Frank's office, and rummaged around in his desk until I found a pad and a ballpoint pen. Then I hurried back to the chemist's aromatic chapel of miracles. He was still waiting in front of the autoclave.

"For Christ's sake, Bailey. I thought you were dead."

"Why?" he asked in an absent tone. Bailey Kramer was obviously not a man easily distracted from his work.

"*Why?!* Because you didn't call, is why. What the hell was I supposed to think? I was *worried* about you."

Now he turned to look at me, and from what I could see of his face he looked genuinely puzzled. "I told you I'd let you know if I couldn't do it. A few days ago I finally cracked the problem, found out I could do it. So I went to work. I've been very busy since our conversation, because I knew there wasn't any time to waste. You said you needed it by Christmas Eve, and that's still a few hours away. We're going to make it."

"Well, if you weren't concerned about putting my mind at rest, what about your expenses?"

He shrugged. "There wasn't a lot of time to worry about accounting. There's hundreds of thousands of dollars' worth of equipment here, Frederickson, and I really don't know of any place where you can rent it. Also, this isn't exactly the kind of operation you can set up in some loft or church basement. As for the prescription drugs, I had to use Frank's DEA number to order them from a pharmaceuticals supply house. Since he was going to find out what I'd been up to in any case, I figured I might as well go ahead and use his charge account. You can settle with him when he gets back. Obviously, since he was so conveniently vacating this very fine laboratory to go away for the holidays, I figured I'd just move in; everything I needed was here." He paused, and from the way the surgical mask covering his mouth and nose moved I thought he might actually be smiling. "Considering the circumstances and all of the other things that are likely to come down on me as a result of this venture, I figured it would be silly to worry about a little thing like Frank firing me."

"You're a pisser, Bailey," I said, shaking my head. "My very own mad scientist. You're everybody's last hope. Do you have any idea what I've been going through?"

"I'm sorry, Frederickson," he said seriously. "I really am. Now that you mention it, I guess I should have called you to let you know where I was and how the work was going. But I told you I didn't know if I could do it until a few days ago, and then I got kind of focused in on the job. When I'm doing something like this, everything else in the world just kind of fades away, doesn't exist for me."

Well, I certainly couldn't complain about that, and so I didn't. The bell on the autoclave chimed, and the red light went off. Bailey donned a pair of heavy, insulated mittens over his surgical gloves, opened the door, and removed a black ceramic plate on which there was a small mound of grayish-blue powder. He set that plate down on the mixing table, then returned to the autoclave and put in the plate with the bubble-gum paste. He shut the door, set the timer, pressed a button, and the red light came on again.

"This is the key ingredient," he continued, pointing to the grayish-blue powder, "the substance I had to replicate in order to make the compound work. The other ingredients are off-the-shelf psychotropics and a tiny amount of binder. I finally broke the chemical code, and then figured out a way to actually make the stuff yesterday afternoon. I've been cooking up the stuff ever since. When you mix all the ingredients in the proper ratios, and then measure it out, you get the brownish powder you see in the proper dosages there at the end of the table. I'm going to show you how to do that. By three or four this afternoon we should have enough dosages of the medication to supply a dozen people for maybe a month. Now that I've figured out how to do it, I can always make more if it's needed. If I'm not in jail, I can probably cook it up in my apartment. You don't need an autoclave; an ordinary kitchen stove will do nicely."

"What about gel capsules to put the dosages in?"

"I'm having three gross delivered at ten."

"Bailey, when was the last time you slept, and for how long?"

"I really don't remember," he replied curtly. "Now, pay attention as I go down the line. When I weigh out each ingredient, you make a note of that weight. Scoop it out with one of the spatulas you'll find in each bin, drop it into one of these little plastic cups, move on to the next ingredient. When you get down to the end of the line you'll have a dose, which you place in a separate pile on the butcher's paper. We'll load them into the gel capsules when they get here. Oh, and add three drops of ether to each dose; it speeds the binding process. Then go back to the other end of the table and start again." He paused, and I could see a glint of amusement in his black-ringed, bloodshot eyes. "It's just like making cookies, Frederickson."

A man's voice behind me said, "The test kitchen's closed, boys."

I wheeled around as I grabbed under my parka at my left armpit—and, just like in the taxicab, there was nothing there but my left armpit. My Beretta and shoulder holster were still home in my safe. The village idiot in me had struck once again. Lulled into compla-cency by the relative inactivity of the past week and a half, distracted by the disaster that was looming closer and closer, and spurred by excitement, I had once again popped out of the brownstone unarmed. Not that it would have made much difference if I'd had a bazooka strapped to my back; the two men who'd come in through the open delivery door and were aiming automatic pistols in our direction clearly had the drop on us, due to the fact that I'd been too absorbed in Bailey's wondrous accomplishment to give a second thought to the many people who might not think that what Bailey had done was so nifty. If my lapse hadn't been so criminally stupid, it would be laughable; while I had been breathlessly chugging along through the early morning streets, the two men who had undoubtedly been sitting in their car across the street from the brownstone had simply put their car into first gear and lazily tooled along behind me at a crawl, undoubtedly most curious as to where I was going in such a hurry at that hour of the morning. They'd walked right in behind me, skulked about while Bailey and I had chatted, and now, *voilà*. At the least, I should have made sure the door was locked behind me. Bailey Kramer wasn't supposed to think of such things; I was. While it was true that, even if I had locked the door, the men would have had us trapped inside, I might have grown a few IQ points by ten o'clock, when the gel capsules were to be delivered, and taken a few precautionary steps. Now it was too late. Now a lot of people could die because of my stupidity. I was within two bullets of snatching defeat from victory, and I found it all very depressing. The fact that the two gunmen were not bothering to cover their faces was not a good sign. Bailey and I stripped off our goggles and pulled down our masks, and I heaved a deep sigh.

They made an odd-looking couple, indeed, like Before and After figures in a diet commercial. They were both about six feet, but one had an enormous belly and must have been over three hundred pounds, while the other was so thin he looked like he might disappear if he turned sideways. After appeared to have what looked like a permanent sneer on his face, while Before's expression could be charitably described as blank. The Glocks they carried were identical twins.

Without a word, Before turned slightly, pressed the trigger of his Glock, and began spraying bullets through the array of bubbling retorts, plastic tubing, and Bunsen burners on two of the three stone-topped tables. Bailey and I both ducked and covered our faces as glass, plastic, and chemicals flew through the air. By the time the fat man had emptied his clip and stopped to reload, there was nothing left on the tables but ruined machines, glass and plastic shards, and one forlorn Bunsen burner that was still bravely burning away as if in memory of its lost companions, having somehow survived the fusillade. I slowly backed away along the length of the mixing table until I came up against a wooden storage rack filled with chemicals in various types of containers. Bailey backed away in the opposite direction as Before approached the table and looked down at the piles of drugs in their plastic bins and the tiny mounds of the pale brown compound Bailey had so carefully prepared. The skinny gunman took up a position to my right, keeping his Glock trained on me while he leaned on one of the glass-strewn worktables and lit a cigar that looked almost as thick as he was from the surviving Bunsen burner.

"Sorry, gentlemen," I said, struggling against the crippling despair I was feeling, "if you're here for the free urine and bad-breath tests, that offer has expired."

"Watch your mouth, Frederickson," After said, puffing on his cigar.

"Who sent you? Lorminix or the CIA? Or are they splitting costs on this one?"

"Where are the others, Frederickson?"

"What others? Other whats?"

It seemed After the talker and Before the shooter were used to working together; without any word of warning or any discernible signal from his partner, the blank-faced fat man half turned and casually pumped a bullet into Bailey's left thigh. Bailey cried out and clutched at his wounded leg as he collapsed into the narrow space between the end of the worktable and the wall. I started toward him, stopped, and retreated to the storage rack when Before swung his gun around and pointed it at my chest.

I said, "Let me put a tourniquet on his leg."

After waved away the suggestion along with the cloud of blue-gray cigar smoke that hung around his head. "You needn't worry about him bleeding to death, pal. If I don't get the right answer this time, you can watch while my associate over there starts shooting your friend to death, one little pop at a time. I imagine the next bullet will go into the other leg, probably in the kneecap."

"Take it easy. Dr. Stephens and two of her patients are back in my house, but you can't get to them. The place is well guarded."

"We didn't see any guards."

"They're inside. There are two of them, and they'll eat you and your guns for breakfast. I'm telling you this because I wouldn't want to see either of you get hurt. I don't know where the rest of the patients are; they're still out somewhere walking around the streets."

"No problem," After said, grinning around his cigar. "We'll just pick them up tonight."

My dismay and disappointment must have shown on my face, for the emaciated man's cigar-punctuated grin grew even wider. "We nabbed one of the loonies," he continued, "and she told us all about the little Christmas Eve reunion. Touching. Now, what were you and the shrink planning to do with the two you've got?"

I glanced back and forth between After, who, apparently satisfied that the situation was under control, had laid his Glock down on the table and was leaning on the marble, enjoying his cigar while he bantered with me, and Before, who still had his gun aimed at my chest. The expression on the fat man's face had gone all the way from blank to bored, and I had the distinct impression that he was waiting for the good part, the killing, to begin.

"Dr. Stephens and I were going to drop them off with the cops before we went to Rockefeller Center to pick up the others and bring them to the cops," I said, watching as the fat man casually brushed his forearm across the butcher's paper at the end of the table, sweeping onto the floor all the dosages Bailey had spent so much time and effort preparing. Then he proceeded to walk the length of the table, giving the same treatment to the plastic bins and their contents; the crashing of the plastic trays on the tile floor was like a fusillade of cannon shots aimed at my heart. Some of the powdered drugs remained suspended in the air, drifting like motes of dust. I pulled my mask up over my nose and mouth, at the same time turning my head slightly to get a glimpse of what was on the storage rack behind me. "The police were going to escort all of us to the hospital. Now, when

I don't show up, Dr. Stephens is going to call the cops and have them come to the house."

"That's pure bullshit," After said, dragging a toe through the fine residue of powder that had fallen at his feet. "If you were planning on going to the cops, you'd have done it before. And you wouldn't have gone to all the trouble of cooking up this shit. I think my associate is going to have to put a slug in your friend's other leg."

As Before brushed powder off the front of his shirt and started to point his gun at Bailey, I cringed and half turned toward the storage rack, at the same time groaning in exaggerated horror as I pointed toward the fat man's powder-coated hands. "Jesus Christ, big guy, if you're going to shoot anybody, you'd better do it fast, while you've still got feeling left in your trigger finger. Didn't anybody tell you not to touch or breathe in any of that stuff you've got all over you? The next time you try to take a shit, it's going to be your balls that fall into the toilet."

The expression on Before's face was no longer blank, or bored. His eyes went wide with real horror as he looked down at his hands and dust-coated belly. Then he turned his attention to the task of vigorously rubbing his left hand on his pants leg. I turned my attention to the rack of chemicals behind me. I grabbed a beaker of ether off the shelf and hurled it at the big man. The glass stopper came out of the beaker as it sailed through the air, and it hit him on the shoulder, spilling its contents over his head and body. Then I quickly ducked down as After grabbed his Glock off the table and fired at me. The bullets flew over my head, smashing the storage rack and everything on it. I was sprayed with a variety of foul-smelling chemicals; I didn't care how bad they smelled, just as long as they weren't as flammable as the ether. Keeping low so that After couldn't see me, I moved along behind the worktable, and then, in a single motion, leaped up, grabbed the single surviving Bunsen burner by its base, and hurled it at the stunned, obese, ether-soaked figure standing a few feet away. The rubber tubing connecting the burner to its gas source popped loose, but the heat at the burner's steel nozzle was sufficient to ignite the ether, and the man suddenly erupted in a plume of bluish flame that rose up and licked at the ceiling. The first sound he'd uttered since walking into the laboratory was a keening scream.

After commenced firing again, but I had already dropped back down behind the solid worktable. I headed back the way I had come, knowing that if I guessed wrong, I was dead. His Glock held a seventeen-shot magazine, and he had to be running low—but it would take only one bullet to kill me. I reached the end, peered around the corner down toward the other end, where the pile of trash Bailey had collected had started to burn. I just caught a glimpse of After's bony rear end as he sneaked around the other end of the two-table setup, looking for me. The fat man's remains were cooking in the middle of the lab floor. The air was filled with the smell of seared flesh and the acrid stench of burning chemicals, which were ablaze in tiny, flaming pools all around the room.

"Hey!"

After popped back around the end of the table, fired off another burst at the spot where my head had been. He was a bit quick on the trigger, but considering the fact that he had to get past me to get out of a room that was rapidly filling with flame and poisonous gases, I could understand his impatience.

We played a few more rounds of ring-around-the-table, with After firing every time I let him see the whites of my eyes, until I finally heard the recoil mechanism on his empty Glock click open. Then I came around my end of the table and walked toward him. He was wide-eyed and his mouth was hanging open, his gaze darting back and forth between me and the flaming corpse of his partner, as he groped inside his jacket pocket for what I presumed was an extra clip of ammunition. What he got was my foot in the face as I leaped into the air and drove the heel of my right sneaker into his larynx. He dropped the gun and sat down hard on the floor, his eyes gaping with horror as he clutched at his throat with its crushed larynx that would no longer admit air into his lungs. He stared back at me as he began to turn blue and die.

The lab itself was heavily insulated, but there was no sprinkler system because water was contraindicated for many chemical fires, and there were enough flammable chemicals in the area to keep things cooking for some time. However, the greater danger at the moment was gas, which seemed to be overpowering the heavy-duty automatic venting system that had cut in. Keeping low, I darted around the flaming, blackened mound that had been the obese gunman. I got to Bailey, who had managed to pull himself to his feet by grabbing the edge of the table next to which he had fallen. He was standing on one foot, gasping for breath. I grabbed hold of his belt, and with him hanging over me we managed to hobble together to the delivery door and out of the lab. I eased him down onto the gravel driveway, then took his right hand and pressed his thumb down on a pressure point just above the bleeding bullet wound in his thigh.

"Just keep pressing here, Bailey," I said. "Don't pass out. I'll be right back."

"Mongo, you can't go back in there! The gases—!"

But I had already bounded back up the steps to the delivery door. I sucked in a deep breath, held it, shut my eyes, and went back in. Relying on my memory of the layout and my sense of touch, I felt my way back along the short corridor to the testing area, stopped when I felt intense heat on my face and heard the wheezy, crackling laughter of flames, almost drowning out the whir of the giant ventilation fans. Still holding my breath, I dropped down to my hands and knees and opened my left eye to a slit. Almost immediately the eye began to sting and tear, but I had seen enough to get my bearings and the lay of this flaming land. I closed my eye again and began to crawl toward what had been the mixing table, which was about fifteen feet away, to my left. When I bumped my head against the table, I put my left shoulder against it and scampered to the far end, where the prepared dosages had been swept to the floor. I put my face close to the floor, opened my right eye slightly. There, literally in front of my nose, was a residue of the light brown powder that meant life to a dozen people, and presumably one more whom I had no interest in saving. I closed the eye as it began to tear, then used both hands to sweep the floor around me, gathering up as much of the compound as I could. I scooped up what amounted to half a handful and put it into my shirt pocket. I had no idea whether the drug would now be effective; it had been "unmixed" and contaminated by other drugs and chemicals, but I figured that what I had collected was better than nothing.

My lungs were bursting, and I knew I had only a few more seconds before I would pass out—and die. I remembered an old diver's trick I had read about, and I swallowed, allowing the tiny amount of air that had been trapped in my throat and larynx to enter my lungs. Then I got to my feet, opened my eyes, and sprinted through the flames and clouds of gas and smoke, down the narrow corridor, and out the back door. I collapsed onto my knees on the gravel, gasping for air while at the same time resisting the impulse to rub my eyes, which were both flooded with tears.

I could hear the wail of approaching police and fire sirens, and I knew I could not afford a lot of recovery time. Still gulping in great drafts of air, I got to my feet. I peered around me until I could see the blurred figure of Bailey Kramer, went over to him.

"Bailey, I've got to get out of here," I croaked, wiping tears from my cheeks but still being careful not to touch my eyes, which were continuing to cleanse themselves quite nicely. "You'll be all right. The bullet didn't hit an artery, and the police and firemen will be here any moment. They'll call an ambulance to get you to a hospital."

He clutched at my sleeve. "Mongo?! What should I tell them?!"

"The truth. Tell them everything that's happened—except about where I am, the patients with me, and the rendezvous at Rockefeller Center. They'll take you to the hospital for treatment before they start questioning you, and that will take some time. When the police do start to question you, ask to speak to Captain MacWhorter personally. He's clued in on most of what's been happening. String him out until dusk, and then you can tell him everything."

"The killers knew about the rendezvous. There could be more of them waiting for you there."

"There'll be a regular contingent of cops at the rink and around the plaza. I'm counting on the hunters not to know what specific individuals to look for, while I will. If there's an army of uniforms over there, I'm afraid it might scare the other patients away. I think MacWhorter will agree. If he does decide to send extra people to the rink, and he almost certainly will, tell him to make sure they're in plainclothes, and they shouldn't interfere while I'm gathering up the patients. I'd also like to see some cops at the hospital, after nightfall. I don't know when we'll be there, but we will be there. Thanks again for everything, Bailey, and I can't tell you how sorry I am for leading those two jokers to you. Talk to you later."

"But Mongo—!"

I didn't wait to see what else Bailey had to say, because I had too much else to do and I didn't want to waste time evading questions from the police and being fussed over by paramedics. I pushed through the knot of people that had gathered at the head of the driveway, reached the sidewalk just as two police cars and a fire truck pulled up to the curb. I headed south, and, with my breathing labored and tears still streaming from my eyes, walked as fast as I could the few blocks to my brownstone. By the time I got there my eyes had stopped stinging and tearing, and I could breathe easier. I hurried through the front entrance, past the open office door. A startled Francisco looked at me and spilled his morning coffee.

"Mongo? What . . . ? Your eyes are all—"

"Call upstairs and tell the women to meet me up in my living room," I said, and started up the stairway.

When I entered my apartment I found Michael, still in his pajamas, sitting stiffly in a chair by the window, staring out through a crack in the blinds. He didn't turn to greet me, and I went directly into the bathroom, where I turned on the tap and began carefully rinsing out my eyes. After a couple of minutes I looked at myself in the mirror; my eyes were still very bloodshot, but I could now see clearly, and I did not think there had been any permanent damage from the gases in the burning laboratory. When I came back out into the living room, Sharon Stephens, Margaret, and Emily were waiting for me, standing in the center of the room next to Michael's sleeping bag, worried expressions on their faces. Michael was still sitting, unmoving and with his back to us, at the window.

Margaret gasped and put a hand to her mouth. "Mongo, what's wrong with your eyes?!"

"I'm all right. Now, listen up. I have good news and I have bad news. The good news is that I found the chemist I told you about, and he's discovered a way to make more of your meds. The bad news is that most of what he'd already made has been destroyed. It will probably be a few days before he can make up another batch, and so you're just going to have to somehow hold out until then. Here's the drill. I—" I paused, turned toward the figure who remained in the chair by the window. "Michael? I hope I'm not boring you. Would you come over here and join us? What I have to say is important."

His answer was to make a dry, rasping sound deep in his throat that sounded like a chuckle but wasn't. It reminded me of rustling leaves.

"Michael? Are you all right?"

The sound came again, this time louder. I hurried across the room and stepped in front of him. What I saw filled me with horror, and I choked off a cry. Blood was running in two steadily streaming rivulets from his nostrils, running down over his lips, dripping off his chin onto the front of his pajamas, which were stained a bright crimson. His eyes were totally vacant, and as I looked on, blood suddenly squirted in a tiny font from the left one, hitting me in the face.

"Get me his capsules!" I shouted to Margaret, wrapping my arms around Michael and easing him off the chair and onto his back on the floor. "They're in the medicine cabinet in the bathroom, bottom shelf! Hurry!"

Margaret rushed out of the room and down the narrow corridor leading to the bathroom as I cradled Michael's head in my arms. The sound of dry, rustling leaves emanating from his chest grew louder, and he was springing deadly crimson leaks everywhere. A dark stain had appeared at his crotch and was spreading down his pajama bottoms as blood flowed from his urethra and anus. Even his high forehead had become spotted; he was sweating blood from his pores.

"They're not there!" Margaret cried as she rushed back into the living room. "Mongo, they're not there!"

I turned to Emily, whose features were clenched in torment. "Get me one of yours or Margaret's, or the extra one! Hurry, Emily!"

For a moment the empath seemed paralyzed by her own terror and horror, but then she suddenly bolted from the room. I heard the door to the apartment slam open, and then her footsteps on the stairs as she raced to the apartment below. I reached into my shirt pocket and took out a large pinch of the adulterated compound I had scraped up from the floor of the laboratory, forced open his mouth with my left hand, and shoved the powder in. It came right back out again, riding the crest of a river of red as he belched blood that flooded out of his mouth, over my hand, and onto the floor. I tried again with a second pinch of powder, but it was useless. I hung my head as Michael shuddered and died.

I heard footsteps, then felt a hand on my shoulder. I looked up into

Emily's stricken face. Margaret and Sharon Stephens stood on either side of her, staring at me intently. In Emily's trembling, outstretched hand was a single black-and-yellow capsule. I shook my head. "He's gone."

"There was an extra capsule in my bag, Mongo," the girl sobbed as tears streamed down her cheeks. "I think Michael must have put it there. He gave up his last med so that Margaret and I could each have one more day."

I nodded, then bent down and kissed the chess master's bloody forehead. And then I wept.

Chapter 14

*S*haron Stephens, who could not stop crying, helped me wrap Michael Stout's corpse, which we would properly attend to at a more propitious time, in a shower curtain. While the women cleaned the floor of the living room, I stripped off my bloody clothes, showered to wash the blood off my face and hands, dressed in clean clothes, and went down to my office. Struggling to put the horror of Michael's death out of my mind, I tried to concentrate on his exquisite and incredibly heroic act, the gift of his life so that two people could live at least another twenty-four hours.

I picked up the phone and began calling the medical specialists I had contacted earlier, double-checking to make sure they would be in the emergency room of the nearest hospital by six o'clock to meet us all when we arrived sometime later in the evening. When I had finished doing that, a tearful Francisco and I went back upstairs to join the others, including the two guards, for our own private memorial service for Michael. When that was over, I scoured Garth's apartment and my own for dark glasses, woolen caps, mufflers, and anything else we could use to provide suitable disguises for the psychiatrist and Emily. At five-thirty, accompanied by Veil, we left the brownstone and, to the sounds of Christmas carols provided by a Salvation Army group and a steel band and a lone violinist stationed along the route, headed through the streets toward Rockefeller Center. A light snow, the first of the season, had begun to fall.

This time out I made sure I was armed, with my Beretta in a shoulder holster and the small Seecamp strapped to my right ankle.

I had Veil and his students escort the three women down to the coffee shop adjacent to the rink, while I stayed up above on the promenade, below the magnificent Christmas tree and above the great, prone figure of Prometheus, checking out the people on the skating rink below me who were whirling about in the snow flurry to the sound of Christmas music. There were hordes of people walking around the promenade, standing around the rink, or gathered to admire the towering, brightly lighted tree behind me. The skaters of both sexes came in all sizes, ages, and races, and there were upwards of three dozen of them, including one understuffed Santa Claus zipping around the rink carrying over his shoulder an understuffed laundry bag with something lumpy in the bottom. There were a number of uniformed policemen patrolling the area, but there didn't seem to be more than the usual contingent. By now I assumed that Bailey had told MacWhorter the whole story, and I wondered how many of the people in the crowd were plainclothes detectives—or killers.

There had been a dozen patients who had originally escaped with Sharon Stephens. Punch and Judy had killed one, and the killers who had come to the laboratory said a woman had been captured, and she was presumably dead by now. Michael Stout was dead, and Emily was with us. That left eight people to round up, and I fervently hoped they were here in the crowd, or soon would be, because there was no time to waste. I had to get them to the hospital so the doctors could examine and start working on them, and then every minute would count in the day or two they had left to them before they ran out of their medication and I had pinched out the last of the precious powder in my pocket.

And then, of course, there was the wild card to consider—Raymond Rogers. Obviously, Rogers had snatched his own supply of the black-and-yellow capsules from the infirmary; when he ran out, he would presumably die. However, from his hidden perch on top of the bus, he may well have overheard the psychiatrist and the other patients making plans to meet on Christmas Eve. If that was the case, he too would be here, somewhere in the crowd, hoping Sharon Stephens had obtained more of the drug, and looking to grab his own lifesaving handout.

In fact, there had been a dramatic decrease in the number of ice-pick killings over the past ten days. Much of that good news was probably attributable to the fact that people in the city had grown eyes in the back of their heads and were extraordinarily cautious in their comings and goings, but I also thought it possible that Rogers was being much more cautious so as not to be caught before Christmas Eve; his description had been printed in all the newspapers, and posters with his likeness and a warning were up all over the city, and at every subway station. There was also the possibility that his medication had run out and he was dead in some alley in a lake of his own blood. But if he was somewhere here in the crowd, watching and waiting, I assumed I would know about it before the end of the evening, and I was going to keep an especially sharp lookout for tall, rangy men.

I watched Santa and the other skaters for a few more minutes to satisfy myself that none of them looked suspicious, then wandered around the promenade, trying very hard to look like your average, everyday New York City dwarf. I felt more than a tad self-conscious, which I thought understandable in light of the fact that Lorminix or Chill Shop assassins in the crowd certainly had my description. I could end up a target marker, a danger to my charges, but it couldn't be helped; I had to be able to communicate with the others. From this point on I intended to stay out of sight, let the psychiatrist and Emily do the spotting, and Margaret and Veil the gathering in of the lost flock.

I went down to the coffee shop. Margaret, Sharon Stephens, and Emily were sitting at a table in a corner in the back, and Veil and his two students were standing in front of them, forming a shield.

"This is how I propose to do this," I said to the women as I pulled up a chair and sat down at the table. Veil immediately moved in front of me to shield me from view. "The tree is on the promenade above us, to our right. It's easy to see the people gathered around it, but it's too open; we can't just stand around up there. I suggest we make this table our home base; it's a relatively closed area, and it's easier for our friends here to keep an eye on everybody. We can't see the tree from here, but we can see the statue and a section of the promenade above it. The people we're looking for will expect to find Dr. Stephens at the tree; when they don't find her there, I think the chances are good that they'll come to the railing to look down at the skaters. Sharon, you and Emily will keep an eye on that railing. If you see one of our people, holler out—in a manner of speaking. Margaret, nobody else knows about you or has your description. If you don't mind, we'll use you as a messenger. You go to the person, tell him or her where we are, and then keep walking. Make sure you don't come back down here together—and when you talk to them, do a lot of pointing at the ice, as if you're talking about the skaters. Can you do that?"

"I certainly can, Mongo," Margaret said in a firm voice. Her pale violet eyes glittered with excitement.

Veil said, "I'll ride shotgun for Margaret every time she goes out. Jack and Moira will stay here on guard."

I nodded. "Once each hour, Veil will take you, Sharon, up to the area around the tree. You'll act like lovers; he'll keep his arm around you so that you can hide your face against his coat and just kind of glance around every once in a while. If you see any of your people, don't approach them. Come back here, and Margaret will go contact them. Okay?"

"Okay," the psychiatrist replied.

"We'll collect as many as come in until ten, and then we'll walk together to the University Medical Center over on the East Side. Maybe I can arrange for a patrol car to escort us. There's a team of medical specialists waiting for us at the hospital. With luck, we'll have everybody at the hospital long before ten. On the other hand, we have to be realistic about no-shows. Considering the importance of this rendezvous, I think it's safe to assume that anybody who doesn't show up by ten o'clock is . . . isn't coming. How does that sound to you folks?"

Sharon Stephens, Margaret, and Emily glanced around the table at each other, and it was the psychiatrist who finally said, "It sounds like a good plan to us."

"Good," I said, leaning back in my chair so that I could see around Veil, toward the front of the coffee shop and out at the great, golden giant on his pedestal across the rink. "Now let's see who shows up."

*   *   *

"There!" Sharon Stephens *said excit-*
edly. "It's Phyllis!"

I grabbed the psychiatrist's arm, pulled it back down to the table.
"Don't point; just describe."

"She's at about two o'clock, on the promenade almost directly
above the head of the statue. She's at the railing looking down at the
skaters. She's wearing a gray hat and coat. There's a young couple
standing to her right."

I glanced around Veil, spotted the woman the psychiatrist had
described, turned to Margaret. "You see her?"

"I see her," Margaret said determinedly, rising from the table as
Veil pulled her chair out for her and took her arm.

"Remember; don't hang around up there. Just deliver the message
while you point to the skaters, and then get back down here. Don't
walk back with her."

"I understand, Mongo."

"Go. Be careful."

I watched as Margaret, with Veil a few steps behind her, walked out
of the coffee shop and disappeared to the left as she headed for the stone
stairs leading up to the promenade. They reappeared in my line of
sight, up on the promenade above Prometheus, a minute or two later.
Veil was still walking behind Margaret, and he stopped to the patient's
left and leaned on the railing as Margaret walked up to the woman and
began speaking—all the while pointing down at the rink as I had told
her. The woman suddenly slumped and would have fallen if Veil had
not quickly grabbed her arm. He led the woman back to the left, while
Margaret continued walking on in the opposite direction. They arrived
back at our table, by their separate routes, at almost the same time.

There was a tearful reunion between the patient named Phyllis and
the other women—a celebration cut short at my insistence because I
didn't want to attract any more attention than we already had.

I rose to get the new arrival some food, and the rest of us another
round of coffee and hot chocolate. I was already feeling exhausted
from tension and anxiety, and the evening's activities were just beginning.

*   *   *

By eight-thirty we had gathered in all but three of the lost flock, not counting the woman Before and After said had been captured, and whom I assumed was dead. I would have allowed myself to begin feeling some measure of elation, or at least satisfaction, were it not for the fact that gathering the survivors was only the beginning; there was still a long and perilous journey to take if this was not to be the last Christmas for these men and women, and there was precious little time in which to take it.

Veil and I kept buying food—a lot of food; all of the patients were half starved, and some were dressed in thin rags that were hanging off them, but at least they were alive. Sharon Stephens had done an excellent job in equitably dividing up the capsules; the people we had gathered in had made it this far, but nobody had more than two capsules left, two people had only one, and I didn't consider the few ounces of nameless powder I had left in my pocket to be any kind of a real buffer. Everything would depend on what the doctors could do, and how fast they could do it, once we reached the hospital.

By nine-fifteen, two more emaciated but excited patients, both men, had been gathered in, and there was only one left to find—one of two middle-aged women. At nine-thirty Veil and Sharon Stephens left for their periodic tour of the area around the Christmas tree. They had been gone less than a minute when Emily grabbed my shoulder and pointed excitedly in the direction of the rink outside.

"That's Alexandra!" Emily said in her small, breathless voice. "She's the woman sitting on the bench on the other side of the rink! She's wearing a blue coat!"

I looked in the direction where Emily was pointing, but my view was momentarily obstructed by a cluster of skaters—all of them new faces, except for the athletic, seemingly indefatigable Santa with his lumpy sack—gliding past. Then there was a gap in the moving bodies, and I could see a black-haired woman who appeared to be in her late forties or early fifties sitting stiffly on one of the wooden benches that had been set up on the walkway surrounding the rink. She had a blank expression on her face as she stared straight ahead of her. All of the other patients had remembered to go to the tree, and I couldn't understand what this one was doing sitting on a bench on the lower level. It didn't feel quite right to me, and I felt my stomach muscles tighten.

"I'll go get her," Margaret said, rising from the table.

I reached out and grabbed for the woman's coat. "Hold on, Margaret. Wait for Veil. He should be back in a couple of minutes."

"Don't be silly, Mongo," Margaret said, pulling out of my grasp. "She's right over there, and I'll just walk around and get her. Nobody knows who I am, but somebody might recognize her, and she's sticking out there like a sore thumb."

"That's the point, Margaret! There's something wrong with—!"

But she had already left the table. As she exited from the restaurant and turned right to walk around the rink, I motioned for the young guard named Jack to follow her. Jack nodded, then quickly walked away. I did not want to leave the second guard, Moira, alone to watch over so many people, but I walked to the glass wall at the front of the coffee shop, where I had a clear view of the entire skating rink. I absently touched the Beretta under my parka, but I knew that the gun was virtually useless in such a crowded area; if any shooting started, a lot of innocent people would surely die.

Presumably only one member of the lost flock was left to gather in, and she was sitting directly across from me, separated by only a few dozen feet of ice. So near, and yet so far. I didn't like the situation, or the look on the woman's face, at all.

I watched tensely as Margaret threaded her way through the people who were standing on the walk on her way toward the woman named Alexandra. Jack was about ten paces behind her. She stopped by the bench where the woman was sitting and began talking to her. Suddenly a man in a gray overcoat who had been standing at the steel railing a few feet away swung around and grabbed both women by the arm. I glanced toward Jack just in time to see a man in a bomber jacket step into his path. The next moment the young man, taken completely by surprise, doubled over, and I knew he had taken a knife in the gut.

The shortest distance between two points is a straight line, and so that was the way I headed, vaulting over the steel railing outside the coffee shop and slip-sliding across the ice toward where Margaret and the woman named Alexandra were struggling with the man in the gray overcoat and the second man in the bomber jacket, who had come over to help. As I slid and staggered on the ice, with startled skaters swerving to avoid me, it occurred to me that these assassins, whether employed by BUHR or Lorminix, had probably been here all evening, mingling with the crowds, waiting and studying our routine while Veil, Sharon Stephens, and Margaret did their work for them, gathering in the lost flock, putting all this living evidence of the horrendous crimes that had been committed into one place where they could be more easily exterminated with a grenade or burst of fire from an automatic weapon. It was Alexandra who had been captured; when Veil had left with Sharon, Alexandra had been used as bait to draw out another guard, thinning our forces further; or, if Margaret hadn't gotten up to go over, it would have been Veil and Sharon who would have been ambushed, and I presumed they were probably being attacked now up on the promenade. And if I hadn't gone to the window to look out, I wouldn't even have known what was happening.

I was aware that it was probably a mistake for me to be scrambling across the ice, knew that my place was back in the coffee shop defending the greater number, but my reaction had been instinctive, and now I was committed to this course of action. Margaret Dutton was the most innocent of innocent bystanders, and she had shown great courage. She was *my* patient, in a manner of speaking, and if it hadn't been for Mama Spit and her faith in me I wouldn't have had a ticket to this dance in the first place. I couldn't turn my back on her when there was the likelihood she was about to be summarily executed along with the woman she had ventured out to rescue.

I was startled when the sounds of laughter and applause suddenly erupted all around me, and then I realized that the hundreds of spectators thought I was part of some special Christmas show, or a drunken dwarf who had seriously lost his way, or both. I kept pumping my arms, struggling to get across the ice to the women and the two men they were struggling with. Margaret was scratching at the eyes of the man in the gray overcoat, and he was drawing back his fist to punch her.

There was a flash of color and movement above them, and then I saw Veil vault over the wall of the promenade, plummet down through the air, and land with his feet on the backs of both men. At almost the same precise moment I felt a strong hand grab me by the seat of my pants and lift me in the air. There was more laughter and applause, but there were also scattered shouts and screams as it dawned on some of the brighter onlookers that this was no show, and that something was seriously amiss on the skating rink at Rockefeller Center.

Dangling rather ignominiously in the firm grip of the very unfriendly skater who held me, I thrashed and tried to get to my Beretta, but it seemed I was about to lose not only face and my free ride but also my race against death, for even as I wrapped my fingers around the stock of the Beretta I could feel the bore of my captor's gun pressing against my rib cage. I was about to take a bullet through the heart.

Then the man cursed, and the gun came away. I looked up and saw Santa, one arm resting behind his back, blithely skating right toward us. My captor cursed again and swerved to avoid the other figure, but Santa just swerved with him and kept coming directly at us. We collided—or, rather, Santa's forearm and my captor's mouth collided. There was the sound of breaking bone and teeth, and my skater and I were suddenly parted, with him going one way and me sliding over the ice on my stomach in the opposite direction.

My trip in that direction didn't last long. I felt like a hockey puck as once again a strong hand grabbed me, this time by the hood of my parka, swung me around, and began pulling me back the way I had come. I caught a flash of red suit and bushy white beard, and realized that now it was Santa who had me. Everything around me was a blur of motion, with panicked skaters racing in all directions. I felt as if I were spinning at the bottom of some old kaleidoscope filled with rapidly shifting images that made me feel dizzy and disoriented, somehow dreamily apart from everything that was going on around me. As Santa continued to slide me across the ice on my belly, I caught a glimpse of Veil across the way. He had knocked unconscious—or probably killed—both men he had jumped on, and they were draped over the steel railing. Now he was leading both Margaret and the woman named Alexandra back around the rink at the same time as he supported Jack, who was holding a hand to the wound in his stomach. We zipped merrily along, past the man whose teeth Santa had knocked out; there was another man, presumably a cop, standing over him and holding a gun to his head. There were other men with guns, but they were all dressed in civilian clothes, making it impossible to tell the good guys from the bad guys.

Sharon Stephens, her eyes wide and her mouth gaping open, was standing up on the promenade, her arm around a woman who was wearing a ragged green woolen cap.

Santa suddenly yanked on the hood of my parka, not quite breaking my neck, lifted me up a foot or so, and then hurled me ahead of him across the ice in the general direction of the coffee shop. I ended up sliding on my bottom until I came up hard against the railing. Santa was following after me at a leisurely pace, but then he abruptly skidded to a stop. His hand went into his suit, and when it came out he was holding a gun, which he proceeded to aim at my head—or a spot just above my head. People behind me screamed as Santa took careful aim and fired. I could actually hear the *thwack* of somebody standing at the railing directly above and behind me being hit by the bullet. There was a strangled groan, and then a man's body pitched over the railing and landed right beside me on his back, snow falling into his blank, unseeing eyes that stared up into the sky. The man, who was wearing boots, green slacks, and a heavy flannel shirt, was tall and gaunt. Even in death he kept a firm grip on the ice pick in his hand, which was embedded in the ice an inch or two from my right thigh; if not for Santa, that ice pick undoubtedly would now be buried in the back of my skull.

There were more screams as people who had been standing at the railing scrambled to get away. Seemingly unmindful of the pandemonium all around, Santa unhurriedly put the gun back into a pocket in his red suit, then picked up the lumpy laundry bag he had dropped on the ice and skated over to me. I found myself looking up over the beard and into a pair of soulful brown eyes that looked very familiar to me.

"Ho, ho, ho, little pilgrim," Santa said. "A Merry Christmas to you."

It was a drop-dead John Wayne imitation, and it meant that this particular Santa Claus was not pleased with me.

"GARTH?!"

Now my brother pulled off his stocking cap, which had covered his wheat-colored hair, stripped off his false white beard and bushy eyebrows. His eyes swam with feeling, both relief and anger, but his John Wayne imitation never faltered. "That outlaw with the steel toothpick has been keeping an eye on you ever since you and your gang got here, Pilgrim. He must have figured you might have something he wanted."

I tried to get up, slipped, and fell back on my rear, so I just sat there, continuing to stare up into the stern face of my brother, thoroughly astonished. "Cut the John Wayne shit, Garth. What are you *doing* here?!"

It was still John Wayne who answered, which meant my brother was *really* angry with me. "Let this be a lesson to you, Pilgrim, not to try to cut me out of something like this. You're real lucky you're not dead, you dumb little dogie. I should have let that ornery cowpoke Rogers put that frog-sticker in your skull; it might have improved your thinking. You think you're the Lone Ranger. Well, let me tell you something; I knew the Lone Ranger, and you're not him."

"Garth, help me up, will you? You've made your point."

His response was to abruptly drop his laundry bag into my lap, where it landed with rustling and clicking sounds as its contents shifted. "Here's a little Christmas present for your friends, Pilgrim. Round 'em up and move 'em out. There's a string of ambulances waiting for you up at the curb on Fifth, and they'll take you all to the sawbones. I'm going to stay here and help Sheriff MacWhorter and his posse clean up this town."

I started to say something else, but Garth abruptly wheeled around and skated back toward the center of the rink, which was still a scene of pandemonium and confusion. However, from what I could make out, the police seemed to have things under control, and they were handcuffing men. I sat on the ice next to Raymond Rogers feeling at once deliriously elated and eminently foolish. I opened the top of the laundry bag and peered down at its contents, what must have been upwards of a thousand large black-and-yellow capsules.

I glanced to my right, where Jack was being attended to by a team of paramedics. On the steps leading up to the promenade, Sharon Stephens and her lost flock were being escorted by Veil, Moira, and a half dozen uniformed police officers. I got to my feet, slung the laundry bag over my shoulder, and went after them.

*T*he Chill Shop was thoroughly burned, and the government's reaction to the story told by the survivors of Rivercliff was refreshingly candid and swift. In less than an hour after the story broke, the President, flanked by both the Secretary of Health and Education and the CIA Director, appeared on national television. The President offered no lame excuses, only an apology to the patients and the entire country for what had been allowed to happen, and a pledge that the patients would be compensated. The CIA Director, in announcing his resignation and that of his immediate deputy, took full responsibility for the activities of the Bureau of Unusual Human Resources. However, he claimed that BUHR's existence had been a closely held secret within the Company itself, an operation kept alive by a few old hands, and he had not, in the three years of his term, ever been told of its existence or activities. The Director's forthright statement and behavior were so untypical of the clouds of smoke that usually belched out of Langley that I tended to believe him, and I listened with at least a measure of sympathy to his plea not to blame the entire American intelligence community for the criminal behavior of a handful of bureaucrats who would be going to prison, probably for life.

Lorminix, while predictably denying all accusations, was having a severe public relations problem, and both Garth and I had been asked if we would agree to serve as consultants to the Swiss authorities as they investigated the drug and chemical cartel. We most certainly would.

The patients had been granted permission to continue on their present, still unnamed medication until such time as a special task force—headed by Bailey Kramer, who was overnight being hailed as a genius, national hero, and scientific pioneer—could build upon the work Bailey had already done and reformulate the compound so as to provide a medication that would be as effective as the original, but without the original compound's deadly side effects. Early predictions were that the compound, for which Bailey had already received certain technical and procedural patents, would revolutionize drug therapy not only for schizophrenics but also for sufferers of other forms of mental illness as well. Frank Lemengello had accepted Bailey's invitation to become his partner in a company that would produce and distribute the new medication, a venture that Wall Street experts estimated would net both men tens of millions of dollars.

And, of course, my name and picture, and Garth's, were in all the newspapers, and we were turning down requests for interviews left and right, referring all book and movie offers to Sharon Stephens and her patients, and especially to Margaret Dutton. There was already a television movie in the works, called *Mama Spit*. I had politely but very firmly refused a request to appear in the film in some cameo role; rumor had it that the producers were trying to get Tom Selleck or Sylvester Stallone to play my part. In return for any cooperation at all, like maybe acting with my brother as a consultant for a ton of money, I insisted that the character of Felix MacWhorter be given a prominent role in the script so as to extol the virtues and valor of the NYPD and his own handling of the situation that had made such a successful outcome possible.

A week after New Year's, a nationally televised memorial service for all of the patients who had died at Rivercliff was held at St. Patrick's Cathedral. Garth, Mary Tree, and I were seated in a relatively private viewing area, which I appreciated since I'd had all the public exposure I wanted for a very long time. The service, presided over by the Cardinal, was quite lovely. No chain of events that involved the deaths of so many people and Michael Stout's sacrifice of his own life could be said to have a happy ending, but I decided it was close. Emily and Margaret had happy beginnings. Eleven of the lost flock and their shepherdess were alive, Garth and I were alive, BUHR had been dismantled, and Lorminix was going to have a lot more trouble than it could handle.

But Garth was still mad at me, which meant I had still not found out how he had found out what was going on, or how he'd obtained the capsules. I was still getting nothing from him but John Wayne homilies, and that meant I was not forgiven.

After the service we walked out and stood together off to the side at the top of the cathedral's great stone steps, looking out on a fine, snow-dusted New York Sunday in the new year.

I said, "Come on, Garth. How long is it going to be before you tell me how you got the capsules?"

"Well, I don't know, little pilgrim," the Duke drawled. "How long were you planning on waiting before calling me to tell me you were up to your ass in Apaches? You had people wanting to plug you, and a couple of them hombres tortured you. I guess you just plumb downright didn't want to bother this old hoss with those details, right? I guess you plumb downright didn't give much of a hoot as to how I'd feel if I came home and found my old pardner had been killed while I was away off up in the mountains."

"Garth, I just didn't think there was anything you could do."

"Then the joke's on you, isn't it, you hardheaded little heifer? It was your trusty old pardner here who got the capsules, and if it wasn't for your trusty old pardner here, you'd have a bullet in the heart, or an ice pick in the brain. It seems to me that it's a good thing for you this hoss crashed the square dance. If you'd been sitting in my saddle and I'd done the same thing to you, not told you what was happening or asked for your help, you'd have come looking to carve out my heart with a rusty bowie knife."

"Look, *Duke*, I'm grateful. Okay? So I made a mistake in not bringing you in. Does that mean I get this crap from you for the rest of my life?"

"Could be, Pilgrim."

"Come on. Gérard called you, didn't he?"

"I can't rightly recollect who it was who told me that my pardner and a dozen other people he was trying to help were in serious danger of winding up on Boot Hill."

I turned to my beautiful and famous sister-in-law. Her long, gray-streaked yellow hair gleamed like gold in the afternoon sun, and her eyes sparkled as she stared back at me. She seemed highly amused by the situation, and I had the strong suspicion that it was all she could do to keep from laughing. I said to her, "You know, don't you?"

Mary Tree's response was an enigmatic, almost apologetic, smile. It meant she knew, but wasn't about to upstage my ham brother, or step on his lines.

John Wayne said, "I hear tell you didn't even let the sheriff back in there know what was going on until it was almost too late. You must have tumbleweed for brains, little pilgrim."

I felt the blood rush to my face. "All right, *Duke*, now you're getting me pissed off. Speaking of brains, it wasn't my mind—or my life—at stake in this thing. I was just a facilitator, *Duke*. I wasn't calling the shots. These people had good reason to be wary of the authorities, medical and legal. If you'd been in my saddle, *Duke*, you'd probably have done the same damn thing. Not only that, but I think it's probably politically incorrect for you to refer to me as being up to my ass in a particular tribe of proud Native Americans. So I don't need to hear any more of your shit."

Garth and Mary exchanged glances, and Mary inclined her head slightly. Garth nodded, then laughed as he put his arm around my shoulders and hugged me. "You did good, Mongo," he said in his normal voice, indicating that John Wayne had finally ridden off into the sunset and I was back in his good graces. "You did real good, and I'm damn proud of you. It was just a little difficult to take, finding out what you'd been trying to deal with alone while I was off falling on my ass on the ski slopes, and you hadn't even bothered to call me. Aside from the fact that I feel an occasional twinge of affection for my brother, it made me feel like a fool. It's my place to be there for you when you need help, just like you've always been there for me. I was really pissed."

"So I noticed. Not contacting you seemed like a good idea at the time, but now I can see your point. I really am sorry. If you hadn't ridden to the rescue, I'd be dead, and probably all the patients as well."

"Apology accepted."

"Gérard filled you in?"

Garth shook his head. "He told me about your call only after I'd learned about your situation from other sources and contacted him again; you'd asked him not to tell me, and he didn't. Once I'd already learned what was happening, his agreement with you was moot, and he filled me in on Punch and Judy."

"Then who got in touch with you?"

"Actually, I got calls from two people. The first was from Felix MacWhorter, who hadn't spoken to me or had a kind word to say in years. It seems you've been doing quite a job of diplomacy with the man, because he thought enough of you to track me down and tell me he was worried about you and thought you could use some help; I'd left a message on my answering machine at the house giving the number where I could be reached in case of an emergency. He also sent me a copy of the Punch and Judy tape, and that told me all I needed to know about Lorminix and Heinrich Muller. I also got a call from Veil."

I grunted, said, "That figures."

"He thought you needed more backup. Also, he knew I'd probably hold him responsible if anything happened to you."

"For Christ's sake," I said, shaking my head. "He never said a word."

"Aha. That's because I asked him not to. I thought it only fitting that I treat you the same way you'd treated me. Besides, I thought there were certain advantages to keeping you in the dark."

"Yeah? Name one."

"It gave me a nice, warm, fuzzy feeling of satisfaction. I think better when I'm feeling good."

"Ho, ho, ho."

"Besides that, I didn't want you distracted and worrying about me. I know that's why you didn't call; you were trying to protect me. You thought you had all the bases covered here, and you didn't want to risk having me get my ass in a wringer over in Switzerland if you told me about Lorminix and the patients' need for more medication. I shouldn't tell you this, but I'm not unappreciative of your motives."

"How the hell did you get the capsules?"

"Simplicity itself. I had Heinrich Muller's name from the Punch and Judy tape, so I just went and asked him for more capsules."

"You're putting me on, right? I can't believe Muller would even agree to talk to you, much less agree to give you the medication."

"He didn't have much choice. I visited him at home; his house didn't have much of a security system. He woke up in the middle of the night to find me sitting on the edge of his bed."

"Ah," I said, rolling my eyes. "The old horse's head gambit."

"Something like that."

"Dare I ask what became of Herr Muller?"

"Never laid a hand on him. I was the soul of sweet reason. The Duke patiently explained the situation to him, and then appealed to his conscience. He finally agreed that the shortage of medication for the patients was an atrocious thing, and something should be done about it. He invited me to come back to his office, where he just happened to have a supply of said capsules in his safe. He insisted that I take all of them, and then he insisted on helping me get through customs with them. Why, the man even insisted on accompanying Mary and me when we flew back to New York in the Lorminix corporate jet. He couldn't have been more cooperative."

"Jesus, you must have scared the shit out of him."

"Well, now that you mention it, the Duke did seem to make him a bit nervous."

Mary laughed, then stepped forward and put her arms around both of us. "Okay, now that the two of you have kissed and made up, let's go get something to eat. I'm starved, and I'm buying."

"Mongo," my brother said to me seriously, "you're never going to make the mistake again of forgetting who loves you, right?"

"Right."

"Right," Garth drawled. "Then let's saddle up and go find ourselves a chuck wagon."